"Good grief, your
eyelashes are

"Really, Mr. Na
enough to thin
sheep yard?" L

"Not the lashes." burst out
laughing. "I meant the color. Never
dreamed that anyone with hair that fair
could have such dark lashes."

"Perhaps you think I bleach my hair, then,"
Letty retorted, Nathaniel's close scrutiny
beginning to unsettle her.

"No, I don't." Nathaniel chuckled. "Even I
can see it's every bit as ash-blond at the
roots, and even the down on your arms is
pale gold."

Letty blushed deeply, meeting his intent
gaze. "Poor Mr. Nathaniel. You were so
determined to find me artificial, you can't
believe any of me is for real. Well, there
are a few shocks ahead for you, believe
me!"

And maybe for you, too, girl!
Letty thought.

New Zealand born **Essie Summers** comes from a long line of storytellers. At eighteen she submitted her writing for publication and soon saw her poems, articles and short stories in print. Essie Summers debuted as a Harlequin author in 1961, has more than forty books to her credit and, as readers around the world will confirm, is one of the best-loved writers.

Books by Essie Summers

Don't miss any of our special offers. Write to us at the following address for information on our newest releases.

Harlequin Reader Service
901 Fuhrmann Blvd., P.O. Box 1397, Buffalo, NY 14240
Canadian address: P.O. Box 603,
Fort Erie, Ont. L2A 5X3

High-Country Governess

Essie Summers

Harlequin Books

TORONTO • NEW YORK • LONDON
AMSTERDAM • PARIS • SYDNEY • HAMBURG
STOCKHOLM • ATHENS • TOKYO • MILAN

Original hardcover edition published in 1987
by Mills & Boon Limited

ISBN 0-373-02883-0

Harlequin Romance first edition January 1988

CHAPTER ONE

LETITIA GREENAWAY could have danced all the way up to Tristan Pengelly's office. This day had come. She was actually going to be free to live her own life. She'd worked in this huge department store for eight long years.

How different it had been from the life she'd planned that first year at Otago University. But when Dad had died so suddenly there had been nothing else for it but to earn money as speedily as possible and to take a permanent job that meant she could stay in Dunedin. There were two younger children to educate. Mother, never a career woman, had been marvellous. She'd faced up to returning to the business world and Letitia had matched her for grit and even for cheerfulness in her daily work, thankful that they had been able to retain their home, continue to pay off the too-large mortgage, make no drastic changes in the children's lives.

Children no longer and Mother no more a widow. It still seemed incredible that Mother had kept that chance of marrying Grayson Moore to herself for five years, because it would have meant uprooting them and going to London. She hadn't thought it would suit them, although she, London-born and bred, must have longed to do just that. She'd had another reason too. She had cared too much for Grayson to add another burden to his life. He'd deserved a freer existence after years of heroic devotion to a crippled wife. But now Mother was free, and the twins, John and Merle, through their own sheer determination, had both achieved overseas scholarships and at this moment were studying at Aberdeen. Nice for Mother to have two of her children in Britain.

Grayson had insisted that their Dunedin home be rented out if Letitia left Pengelly's, so that Letitia could have some

financial security yet not be tied there. Tristan Pengelly had
known for some time she would be leaving, though he'd
kept it to himself, the dear old curmudgeon, as she always
called him, secretly. He'd sent her off to other centres to
find, as he was stubbornly sure she would, another expert
cosmetician for her counter, also with a name beginning
with L. He had this mania for alliteration.

His departments were charmingly set out and renowned
for quality. They were entered through arches bearing
names, *Ursula for Underwear, Alicia for Accessories,
Barbara for Babyware, Madeleine for Millinery*, and, oh
horrors, her own cosmetic counter, *Letitia for Loveliness!*
Letitia hated it now as much as she had on her first rebel-
lious day in charge. She'd pleaded then with Tristan to
allow her to stay as second-in-charge of the babywear,
where initials didn't matter, but he'd been determined and,
knowing she needed a bigger wage, he offered one that,
because of their straitened circumstances, her conscience
wouldn't allow her to refuse.

When she had departed on her quest she'd said darkly,
'For just once, Mr Pengelly, you might miss out on an
excellent saleswoman for the sake of this . . . er . . .
kink. Not everyone would consent to change their name
for work hours like Rita Lawson when she became the
second Madeleine.'

He had laughed. 'I heard her say recently that even her
husband calls her Madeleine now. Thinks it suits her
better.'

'It had been a minor feather in Letitia's cap when she'd
returned to say, 'You've got to skip the "L", Mr Pengelly.
But I'm sure you'll settle for something much more suitable. *Letitia for Loveliness* sounds so contrived. This one
is a first-class buyer, saleswoman, a superb looker and
above all, wants to come to Dunedin. What do you think
of *Chloe for Cosmetics*? Here's her photo.'

He'd fallen for it, of course, and even more when he met
her in the flesh. Now Chloe was arriving in three days'
time, not ten as had been arranged at first. She'd rung
Letitia last night, at home, from Wellington, when she
hadn't been able to raise Mr Pengelly at his home.

Now Letitia could place the advert that she hoped would bring her the position she craved. She didn't feel like facing university again. Too many years had already been whisked away from her and her goal had always been teaching, anyway. Her other love had been for the outdoor life, the mountains, the great silences . . . now she dreamed of becoming a governess on one of the great sheep-stations in the high-country, where the children were on correspondence lessons. It wouldn't be difficult to obtain. Governesses were hard to come by; not many girls liked the isolated life and many mothers in such situations were desperate for help. It was a good time of year, January, the long summer holiday in New Zealand.

Tristan Pengelly was here so early, so often, long before his office staff. She hoped to catch him to discuss Chloe's earlier arrival before the inevitable interruptions of the life serving the public took over. Oh, his office blinds between that and the main office were still down. She'd beaten him to it. His car had been in the car park, though. He'd be in one of the reserves, probably; that crew started earlier. Letitia looked at the notes in her hand, setting out all that Chloe had told her, and decided to leave them on his desk, and just scrawl beneath, 'Please send for me when convenient.'

She was about to leave when a sound caught her ear, from the inner office that Tristan called his *Sanctum Sanctorum*. Startled, she lifted her head, listened. There it was again, a bang and a rustle. What on earth——? A slightly eerie feeling feathered over her skin, raising goose-pimples. What if Tristan *was* in, had taken some sort of turn? He could, at his age. She went swiftly to the door, thrust it open, then just as quickly closed it.

That's what came of Tristan feeding his tame pigeon, on his broad window-ledge. Just as well this was seven storeys up, because that window must have been open all night. Popeye had had a marvellous time among the papers, annoyed, probably, because there wasn't a crumb in sight. She must get him out as soon as possible. Fortunately he was very tame.

Letitia began making crooning noises in between beseeching him to 'come along over here . . . now, now . . . attaboy . . . Oh, you *are* naughty! This way . . . ' Finally Popeye hopped on to her shoulder, she made a grab with her other hand and he was out of the window and she had it shut.

She straightened up the papers, picked up umpteen paperclips from the floor, removed evidence of Popeye's visit from blotting pad and an ornate inkstand that was never used, and bent to rescue the ballpoints from under the desk. Her head was still underneath it when she heard voices and the shutting of the outer office door. Tristan's voice, for sure, and whose——? Oh, Mr Nathaniel's, his younger son, the one who hated drapery. He'd had to return to it though, while his brother James was spending Christmas in Canada. She hoped they wouldn't jump out of their skins when she emerged. She began to back out from under the desk. She'd better raise herself up slowly, not pop up, because they would see her through the pebbled glass. And give a warning cough.

The cough was strangled at birth as she heard her name in withering tones from Mr Nathaniel. 'What? Me offer a job like that to *Letitia for Loveliness*? Dad, you've got to be joking! I'd just as soon offer it to a film star! Take *her* up to The Wilderness? My great-great-grandmother would turn in her grave! She wouldn't know B from a bull's foot about life on a sheep-station—life's real up there, not artificial. I want the sort of governess who wouldn't turn a hair if she had to help with tailing in an emergency . . . not go round smothered in make-up, blinking false eyelashes at me and looking like something out of a sheikh's harem!'

Letitia stayed on her hands and knees, frozen with indignation. 'Ohhhh! Just wait, Nathaniel Pengelly . . . in the next ten seconds you're going to have the shock of your life. Your eyes are going to bulge and your ears are going to be mentally boxed. I can guarantee they'll tingle more than if I physically assulted you!'

There was a roar of laughter from old Tristan. 'Nat, you don't know what you're talking about. You never go near that department. She's leaving us. Her mother got married again—before you came down—and has gone to England. The lovely Letitia couldn't leave us quickly enough. Her first ambition was to go teaching, but she left after one year at university. So now she's pulling up the roots and tells me she's going to advertise for a position governessing in the high-country.'

This time it was Nathaniel who roared with laughter. That made Letitia clench her fists. 'Fat hope she'll have. Any high-country wife and mother would take one look at that walking example of artificiality and allure and turn her down. She'd make more mischief in the high-country than a flock of *keas*, believe me. No wife would risk it . . . imagine risking a husband . . . or shepherds, with that sort of menace!'

Tristan said, 'I've never heard such a bigoted opinion in all my life. You know absolutely nothing about her whatever.'

Letitia heard a snort, then Nathaniel's voice again. 'I don't have to. Any girl who takes up a job like hers here has nothing to do with the reality of life lived in the wop-wops. There are plenty other careers even if she was a drop-out from Varsity. Even less glam sections of Pengelly's, I imagine, but she had to pick that!'

'You're off-beam, son. She was in the baby department to begin with and loved that. But you know me . . . her name began with L and I was all for having a department called *Letitia for Loveliness*. She didn't want to take it.'

Another snort. 'Well, I know you. You're a tough old hombre but fair. You wouldn't have sacked her. You'd have probably admired her the more for having guts if she'd refused.'

'But I offered her a huge rise. So she took it. No, don't curl your lip, Nat. Let me tell you that to start with she was no drop-out. Her mother was widowed, they had a hefty mortgage, and two children quite young. Thanks to Letitia they've been able to make it to university and done well. Studying at Aberdeen now. She's a free agent at last and is off to do something similar to what she wanted in the first place. I offered her a rise to keep her, but she just grinned and said, "Nothing doing".'

'Can't imagine her on speaking terms with a *grin*. I *can* imagine a *supercilious smile*.'

Letitia's blood pressure rose.

Nathaniel Pengelly added, 'Well, granted she seemed to have reasons for taking on that job, but believe me, she's not coming to The Wilderness! Can't stand the sight of her. We get enough cold weather in the valley in winter without introducing a human icicle! Now don't push it, Dad. No amount of sugar would sweeten that pill! I can't think what's got into you. You must know she's unsuitable.'

For Tristan, his tone was mild. 'H'm. Pity. I've been thinking lately she's the sort of girl I'd like for a daughter-in-law.'

This time Letitia's eyebrows rose.

Nathaniel's voice rose in squeak of surprise. '*Daughter-in-law?* Good God, you've got to mean me! James is married.'

Letitia imagined Tristan was smiling devilishly at his son in a way he had, but he said nothing. Nathaniel added explosively, 'This is the maddest conversation I've ever had with you, and I've had some. What in the world would make you believe I'd cast a flicker of an eye in *her* direction?'

Tristan gave a funny sort of chuckle, an almost deprecatory one. 'Now you'll really think I'm an old fool. But I'll tell you why . . . because I discovered in myself an odd sort of tenderness for the girl. If I was twenty or more years younger I'd have a shot for her myself.'

Nathaniel was evidently winded. Letitia felt the acid of frustrated fury ebb out of her. She blinked tears away; the old sweetie . . . the old sweetie. But who'd have thought it?

Nathaniel managed to recover himself. 'Well, perhaps James and I should be thankful for those twenty years. I've heard of such things, but——'

'But you never dreamed it of your father. You're probably thinking as most sons would in such circumstances, that I'm getting senile, that there's no fool like an old fool.' Another chuckle, this time a derisive one. 'But there are young fools too, don't forget, and the company you've been seen round in lately doesn't make me credit you with much discrimination. What makes you think Portia Latimer would suit a high-country man?'

Nathaniel's laugh was just as derisive. 'When I'm considering her as a wife I'll let you know, Dad. Look, this conversation is getting us nowhere. I've given you this month when James was away, but I've got to get back to my own property. I've got a good man and I'll keep him if I can get someone to take over the lessons for the children. He thought his wife was a bit run down coping with the baby and correspondence lessons, besides everything else. She's marvellous too and I don't want to lose either. It's up to me to get someone.'

Tristan's tone changed. 'If it's any help and you can get someone by offering them extra-high wages, I'll pay them. You were too stiff-necked to take an interest-free loan from me when you bought the run. I can't see why. That's how James bought his house and——'

'No, Dad. You and Mother had your struggles in your young days building a great business up. I want to do the same with my property. And without strings attached. You wily old beggar . . . you'd probably make it conditional on marrying to please you.'

Tristan's response sounded as if he'd been complimented, not insulted. 'Not a bad idea! On those conditions I'd make the mortgage a wedding gift, not an interest-free loan.'

Nathaniel laughed. 'Dad, this is sheer Victorian melodrama, only topsy-turvy. It was usually the heroine marrying a man she hated, to save her parents from penury. I wouldn't consider it even if you promised to push a road through the Big Slip.'

Letitia's blood boiled again.

'My dear Papa, I'm giving myself the rest of the week to advertise for a governess. If nobody offers I'll stay in Queenstown a day or two on the way back and see if the old grapevine can come up with a name or two. Old Mattie is still going strong, you know. She may know of someone. Wish we could get someone like her, but that breed doesn't come any more. Well, I want to see Jock in the reserves

about letting the haberdashery department have some
different fixtures, so I'd better get on. It'll be a tussle. I'd
rather be dipping lambs, and *they* can be contrary!'

Letitia was still crouched. Thank heaven he was going.
It was inevitable that Tristan would discover her, but
although she'd longed a few hot seconds ago to confront
the unspeakable Nathaniel, now she knew that if she did
she'd go clean up in smoke and it would spoil her last days
at Pengelly's and her memories of a very fine boss would
be shadowed.

Blessedly Tristan said, 'I'll come with you. Jock'll be
managed easily enough, but whoever has the fixtures
adjoining the haby might be a harder nut to crack.'

That would be true, thought Letitia viciously to herself.
The cosmetics ones were right next to the haby ones! But
what a relief. Tristan need never know she'd overheard all.

She emerged cautiously. The office staff were arriving.
She merely said good morning, offered no reason for being
in Tristan's office by herself and took the main stairs, not
the reserve ones.

It was all of eleven before she simmered down, because
she couldn't stop her mind seething with all she'd *like* to
say to Nathaniel Pengelly. She just couldn't admit to
hearing what she had. She'd rather die. She tried to be
philosophical, apply the things life had already taught
her . . . like 'This too will pass' and 'Just remember that
in twelve months' time this won't even be a ripple on the
water'. It was hopeless. She still boiled.

There was nothing she could do about it. *Nothing.*
Instantly her mind presented her with examples of poetic
justice; in a play now, Nathaniel would, against his will,
fall headlong in love with her, beg her to marry him and
be spurned most dramatically. Oh, stop it, Letitia, that's
kids' stuff, the sort of thing you would have dreamed up
in your early teens. Get on with your work—heaven knows
there's enough of it to get through before Chloe arrives.
Certainly she had already made a visit by plane, and had
spent three days in the department with Letitia, though the
staff had merely thought she was to be a deputy, but now

Letitia must make full and detailed notes for her concerning indent orders, dates of demonstrations, and so on, and double-check with the hairdressing salon, whose programmes were always inter-related.

She told an assistant what was happening, now, and said, 'I'll disappear for the morning into my office. As few interruptions as possible, please.'

Nevertheless it took time to get her mind fully on her work. At last, after much telephoning, the contacts with other business personnel began to steady her. After all, what did it matter? This time next week the cosmetics department wouldn't mean a thing to her, and she might never see the Pengellys again, father or son. The entire high-country would be her world then. Somewhere in the remote sheep-stations or cattle-runs or deer ranches tucked into the folds of the mountains beyond the great lakes of Central Otago or South Canterbury, she would find a niche for herself, far beyond that other world of hairstylists, beauticians, sales reps. She worked on.

There was a discreet tap. Well, Anita had till now kept everyone away, and interruptions wouldn't matter so much now she had her temper under control. 'Come in,' she said, and looked up. Nathaniel Pengelly!

Letitia managed to keep her face impassive. She was glad to be behind a desk, it gave you a feeling of authority, impersonal and efficient. Her voice remained steady. 'Oh, good morning, Mr Nathaniel. What can I do for you?' She gestured him to the seat opposite the desk.

He said, 'I'd better come round there with you. I've some sketches I'd like you to see. Hard to explain otherwise.' He whisked the chair round to her side. Pity. So much for authority.

'Oh yes? Then I'll make room for them. No . . . don't dare touch those papers. I must keep them in sequence. I'll move them.'

She placed them on a trolley nearby, shuffling them carefully. 'I've a lot to get through the next few days. Your father may have said my successor is arriving sooner than planned and I don't want her to face any disruptions right away. Will what you want to show me really concern me? Mightn't it be policy to show them to the next head of department?'

Considering the way she'd heard him speaking about her earlier, he gave her what she considered a very cheeky grin, then said, 'It will suit me better to have you decide, then Miss Chloe Denham will be faced with a *fait accompli*. In the few times I've had to spend time in the shop I've noticed that it's a red rag to a bull if any head is approached re giving up window space, floor space, or advertising prominence. So I thought it would cause less hoo-ha all round this way.'

She looked at him like the icicle he'd called her, raised one well-groomed eyebrow, said, 'And you think I'd care so little about the continuing success of this department and the welfare of my successor that I'd simply agree?'

His hand, far rougher and browner than most drapers' hands, made an impatient gesture. 'Oh, come, aren't you making too much of this? You don't even know what it's about. I'm not asking you to give up a display counter or one of your elegant stands, it's just a matter of a few reserve fixtures being placed elsewhere to give the haberdashery stock some more shallow shelves. Their stuff carries so many lines the deeper shelves are treble-banked so they spend far too much time labelling them to indicate what's behind other lines. Your fixtures, shallower, would be ideal.'

Her tone was dry. 'No doubt, but my lines are also small and numerous. But what had you in mind for me, should mine be moved?'

'That's better, I thought you were going to be like all the rest, not willing to budge an inch.'

She said coolly, 'Mr Nathaniel, I don't doubt that, in the world of sheep and shearing, woolsheds and stockyards, you're very knowledgeable and you are your own boss. Every one of the heads of department here has to make her own section pay and she can't if she's spineless enough to let herself be pushed around because another head is more aggressive. When I first started in Pengelly's in the babylinen, we were asked to move back near the old cash-desks to allow the jewellery department to go by the west door instead of us. This costume jewellery caught the light more. In an endeavour not to appear obstructive, and seeing the point of this, we agreed. We dropped thirty per cent in four months, due to missing out on casual sales from customers passing by. Those with definite needs came through, prams and all, but fond grannies and aunts weren't caught by something they'd love to buy. Your father realised it and a compromise was made. So don't misjudge the chiefs you probably regard as battleaxes. They've got their jobs to do. What are you looking at me like that for?' Didn't matter what she said now.

The tawny eyes so close to hers blinked. 'Just surprise. Didn't expect you to get on a soapbox about this when you're leaving.'

The eyes opposite his were green with hazel flecks, rather too heavily made-up for his taste, but they were emitting sparks. She continued, 'I do like to see fairness done. But I am also quite unbiased, so if it's possible to concede those fixtures I will. I've always thought those others weren't the best for the baby. The stacks of dressmaking accessories are always tumbling. But I'll want to be sure the alternative accommodation for our wares is suitable. Let me see your sketches.'

She took a mental check on herself. It was only natural she'd like to block him, but she mustn't let what she'd overheard make her petty. Heaven send she didn't have to be too obstructive.

He spread out the sketches. They were very well done; Letitia made herself say so. He said, 'I'm more used to designing covered yards or pulling an old house to pieces and reconstructing it, and where I live there's too much travelling involved to get men up to give preliminary estimates and it's too costly, so I do my own and take them in to Queenstown. Now, if you gave up these in the second row back, and we got the joiner to make you identical ones here . . . and there . . . how would that be?'

She took them, studied them. 'H'mm. These here would be okay, but the ones there I'm doubtful about. I'll have to come up before I can decide as——'

He interrupted her. 'Surely there can't be a snag there? It's not all that much further away. The time involved in bringing stock forward wouldn't justify a veto, surely?'

She said crisply but not impatiently, 'You've sketched the floor space and the height of the fixtures but haven't paid attention to the ceiling. Now——'

'Ceiling? What's that to do with anything? I——'

She held up an exquisitely manicured hand. 'Everything to do with it. Don't feel badly, Mr Nathaniel. Your father would have noticed it instantly, or Mr James. The light-well is almost above it and a lot of the day the sun would slant down on those, striking right across the front of the containers. The contents couldn't fade as they are well packed but while the baby lines would be fine there, mine couldn't stand the dryness. We'd have complaints galore, and rightly so. Why not give those to the baby and let me retain half of what you want to move?'

He was silent, and she knew an inner exultation. She couldn't take him up on what she'd overheard, but if he argued, she'd jolly well enjoy the clash. She was sure of winning her point because Tristan Pengelly would merely say, 'Of course.'

To her surprise Nathaniel agreed, a note of astonishment in his voice. 'You're dead right. I hadn't thought there was so much to cosmetics. I know about textiles fading and goods in the windows. I've had that drummed into me since I worked here as a schoolboy in the holidays, long before your time, of course. Well, fair enough. I approve of compromises. Half their goods can be moved and half yours. Happy about that, Miss Greenaway?'

She nodded. 'Wonder your father didn't point out the position of the light-well to you.' She realised she shouldn't have known Tristan had been with his son. She added quickly, 'Or wasn't he with you? He usually likes the final say-so in such things.' Phew!

Nathaniel didn't notice. He grinned, lines carving themselves down his somewhat weather-beaten cheeks. 'He'd know all right, the wily old fox. He likes me to find out things. Tells me running a shop is as much a science as farming. I reckon he wanted me to see that even the head of the cosmetics department knows her onions.'

Even! She could have shot him, but she looked at him levelly. 'It isn't just a case of getting behind a counter heavily made-up, you know, and automatically selling products. All my girls attend good seminars. It's not merely presenting an artificial façade—we do a real service in helping self-conscious teenagers hide acne, improve their grooming, make the best of themselves; and occasionally when a woman has let herself slip because she's got so little time to spend on herself and she's losing confidence and perhaps putting her marriage in jeopardy, we do as much for her as the psychologist. Most women need a little glamour, not just the basics of clothes and footwear. I'm on my soap-box again, I know, but I don't like the boss's son or anyone else to be patronising about my department, even if it was never my favourite one.' There, she felt a whole heap better!

She was most disconcerted when he burst out laughing. The laugh of a man used to great open spaces. To cover up she said, 'Shhh! We're right up against one of the showroom fitting-rooms. These walls are paper-thin. Doesn't matter usually because I rarely have interviews here. It's more a place to stow my order forms and indents.'

'Just as well . . . those two women seem to have been there for ages, trying on frocks, I suppose. Hope they mean to buy one. The saleswoman must be nearly going mad.'

Letitia said, 'Unfortunately it's only too common. All the girls would rather have a customer on her own. Some so-called friends are deliberately off-putting, out of jealousy at the way another woman looks, or that she can afford it, and a few don't even intend to buy, they're just passing the time. It's well known that the showroom staff suffer more mental fatigue than the ones behind the counter selling less costly stuff. Some customers are delightful of course, we get quite fond of them, but *some*!'

He replied in the same low voice, 'I can understand that. I've been conscious for the last ten minutes or so that those two are first-class snags. Oh, well, it takes all sorts, I guess.'

Letitia was just about to ask if he wanted to see her upstairs now, or after lunch, when into the silence came the customer's voice. 'I'll have that one. I always get a discount. A considerable one.'

The two in the office listened instinctively. The saleswoman said, 'Very well, I'll just contact the office. What name, madam?'

Then, devastatingly clearly, 'Miss Portia Latimer. And you won't need to contact the office. Just ask Mr Nathaniel Pengelly.'

Cora Hart said pleasantly, 'Very well, that may take a little while. I mean finding him. Perhaps when you're dressed again, you might like to take seats by the showroom counter? I did see him downstairs before, but he's probably away up again. Or would you prefer to have a look around some other department and come back?'

'No, thanks. We'll wait. In fact I might just try on that blue one again. Then if Nat's generous enough I might take the two.'

Cora said uncertainly, 'Is it not just a percentage?'

Portia's voice was down-putting. 'Heavens, no, my dear girl. He could even let me have it at practically cost. It's happened before. Run along.'

Nathaniel had risen, ready to go out to save Cora looking for him, but now he paused and Letitia saw a dark red rise from his collar into the bronzed cheeks. He motioned her to sit down again. He kept his voice very low but his eyes were glinting. 'Let her look for me for the moment, till I decide how to handle this. I think she's taking too much for granted. And keep quiet, I'd like to know how her friend responds to this.'

Letitia felt most uncomfortable. True, she herself had been an eavesdropper earlier, but unwillingly, and she'd only not revealed herself because she didn't want to embarrass the boss who'd been such an understanding one, and generous too.

They knew soon enough. The friend's voice was admiring, tinged with envy. 'Aren't you the cool one! And you certainly know the right people. Cost price! But tell me, you said he's most of the time away in an outlandish spot. Will you be able to get this concession when he's not here?'

'I shouldn't think so. Old Tristan Pengelly is a toughie. He strongly suspects me of having an eye to the main chance. But I do quite fancy Nat, apart from his quaint idea of taking on this derelict old homestead in the way-outs, that belonged to some crude old pioneer ancestors on his mother's side. I'm surprised he's stuck it for two years. But he'll get sick of it soon, with farming not what it was. It's ridiculous. He's finding it hard to keep staff. That should bring him to his senses. The access road is like a mule-track . . . no school bus and no likelihood of it, and governesses aren't exactly thick on the ground these days. If I play my cards right, he could stay in the business here, like James. You ought to see James's house. I bet the old man paid for it—much more profitable. Nat even arranged a loan independently, to finance the sale. His father would have advanced it, interest-free. What a fool! I reckon if this family he's got up there walks out on him because of the isolation, he'll pack it in. I hope they do. It'll take years for him to make the sheep-run pay. What do you think of this blue one, Marty?'

Nathaniel's colour had ebbed again. He looked at Letitia, as if he were challenging her to say something. She didn't know what to say. One moment she was desperately sorry for him, for *his* humiliation, the next she was remembering, inevitably, the contempt he had heaped on *her* that morning.

His jaw set and his voice, though pitched low, held real fury. 'What do you think of that, Miss Greenaway? How'd you like to overhear such a thing about yourself?'

She had to hold back what she'd have liked to have said, about what *she'd* overheard, and she didn't find it easy, so she said the first thing that shot into her head. 'Might depend how much I cared about the speaker's opinion. Hard cheese for her that we happened to hear. But she may not really mean it. She could be putting on a tough act in front of a friend she wants to impress. Ignore it.' Then, when he didn't speak, 'After all, it's an accident of fate . . . don't you know it's Eavesdroppers' Day? I myself——' She caught the words back—no, she mustn't.

It deflected his wrath, he said, 'What do you mean . . . Eavesdroppers' Day? Never heard of it.'

She said, rather flippantly, 'I dare say there are lots of days you've never heard of. Like Lazybones' Day, for instance, in Holland.'

He was staring at her. Still shocked, she supposed, so she added, '*I* didn't know of it till last year when cousins of ours came from Holland to visit us. I believe it's in May. Not a popular custom, I gather. Groups of young people drive round very early in the morning shouting to those still in bed to get up. But *this* is Eavesdroppers' Day for sure!'

He stood up as he heard Cora Hart say to someone, 'Have you seen Mr Nathaniel? They said he was down here with Miss Greenaway, but I can't see her either.'

Nathaniel Pengelly stood up, seized Letitia by the wrist, dragged her to the door, then said, retaining his grip, his voice loud and clear, 'We're right here in her office, Miss Hart. I'll see to this personally.'

At that moment the two women emerged from the fitting-room. As Nathaniel uttered his last sentence they both looked aghast. Also, it was patent, they were hoping against hope he'd not been there long.

Portia Latimer did try. She moistened her lips, gave an audible swallow, then said, 'Oh, fancy, if that girl had known, it would have saved her looking for you, Have you been——'

It wasn't a nice smile on Nathaniel Pengelly's face. He said, quietly but between his teeth, 'I think you want to ask me have I been here long? Yes, from the very start. *You'll be paying full price for that frock. If you still want it.*'

Cora Hart had disappeared. Very wise. She had simply melted into invisibility between the circular racks of frocks. Letitia couldn't because the iron grip on her wrist still held. Portia's friend tried to back into the fitting-room, but Nathaniel's voice arrested her. 'Oh, don't try to efface yourself, Marty, you might as well get the situation clear too. No discount now or ever, and no more efforts to try to persuade me to change my way of life. It was never anything to do with you, anyway, Portia, I'm not as mad as that. And the difficulties you spoke of no longer exist. My father solved them for me this morning. All unknown to me, Miss Greenaway here, whom you probably know as *Letitia for Loveliness*, is very qualified to supervise Hope Maybury's children's lessons. You mightn't think it to look at so glamorous a creature, but the dream of her life is to be a governess on a high-country station. I'm helping her realise that dream. How lucky can a man get? We're taking off on Tuesday morning. If you don't want to face our Miss Hart after this, I'll simply cancel the docket myself. I'm sure Pengelly's can stand the loss of a sale.'

Portia Latimer had gone scarlet and white by turns. At that she wheeled round, not looking to see if her friend was following, and swept out of the showroom in the direction of one of the exits. Her friend put her head down and positively scuttled after her.

Nathaniel Pengelly made a magnificent gesture towards Letitia's open door, said, 'In there! I'll be back in a moment. I'll just cancel this entry in Miss Hart's docket book.'

It was just a moment. Letitia was behind her desk again, feeling for the second time that morning as if a steam-roller had run over her. In all her eight years here she'd never known a morning like this.

She dreaded his return. No man would like to be spoken of in that way, made to feel a fool. What Nathaniel had said was sheer poetic retaliation, of course, not to be taken seriously. Thank heaven she was leaving and starting a new life free of Pengelly's.

He came in, shut the door, leaned over her desk, said, *'That's it, then.* You're coming to The Wilderness with me. It's what you want, what you were going to advertise for, from what Dad told me earlier. Do you know where it is? A valley between Queenstown and Glenorchy. With a mule-track out in one direction, and an immovable landslip in the other. Named not only for its isolation but also for the first woman to live there, whose name before she married was Ellen Wildernesse. Can you be ready to go Tuesday morning? I can't delay any longer.'

CHAPTER TWO

LETITIA drew in a deep breath to steady herself. It worked. She said, levelly, 'I make allowance for the fact that the last few moments have been extremely traumatic for you, but I take great exception to your . . . your effrontery in assuming you have the right to order my movements . . . in fact to attempt to order my life, merely because *you* need a governess and *I'm* looking for a situation. I realise you couldn't resist the chance of scoring off Miss Latimer. You were presented with a triumph that was surely in the poetic justice line, because it seems your father told you I'm looking for just such a position, so I forgive you that, *but it doesn't mean I'm going to agree!*'

He still loomed over her but didn't rush into argument. Then he slapped his leg and said, 'Well, it beats all. I'd never have believed it of *Letitia for Loveliness*. I'm blest if, in addition to having a soap-box complex, you don't talk in the same fashion as a governess I knew when I was very small. Miss Mattie, who taught the children at Mount Olivet House, near Paradise. We used to spend holidays up there. Well, if you're as good a governess as she was, you'll do us. I don't think I've ever heard anyone of my own generation use that word "effrontery". Really, the way you brought it out! It's priceless!'

He stopped and for the first time looked less sure of himself. His listener was looking at him with dislike. He said ruefully, 'I'm putting my foot in it. Perhaps I should take a leaf out of your book and say, "Dear Madam, we are most impressed with your application and, without further ado, beg you to honour our far-off estate with your undoubted gifts for fulfilling our needs. We know that it may be a sacrifice to bury yourself so far from the haunts of civilisation, but our need is great and we can but hope that the extreme beauty of our surroundings may compensate you for our lack of finesse in our first approach to the situation." How's that?'

This was undoubtedly the moment for Letitia to rise with dignity and say, 'I'm sorry, but I would far rather work for a stranger,' and sweep out of the office. But this extraordinary speech, delivered with such solemnity, was too much for her. She felt the corners of her mouth crumbling, laughter welling up within her, so that waves of it beat against her ribs and the refusal died on her lips in a gasp of mirth.

'Well, thank heaven,' he said and sat down on the corner of her desk and joined in the laughter. Finally she pulled herself together, said, 'I—I think you'd better put me in the picture. Have you a proper schoolroom? How many children on the estate? What grades are they in? Have they been on correspondence lessons before?'

'Of course. Now we're getting somewhere. You need to know these things. Do you know the Lake Wakatipu area at all, apart from Queenstown, I mean? Most Dunedin people know that, but not much beyond it.'

'I've had holidays there and on one went up to Glenorchy on the *SS Earnslaw,* went right on as far as Paradise on a sightseeing coach and came back with it by road, a fearsome road!'

'Not half as fearsome as ours. I take it that you know the old estate is off the Glenorchy road, between Closeburn and Creighton Stations? Some of the staff do.'

'I couldn't have pinpointed it. I just knew it had belonged to your mother's family and hadn't been worked much for years. But if it's there, doesn't the Glenorchy road serve you?'

'Many people assume that and thought when the road was pushed past Closeburn it would give access to our valley but don't realise how extensive Big Slip is. Unsurmountable for me. Oh, I know we've got fantastic earthmoving machinery these days, but the cost for access to one rundown estate isn't viable. Before the landslip occurred, back in the earliest days, they used to ship their wool out by whale-boat to Queenstown, and bring their supplies in that way, from Kingston at the foot of the lake. Now ours goes out over what Portia called a mule-track. If Big Slip wasn't there, it would be a mere twelve miles to Queenstown on the road by the lake. But the mule-track takes a tortuous way round riverbeds and bluffs for some twenty-five to thirty miles, till it reaches the Drumlogie Guest House on the Gorge Road. Know it? They give us access through there.'

'I've never stayed at Drumlogie, but know roughly where it is. Near the Ben Lomond Station, isn't it?'

'Yes. Well, during the time the homestead was abandoned, due partly to the Slip, partly to the rabbit menace which forced so many big landowners to walk off properties, it was just leased out for grazing for hardy animals and neglected. Only access on horseback. I had to have that access road, such as it is, bulldozed out. That's why I had to take on a huge mortgage. I wouldn't let Dad pay for it because he thought I was stark raving mad as it was and if he had done, he'd have run it his way, not mine. And stood to lose a pile.

'We go in by four-wheel drive army truck, but there are still times when, in very heavy rain or after snow, we're cut off. I'd never have got Hope Maybury up there if it wasn't for the helicopter rescue service. Makes her feel safer about the children. I don't blame her. I'm running deer, sheep, cattle and, if prices don't go altogether haywire and the economy improves, I should be able to provide decent all-weather access in a dozen years or so. But I've got to have a governess. Not fair otherwise. Could you stand it? If you can't, if it's too rough, you can pack it in, in three months if you like, and no hard feelings. In fact Dad would have you back like a shot, any time.'

That did it. He thought she couldn't take it. Letitia stood up, and he rose with her. 'Mr Nathaniel, you needn't make concessions. I *won't* be coming back to shop-life. I've had it. I think you'll find I can take it. Now, I *must* go to the counter. They need me in the lunch-hour. Could I see you, in one of the upstairs offices, say three-thirty, to discuss details? Yes? See you then.'

The rest of the day was a lull, emotionally. At three-thirty Letitia made her way up to Tristan's office. Tristan had a twinkle in his eye that his companions disregarded. It held a hint of mischief, a hint of blandness, and more than a hint of triumph.

Letitia surmised that Nathaniel had told his father what he'd overheard and guessed he'd watered down his decidedly bullying tactics in getting her to accept the position, because just before Nathaniel arrived in, Tristan said, beaming Jove-like on her, 'I suppose you were so indignant at what you heard that Latimer woman say, you offered to take on the schoolroom at The Wilderness right there and then?'

She said, 'Something like that,' and let it go.

Nathaniel was surprised to find out how much his father knew about Letitia's arrangements for leaving. 'Very fortunate,' Tristan remarked, 'that those tenants are coming soon. Means you're not leaving it empty, which is always risky. And knowing your passion for organising, you'll want everything immaculate for their takeover, every speck of dust banished, the last blade of grass mown. I'm glad their references were so good, but I'll have our accountant keep an eye on things just the same. He'll check with the bank.'

Nathaniel looked astounded. 'How come you know so much about the arrangements, sir?' He always called his father that, not Dad, in front of the staff.

His father, if possible, looked slyer than ever. 'I offered to vet the tenants for her. The firm is noted for keeping an eye on the affairs of its long-term employees.'

Nathaniel said, 'That makes her sound in the sere and yellow, long in the tooth and all that. Not like *Letitia for Loveliness.*'

Letitia felt if he called her that just once more she'd heave that jar of ballpoints at him. But she said crisply, 'It couldn't be better. When those folk asked could they come sooner, I knew I'd have to get on pronto with advertising, but if no answers came quickly, instead of staying with my neighbour, I decided to go up to the Lake District and hunt around, so I can come Tuesday as you suggest. It's only the fifteenth of January, so that gives us two weeks to the beginning of the new school year. It'll give me time to work out a time-table to suit Mrs Maybury, arrange the school-room, and digest the work the Correspondence School sends up. And get to know the children. How old are they?'

'Roberta is ten, Damien eight. Both very quick in the uptake, biddable but full of high spirits, and the baby, small Josselyn, must be eight or nine months. They've a new house on the estate. That was a must. It's very convenient. The schoolroom is at the old homestead—and, Miss Greenaway, if you've any super-efficient ideas about the specks of dust and blades of grass, forget them. The homestead is by no means redecorated yet, so don't turn up that Grecian nose at it.'

Automatically her hand went to her nose. 'Is it Grecian? I wouldn't know . . . and I think you'd better stop associating me with the cosmetics counter. Think of me as a high-country governess.'

Tristan snorted, 'Nat, no wonder you didn't go into drapery! In fact thank God you didn't. You're too tact-less. Here, the customer is always right. In a sense Miss Greenaway is your customer. She can take it or leave it. And if you keep on being off-putting like this I wouldn't expect her to attempt it.' He turned to Letitia. 'My dear, to be more business-like, you'll get your days off. True, you won't have your own transport, because that road in needs a four-wheel drive, but providing the weather's suitable, they're in and out to Queenstown reasonably often. Take several off-days together to give yourself a long weekend.'

Nathaniel roared, 'Sir . . . she'll be my employee, not yours! You can't help it, can you?'

Tristan disregarded him. 'There's a dear soul in Queens-town, Miss Mattie Clutterbone, which, as Gideon Darroch always says, sounds like something out of *Cranford*. She housekeeps a place there for the Mount Olivet family and oddly enough she's fond of Nathaniel. She'll see you get some breaks. Queenstown is a pretty lively place with its tourist attractions and cosmopolitan atmosphere, and I tell you what . . . It'll be best if you go all the way on Tuesday with Nat, to give you a chance to get to know each other, seeing he's avoided the cosmetics counter like the plague, but in a month or so I'll drive your car up, leave it at Miss Mattie's for you, and fly home. Give you a chance to explore the Lake District.'

His son gave an exasperated bellow of laughter. Looking at Letitia, he said, waving a hand at his father, 'Do you wonder I bury myself in the back of beyond? He's even trying to run *my* staff now! That's enough, sir. I admit it's a good idea, but stop bulldozing. Miss Greenaway and I will sort ourselves out. Now, Miss Greenaway, I'll take you out to dinner tonight and fill you in with the rest of it without your former boss butting in at every opportunity. I can see it's the only way.'

Letitia stood up. 'No, you won't take me to dinner tonight, Mr Nathaniel. *I* don't take kindly to being bull-dozed either. Did it ever occur to you you're a chip off the old block yourself? I'll be available in shop hours till I leave Saturday morning. I've a few private things to attend to in my spare time. Till then, and as your father said, we'll have time for discussion on the way up. I'll be ready any time, however early Tuesday morning. Now I must get back to my department.' And she swept out, Tristan's delighted and mischievous chuckle following her.

It wasn't till she was in bed that night that Letitia analysed her reasons for letting Nathaniel, in the first place, bull-doze her into accepting the position . . . *seemingly* let her objections be overruled. *She wanted to go. She wanted to have Nathaniel Pengelly eat his words.* He would never know she'd overheard, but she wanted him to completely reverse that devastating opinion of her. She seethed all over again at the memory. Artificial! An icicle! Looking like something out of a sheikh's harem! Make more mischief than a flock of *keas!* Couldn't imagine her on speaking terms with a grin but conceded she might manage a super-cilious smile! Grrrrr! Her blood pressure rose again at the thought.

But what stung most was his reception of his father's admittedly outrageous suggestion of her as a high-country wife. That detestable Nathaniel had averred that nothing could sugar the pill to make him consider that. What made that insufferable male imagine for a single instant he'd have had half a chance? Suddenly she giggled. Tristan really had been awful. Talk about Gothic! Though what he'd said also had been most disarming. What exactly had he said . . . ? He'd discovered within himself an odd tenderness for her. Yes, that was it. Older men certainly had something. They were articulate. Tristan's wife had been a wonderful woman, delightful to serve so that the whole staff loved her. She remembered Tristan saying shortly after she died, 'She was the one love of my life.' He hadn't minded saying that to someone who was, after all, just an employee.

Fleetingly Letitia remembered that for a few over-charged moments she had been sorry for Nathaniel who'd had to overhear, in company with a staff member he didn't even like, those revealing comments from Portia Latimer. She shook the thought away. He'd said far worse of her. She must remember every scathing comment he'd made and not soften towards him. Besides, *he was going to reverse every one*. She was going to make him recognise her as the stuff of which high-country wives were made. She was going to wipe out the impression he had of her as the head cosmetician of Pengelly's. Then, when she'd made herself indispensable or, at the very least, damned hard to replace, she'd wave an airy goodbye and seek some other high-country post. Not a derelict old homestead, but one of the famous ones. Then, and only then, would he be told he'd cooked his goose long before.

As she got ready for work next morning she grinned at her own reflection. It wouldn't be like that much longer. She swept up the last wayward strand of ash-blonde hair into its retaining Juliet band, sprayed the tendrils in front of her ears, made sure each eye matched for the shad-owing, inspected her nails, touched one up yet again with that new shell-colour with the hint of violet, plucked another couple of hairs from her left eyebrow. She made a face at herself. It would be wonderful to have her hair free again, the wind stirring through it as she rode. She hoped there would be horses up there. Oh, there must. Some mustering might have to be done on foot, but the lowlands on horseback, surely. Well, there were some shocks ahead of Mr Nathaniel Pengelly.

Her resolve was so iron-hard, so much occupying her conscious thoughts that it was with surprise she experienced a moment of real magic when she said goodbye to Tristan on the Saturday closing hour. The staff had given her a farewell the evening before, the late-night opening. Letitia had expected that Tristan, as usual, would have given a generous donation to the staff's parting gift. But now he called her into the *Sanctum Sanctorum* and motioned her to a chair. At that moment the door opened to admit Nathaniel. He looked surprised to see Letitia there. He said, 'You wanted me now, sir? Or should I come back later?'

'No, sit down.' Tristan took a book from his drawer. It was beautifully bound in soft blue leather and was Palgrave's *Golden Treasury* of verse. Letitia saw, as he handed it to her, low down on the right-hand lower corner, engraved in gilt, 'Letitia Greenaway'. She gave a cry of delight, and an unorthodox exclamation escaped her, 'Oh, you old sweetie! My school copy is so old and so much read it's falling to pieces. How could you know?'

'Saw you reading it once, in your lunch hour. Nancy, Nat and James's mother, loved her Palgrave's *Treasury*. She always kept it by our bed. She used to read bits out.'

Letitia rose swiftly in a spontaneous gesture, crossed to him and bent, kissed first one cheek, then the other. Then she said, in a bewildered tone, 'I—I could never, when I was a raw junior, have imagined myself kissing my boss. But it's the only way to thank you properly.' The shine of unshed tears glimmered for a moment. She steadied herself, said, 'I do hope you've inscribed it to mark the occasion.' She opened it and saw he had, but next moment was staring at a very generous cheque. She bit her lip, overcome. Tristan, pink with pleasure, said, 'You deserve every bit of it, lass, for the past years, *and* for going up to The Wilderness.' Then he looked roguish again. 'And your method of thanking me makes me feel like long-ago Leigh Hunt in that volume.'

Letitia wrinkled her brow, thought. Nathaniel might just as well not have been there. Then her brow cleared. 'Got it! Thank you. The age of chivalry and all that. I think I'd better go. I'm having trouble with my tear-ducts. Thank you and goodbye. You'll be picking me up at eight-thirty, Mr Nathaniel? Goodbye till then,' and she flashed out.

Letitia had a busy weekend tying up the ends. She kept her heart hardened against Mr Nathaniel. She wouldn't let herself look forward gladly to this new experience. It was to be merely a stepping-stone to other places. She owed it to these Maybury children to stay a year, that would be all.

On Saturday night as usual she went to Knox Church. It did something to restoring her tranquillity . . . that is, except for one sentence in the last prayer when the minister prayed for himself and for his people, 'Deliver us, O God, from triviality of thought, poverty of desire, waywardness of spirit and meanness of motive.'

Meanness of motive? That came uncomfortably close to the bone. Perhaps it *was* mean to long for Nathaniel Pengelly to be forced to eat his words? But then, she began to excuse herself, it was only natural to want him to admit she wasn't artificial, to find out she had what it took for the high-country. To find out too that she was no icicle! Wow! She shied away from what that implied. She had been misjudged, she thought hurriedly, misunderstood . . . anger rose within her, swamping the truth in that prayer . . . *save us from meanness of motive.*

The sweetest triumph of all, of course, would be to have him fall for her, head over heels, to have him *beg* her to marry him. The absurdity of it struck her as she drove home. No likelihood of that. Poetic justice didn't often happen as it had when they had overheard Portia Latimer's unconsidered words. Letitia shut her mind to that. It was enough to be going to the high-country. Roll on, Tuesday morning!

It was Monday morning, however, when Nathaniel Pengelly unlatched a gate surrounded by trees in a quiet

Maori Hill street. Quite charming. There was a glimpse of a grey-gabled house beyond lawns to the right. An immense and shady oak towered over him to the left. A loud, impatient young voice above him said, 'For goodness' sake, Betty, let yourself go. What a dill you are! I never dreamed you'd be so chicken. It's no height. Gosh, you ought to have taken that Outward Bound course at Anikawa. It's no place for greenhorns where you're going. After all, there's no river below you here and this rope would hold a battleship. If you don't go I'll push you off, so help me . . . *there* . . . !'

The next minute Mr Nathaniel Pengelly got a fearful whack in the chest, something gripped round his waist in a convulsive scissor movement . . . somebody's legs, he thought . . . there was a piercing female scream and then he was flat on his back on the path with the demon attacker on top of him. Instinctively his hands came up, he grabbed a pair of shoulders, pushed at them and said windedly, 'What the hell——?'

The figure sat bolt upright, astride him, yelled out, 'Now look what you've done, Tim! I could have killed this person.'

Nathaniel, dazed, surveyed the face above him, shiny, freckled, with a fringe of slanting ash-blonde hair across green eyes that were somehow familiar, and gasped, 'Are you a young sister of Letitia's, for goodness' sake?'

The eyes surveyed him, widened, looked unbelieving, then the voice gasped, 'Mr Nathaniel! No, of course not. I *am* Letitia. What's the matter with you?'

He blinked, put up a hand as if to clear his vision, said, 'I can't be seeing straight. But anyway, that voice said, "Betty".'

She was still gazing at him unbelievingly, but she said scornfully, 'Not Betty. *Letty.* I'm never called Letitia outside business hours.'

He said feebly, although accusingly, 'And you've got freckles. How could I recognise you? And what have you done to your hair?'

'Cut it, that's all. Hate it long. That style needs a hair-dresser right on hand. And as for freckles, that's what cosmetics are all about—to hide blemishes. But look . . . don't let's carry on like this. Are you all right? Tim gave me a terrific push. You could have concussion, or a slipped disc or something.'

He said, 'I've got skinned elbows, that I do know, but I doubt I've suffered any serious damage.'

A voice from up the tree said uncertainly, 'Then is it safe to come down? I mean you won't clock me one, will you . . . er . . . sir?'

'No. Letitia, if you'd stop straddling me, I'd try to get up.'

She went scarlet and scrambled up. 'Well, you see, I couldn't take it in. That I'd hit someone and that that someone was you. Sorry. That's why I didn't get off right away.'

He grinned. 'Oh, don't apologise for that. It wasn't unpleasant. But tell me, do you mean you'd rather have laid someone else out?'

She said helplessly, 'Yes. At least . . . no. Oh, I don't know. What sort of a question is that? *Are* you hurt?'

He turned over and sprang up, lithely enough, dusted himself down, rubbed each elbow in turn, said, 'I think I'm all in one piece, but I've sure lost some skin.' His hands came away red and blood began to drip on to his tan-coloured shorts.

Letitia began to utter squawks of dismay. She grabbed at his hands to hold them away from his clothes. 'Come on up to the house and I'll mop you up and put plasters on. Timothy, you'd better scoot ahead and get the first-aid box out from under the bathroom basin.'

A boy of about eleven dropped to the ground and wasted no time getting ahead of them. Nathaniel said, 'Not your brother? Oh, no, didn't Dad say the rest of the family are in Britain?'

'Just the boy next door. I go tramping with his parents a lot. I've known him since he was in nappies.' Tim turned round and glared at her.

Nathaniel chuckled. 'What an untactful speech! Girls are the limit, aren't they, Tim? Especially to a doughty warrior of the Outward Bound School. Do you mind telling me what it was in aid of?'

Tim dropped back. 'Well, I thought when she was going away up into the boo-hai, she'd better learn a thing or two, sort of crash survival course. Like if she got marooned away up in the hills and the stream was too deep to wade through because there was a flash flood, she'd better know how to cross it by swinging on a rope from a tree, but she got all scared on me, and hadn't the guts to let herself go. It was a good practice idea if only you hadn't arrived.'

'I'll endorse that,' said Nathaniel devoutly. 'Well, thanks for your good work. Letitia, you must never go exploring without a rope coiled round your waist.'

As they reached the door Tim produced a doubtful-looking handkerchief from his pocket and clapped it on one elbow and told Nathaniel to use his for the other. 'Only because Letty's got the house really up to the mark and won't want you dripping blood all over. The tenants move in tonight. She's spending it at our place. I'll miss her. She's not always such a duffer—in fact she's pretty good for a girl. Yours must be a beaut place. I know you couldn't have me in what's left of these hols, but I wouldn't mind coming up in May if it's not too much cheek?'

'Timothy!' wailed Letitia. To her relief her boss simply said, 'It would be a great idea if you're prepared to buckle in. No time for tourists at The Wilderness.'

Tim was nonchalant. 'Thanks. Jolly good of you, seeing we scuppered you in the gateway. I say you aren't a haemophil—phil—something, are you? I've never seen anyone bleed as much.'

'Haemophiliac? No, sorry about that. Nothing so exciting. I'm sure you'd have been slapping tourniquets on right, left, and centre. Blood always looks more than the same quantity of water. Because it's red, I suppose.'

Tim conceded the point. 'That's interesting. Pity we couldn't measure it.'

Letitia said severely, 'That sounds callous. Run some water in the basin, tip some disinfectant in and while I'm dabbling, hand down the iodine.'

Nathaniel said hastily, 'The disinfectant will do, thanks.'

She sighed. 'Men are cowards when it comes to iodine. But it's going on just the same. A friend arrived yesterday afternoon with some horse manure. He tipped the wheelbarrow over on the path. Have you had an up-to-date tetanus injection? Oh, all right. Otherwise I was going to whisk you off to Out-patients.'

He said sourly, 'I thought *I* was the boss.' Then his eye gleamed. 'As soon as you're finished, *Letitia for Loveliness,* you're going to take my seat and it's you for the iodine. You've grazed your knee.'

She had ancient denim shorts on. She said crossly, 'It's only a shaving of skin, not a speck of blood.'

Tim giggled, 'Letty, he means business. Better let him.'

The plaster fixed, she said, 'What brings you here today?'

'I wondered if maybe we could start after lunch *today.* I've got a bit of business in Alexandra, and it'll be dark when we get to Queenstown, so we'd stay the night, but it would give us an early start tomorrow and I could get there in time to help Owen with the dagging. No pressure; if you can't make it, okay, but——?'

Here was a chance to show him she could take changes in plans. 'Yes, no problem. Tim's mother could hand over the keys to the tenants and she's going to garage my car till your father brings it to Queenstown. Of course only if you approve of him doing that. I could be ready by one-thirty. How about that? Would that give you time for your call at Alex? But you must have a coffee after that fall, then I'd be glad if you clear off. I'll scamper through the rest of the chores. Tim'll help.'

'Is there anything I can do?'

She considered that. 'M'm. I've some stuff to go to my cousin's at Macandrew Bay. His wife will be at home. It would save a fair bit of time. She wouldn't keep you chatting as long.'

Nathaniel departed with two trunks in his station wagon and several cartons. When he'd gone Tim said in a tone of great respect, 'Crumbs, you don't half order him round. He's your boss!'

She said briefly, 'He's in a cleft stick. Governesses are as scarce as hens' teeth. I've got him exactly where I want him.'

Tim looked surprised. 'Whaddye mean? Where *do* you want him?'

'That'd be telling. Dancing to my piping will be the least of it.'

Tim positively stared. Letitia said, 'Now, I've got to hustle. Sorry our day is cut short, but you've got a choice: either you go home now or you help me finish packing. Then I'll ring the tenants in case they want to see me today now I'm going earlier. I want to be ready and waiting for his high-and-mightiness.'

She was, even though Nathaniel was ahead of time. He raised his brows at the luggage neatly strapped on the porch. 'I came early in case you needed a hand, but it looks as if you don't.'

She said crisply, 'Don't think those are all clothes. Four cartons are books and heavy. I've no idea how well-stocked the schoolroom is and in any case I'd feel lost without some of these.'

He nodded approval. 'Do you happen to ski?'

'No, why? It's too expensive a sport.'

'Just that I was going to say bring your gear if you did. We don't have to go to Coronet Peak. We can ski round our own paddocks and hills at times during winter. There are plenty skis at The Wilderness and it won't cost you a penny. All part of the life.'

She couldn't help sparkling. 'Best way ever to learn, as a necessity rather than a sport. I'm not in the least competitive.'

He looked at her keenly. 'Do you mean you prefer being a loner to being in team sports?'

'Not really.' Her voice had an edge to it. 'That makes me sound as if I can't work in with people. I was thinking of the drapery world, the bit I didn't like. Scanning the papers every day to see what the other firms were offering, trying to be one jump ahead of the other fellow. Cutting prices where possible. Timing sales to get in first. Even

spending part of one's dinner-hour checking on rivals'
windows. Analysing dropping sales, or surges. I'd rather
far be doing necessary things as part of existence. I know
the other's vital to business and to some it's the breath of
life——' She stopped.

Nathaniel pulled a face. 'Say it. As it is to my father.
Yet I'm glad he enjoys it. His life since we lost Mother
would be so empty otherwise. He thrives on competition.'

For a moment that understanding comment weakened
the animosity Letitia felt towards this man. The next she
resented that weakening. She bent to pick up two cases and
began loading them. The station wagon bore every sign of
rough country usage, yet he'd said they always left it at
Drumlogie. He had two cases himself, but there was a huge
box labelled Pengelly's, piled with winter jerseys, slacks,
pullovers, socks, all in their polythene wrappers. He
gestured. 'Couldn't stop Dad piling those in, for the staff
family. Said it would help keep them contented in the wop-
wops. There's some there for you and whatever happens
don't turn it down. Have you delivered the keys?
Good . . . then Wilderness here we come!'

They headed out on the Main South Road, leaving the
steep hills of Dunedin behind them but running through
rolling country, to the left here and there a glimpse of the
curving bays of the Pacific, on the right the narrow Taieri
Plains, the airport control tower silhouetted against the
contours of the Maungatuas. They crossed the Taieri and
Waihola Rivers, curved close to Lake Waihola, its grey
waters so different from the blue snow-fed waters of the
lakes they would come to in the west against the mountains, after they struck off at right angles past Milton. Here,
on this hot January day, children paddled in canoes at the
grey water's edge and speed-boats carved shimmering white
lines in their wakes, with water-skiers braced behind them.

Till now the hills had been green and lush, for the
summer near the coast had been blessed with generous
rainfall, but after turning west they took on the familiar
lion-gold of Central Otago. Through Lawrence, girdled
with trees and ribboned with the rainbow colours of wild
lupins, its streets still reminiscent of the gold-rush days

when every second building was a tavern. Now it dreamed sleepily, and encouraged tourists with those buildings turned into pottery studios, art shops, souvenir shops.

At Beaumont they had their first glimpse of a river that had truly caught the refracted light crystals from melted snows back in those towering mountains beyond, and swirled round its rugged islands of water-worn rocks in the true peacock-greeny-blue of the roaring Clutha. The road, of course, was determined largely by the course of the river and the contours of the hills, taking mostly the easiest way through, with here and there evidences of man's desire to shorten the miles by carving through formidable bluffs. There were already honesty stalls at the orchard gates with early plums displayed, a few peaches. Lashings of cherries, strawberries, boysenberries, raspberries and tomatoes. Not many apples yet.

Nathaniel said, 'I'll buy a modest amount of berries nearer home. If I take too much, Hope and Jamesina will wear themselves out jam-making and preserving.'

'Jamesina? That's an unusual name. You mean Mrs Forbes, your housekeeper?'

'Yes, and I'd better warn you, she likes the full name, doesn't like to be called Jamesy or Jamie. Yet she likes the children to use her Christian name. She's getting on but scared stiff anyone realises it. In fact, if she wasn't so keen on covering up her age, we'd never guess there was anything to hide. She hasn't a grey hair. It's still a shining brown.'

'That doesn't mean a thing. She probably tints it.'

His laugh was pure derision. 'There speaks *Letitia for Loveliness!* Not Jamesina. She wouldn't be on even speaking terms with hair tint. And she's still got the English complexion my father vows she had when he knew her thirty years ago.'

Letitia didn't dare say that too could come out of a box. She felt if he was going to make a habit of referring to her by her counter name, she'd probably grind her teeth down like an aged ewe's!

He continued, 'She lost Sam, her husband, about fifteen years ago, when they were farming at Glenorchy. In her first years at the Head of the Lake, of course, there wasn't even a road, just the steamer. Her family wouldn't hear of her staying up there in what was still relative isolation, so brought her down to Queenstown and she bought a retirement unit. Nearly drove her mad. So she took to going to certain sheep-stations she knew well to give them a hand at busy times. Bit of luck for me to get her as a housekeeper. She's in her element. Her own boss, a free hand.'

'Poor Jamesina! She mightn't appreciate another woman in the house. I'll keep myself out of her way as much as possible. Pity the married couple's place isn't big enough to take me.'

His reaction was to snort. 'Break it down! You're surely not as naïve as that. Worst thing possible for a married couple to have someone like you in the house. Hope and Owen are an ideal couple and I want it to stay that way. You mightn't be exactly Jamesina's type, but I'm sure this is the lesser of two evils.'

She said calmly, 'You put things so charmingly. You're doing nothing for my confidence. I'd be a danger to the married couple's bliss and an irritation to the housekeeper. Tell me, why do you think I've let my freckles appear and chopped my hair off? Isn't it because I don't want to apear the *femme fatale* you persist in regarding me as?'

To her chagrin he burst out laughing. 'A few more remarks like that and I won't regard you as a menace; you're about as blunt as Mrs Forbes herself!' He continued to chuckle.

She said, 'And I've no doubt that on reflection you'll begin to wonder if two blunt people could possibly get on. I'll make myself as unobtrusive as possible in every way. You said my room was at the schoolroom end. Good, I'll spend as much time there as I can. Though I'm prepared to help with dishes and a few chores in my spare time so the aforesaid housekeeper doesn't feel she has to wait on me. Heavens, this is a sort of *Upstairs, Downstairs* situation. In all the Victorian novels I'm so fond of, there was always trouble between the governess and the servants. And by the same token she wasn't on an equality with the family!'

It didn't even dent his complacency. He said, 'This is fascinating. Never in my wildest dreams could I have imagined having such a conversation with *Letitia for Loveliness*.'

She said, between her teeth, 'Evidently Mrs Forbes is free to state her preference for what she's called. So I'll insist on that too. I don't want you calling me that again, and certainly not at The Wilderness, or Hope Maybury won't see me as a freckle-faced governess who likes the high-country life, she'll see me as a threat. She needn't even know I was a cosmetician. Just that I was behind the counter in your father's shop. The years I *liked* at the shop were spent in the babylinen and children's wear departments. I'm a run-of-the-mill shopgirl who once aspired to teaching and am partly qualified. I'm to be known as Letty. Now, tell me where we're spending the night?'

'Just past Queenstown, my dear Letty. On the Gorge Road, at Drumlogie, the guest house I told you of, where our track leads off into the wild back country. It's run by the Adairs and the Logies. They're giving us dinner in their private quarters so we won't have to go across to the restaurant. That's run by Chris and Kirsty Adair, Stella's son and daughter-in-law. When I rang I also asked Stella to let them know at home that we'll be in earlier on Tuesday than we first thought. I couldn't get them myself. Stella said there was a fault on their line. Probably a tree down, but the department would fix it as soon as they find it. I hate that. It happens with snow sometimes but rarely in summer. The telephone is our life-line in times of emergency. I guess it'll be on again by the time we get there.'

Letty was glad they were back on less personal exchanges. She said, 'Isn't Alexandra beautiful with that pinkish haze all over the otherwise bare rock faces, with the wild thyme? Oh, look, the herb-gatherers are out. And look at the gardens. Before a township sprang up here it must have been all bare pitiless rocks above the bright river. Grand in its own way, I suppose, but almost like a

desert. The winds must have whistled across here devastatingly.'

Nathaniel nodded. 'The desert. Dad would agree with
you. He once said the hills around here . . . mountains
really . . . reminded him of the barren rocks of Aden,
then added that man had made it blossom like the rose.
The colours in these gardens almost hurt the eyes.'

He drew up at the civic buildings, fronted by glorious
trees, said, 'I won't be very long. Perhaps you could browse
round the library.'

Soon they were through the town, threading through
groves of pines, and in six short miles were at Clyde, at the
entrance to the Cromwell Gorge where the immense scars
of the dam-building grooved into the hillsides and massive
concrete structures dropped down below them.

'They've made a Lookout with a viewing platform; care
to see it?' asked Nathaniel.

'Yes, very much if you've time. I'm not here to sightsee.'

'Oh, a pity to miss it at this stage, with those tractors
below looking like matchbox cars. You can't help a pang
at the thought of all that beautiful orchard-land for ever
below the waters, and some properties, generations old,
having to be relinquished. But I suppose all that power
must be harnessed. Hard, though, to view it objectively.
Imagine how I'd feel if my property was taken over for
something like this, or even turned into a tourist attraction
of some kind. They'll landscape the surrounds, of course,
and if they make it as beautiful as the man-made lake at
Benmore, we could grow to appreciate it. We'll have a cup
of coffee here. I picked up a flask and sandwiches at the
shop when I said goodbye to Dad. If we stop at a café it'll
take too long with so many tourists about.'

On again through the Gorge, and across the old bridge
spanning the confluence of the Kawarau and the Clutha,
one draining Lake Wakatipu, the other Lake Wanaka,
knowing a natural pang of regret that soon this remarkable feature of two rivers running so swiftly they didn't
mingle till well downstream would also lie submerged with
so many buildings that belonged to the old gold-mining
days of the Junction. The division was most apparent

today, because the Wanaka area must have had rain, and the water from there was discoloured.

When they turned into the steep-sided Kawarau Gorge they were into more awesome scenery, the Roaring Meg's waters and the Gentle Annie's pouring from the heights above, disappearing under the road, to mingle with the white water that made the jet-boating such a thrill. Across the Battling Betty bridge, named for the engineer's wife, and then beyond gentle tree-rimmed Lake Hayes, crossing the Shotover River to run beside Wakatipu, the Trough-of-the-Goblin, the Water-Swallower, to enter the incredible alpine beauty of Queenstown, nestled in a triangle between great shoulders of mountains, with beautifully sculpted mountains on the far side of the sapphire waters, and downlake the vertical and jagged peaks of the Remarkables, the New Zealand Dolomites in appearance. Back against the seemingly uncaring heights of the little town were the less beautiful heights of high-rise accommodation. God send they kept them back from the more Lilliputian charm of the lower houses clustered round Queenstown Bay.

They didn't linger but swept through, turned right, went over the Shotover again at the Edith Cavell Bridge at Arthur's Point where much gold had once been found, then, before they reached the road up to the famous Coronet Peak of skiing fame, they swung left under a rustic rough-barked gateway that said, *Drumlogie*.

CHAPTER THREE

DRUMLOGIE was a blaze of colour against the tawny hills; this was how loving attention and watering and judicious planting could put plus-marks to existing beauty. Geraniums blazed under the eaves, and the garden that looked like a creation of a landscaper wasn't really, Nathaniel informed Letitia, but was merely a case of each generation following the natural contours of the land and partly covering the myriad outcroppings of rock on the hillside with hardy creepers and iceplants. In the pockets of soil on the terraces that looked like something out of a village in Provence, richer soil had been built up, out of which foamed pools of aubrietia, spilling over into blue and purple cascades, and above them waved a mass of lark-spur, delphiniums, cornflowers blue and rose-coloured, and great bushes of daisies white and yellow were starred with bloom, and pink shastas, and everywhere dahlias splashed oriental colours.

The stones of the hillsides had been formed into steps tempting feet to wander and explore through rough-barked *manuka* arches, covered with fragrant roses, and pinks spread clove-like scent. There were trees in every hollow, that would make autumn vividly gold and russet: oaks, birches, poplars, liquidambars, maples, sumacs and scores of poplars.

Letty forgot her enmity and said, 'Oh, Mr Nathaniel, please stop! I can't bear to rush through it, it seems criminal. Oh, let me drink it in.'

He glanced at her sideways as he halted. She wasn't aware of him at all, right then. She stepped out, swept the whole scene with her eyes, lingered on certain features, lips parted, delight in every part of her.

Happy sounds of children's laughter came from a play area, dogs barked, hens clucked contentedly, and through it all birdsong lilted, mingling with the silver sound of a small hidden stream.

Over to the right a boy of about seven leapt on to a huge rock, lifted up his arms and cried exultantly, 'I'm the king of the castle!' There was sheer joy in it. Letty's answering laugh held that joy too. She turned, got in, and said in the most natural tone, 'I hope that child remembers this moment all his life, whatever time does to him. There was all happiness in that sound.' Then she coloured up. 'You'll think me a sentimental twit!'

He said, 'Don't spoil it. I hope so, too,' then he added, 'Someday I hope to restore my place to something approaching this. It will take time, but I believe Ellen Nathaniel created great beauty on my—her—hillsides. I must cast about for a wife with green fingers.'

Letty looked away. She'd have liked to say something provocative like, 'How about settling for a governess who loves gardening?' but she mustn't be too obvious.

They ran the car into a row of carports. He must be here often and welcome. 'It looks as if the guests are at dinner,' he gestured to the restaurant. 'Good. That means we'll have the others to ourselves. We'll go to the house.'

Half-way there they were met by hastening figures, the older ones, Stella and Rob Adair, and Giles, Stella's nephew who farmed the property, and Lucinda his wife, who was responsible for most of the gardening. There was kissing all round. Nathaniel was evidently a favourite. Letty felt slightly dazed—could this be the unapproachable boss's son who disliked the shop and especially her department?

Lucinda, with peaty-brown eyes and dark hair, chuckled. 'Letty, you'll find us overwhelming. We're all extroverts here . . . sort of exuberant and effervescent. But it's nice to have friends, not just guests.'

Giles, a tawny man much Nathaniel's type, grinned. 'Effervescent? You make us sound like fruit salts, my love! Don't worry, Letty, Rob and I scarcely fizz at all. Neither does Chris. You'll find it's our womenfolk who do that. They rush round as if one lifetime's too short to cram everything in, but they'll have a darned good try. One of these days, Nat, we'll take off and land up at your place to give ourselves a chance to simmer down.' He cocked an eye at Letty.

She grinned. 'I detect a note of pride, nevertheless. I think you love them like this.'

Stella sparkled. 'That marks you for a kindred soul. Oh, how lovely, you may be as mad as us. It makes life such fun.'

Letty glowed. 'I hope so. I've always wanted an adventurous life in the back of beyond and haven't achieved it till now.'

'What did you do? I mean where did you teach?'

Letty hesitated because Nathaniel had started to speak, then stopped. Then she said, 'That was my first ambition, but my training was interrupted when my dad died, so I worked for Mr Nathaniel's father. For years.' She'd kill Mr Nathaniel if he mentioned what department.

He caught on. 'She liked the children's department best. If she couldn't teach 'em, she dressed 'em. You'll notice she can't get out of the habit of calling me Mr Nathaniel. But it won't last in the atmosphere of The Wilderness.'

Stella said, 'Well, come in, the meal's all ready. It's so simple to entertain here. We just go across to the restaurant, pick out what we want, and keep it hot or cold as desired.'

It seemed Lucinda and Giles had two children: Kenneth, three, and Marguerite, just a year. They'd had nursery tea and were now bedded down, fast asleep, 'Worn out with a day of their usual deviltry,' said Giles, albeit proudly. Talk flowed and for the first time Letty began to unwind. These folk didn't see her as an artificial creature and didn't know Nathaniel was taking her to his estate only because governesses were an endangered species and he'd had to take what he could get.

She was surprised to know that at this distance from Queenstown, they could get a view of the lake from behind the house. It was known as the Half-Million-Dollar View because it was half as high as the famed Million-Dollar View. 'But ours has something the Million-Dollar hasn't,' said Giles Logie, and his eye flickered meaningly towards his wife for a fraction of a second. Lucinda nodded, warmth in her voice. 'Of course. *Our* view can be seen from the Moon-Gate. It looks across to my favourite view of all, to Walter Peak. It's so classical a peak. Lovely by day, beautiful by starlight and by moonlight, sheer enchantment. Goodness . . . didn't that sound poetical? And all about you as you walk through the Moon-Gate is Giles's father's night garden . . . all white flowers. Angus, my father-in-law, isn't an extrovert like his son. He's rather inarticulate, so he said it with flowers for his own Marguerite.'

'A Moon-Gate?' said Letty. 'I've never heard of one, much less seen one. Could it be circular, in a wall?'

Giles nodded. 'I'm glad you're staying the night, Letty. There's a long twilight at present down here, but we never go to bed early. You can go through when most of the guests have retired.' He turned to Nathaniel. 'It's a must, Nat. You'll want to grapple this *rara avis*, a real live governess, to The Wilderness with hooks of steel . . . '

Letty and Nathaniel stared at him. He answered the look. 'It's this legend, you know. A legend all Moon-Gates have. If you see the moon through it, it casts a spell upon you and you never leave the lake again.' He added hastily, 'Of course if it's a Moon-Gate in a desert oasis, then you never leave the mysterious east.'

Lucinda tried not to laugh as she saw Nathaniel's suspicious look and Letty's disbelieving one, but it burst out of her. 'Your memory's failing you, Giles. When you first told me that, it had to be a full moon because I'd seen it through the Moon-Gate at the full.'

Giles pulled a face at her. 'Now you've spoiled it. I couldn't remember whether it had to be full or not and what's happening to the moon at the moment.'

Lucinda said severely, 'What you really mean is you can't remember what you said the night you invented the legend.'

He grinned. 'Well, you fell for it . . . and for me . . . so who cares? All legends have got to start somewhere.'

Stella said, 'Now Letty knows we're all mad. But seriously, Letty, The Wilderness needs you. The wife of anyone employed up there wouldn't stay if she had to teach three children as well as run her own house and garden. Hope is marvellous, but it will make it much more probable that Nat's got a permanent couple there if Letty stays.'

Lucinda said, 'Whereas that cunning Giles wanted a girl-gardener to take that chore off his aunt's shoulder's.'

Rob Adair looked up from his roast beef. 'I beg to differ. Giles wanted a wife.'

There was an odd silence as if the same idea had hit all of them. Letty said coolly, spearing a piece of roast pumpkin, 'Well, a governess would suit Mr Nathaniel much better than a wife. Governesses are hard to come by. I think, though, I'll keep away from the Moon-Gate. I'd like a varied experience of high-country life. South Canterbury appeals to me. Perhaps a year or two here, then off to some place like Dragonshill, or Thor's Hill, or Craigievar. The ones that haven't even an access track really appeal. The ones you have to cross a river to reach. Now that would be *really* adventuresome.'

Nathaniel's voice was dry. 'There speaks one who's been behind a city counter all her life! My dear Letitia, I think you'd be wise to try our brand of the wop-wops first.'

There was quite an edge to Letty's tongue. 'Poor Mr Nathaniel, he can't get over the fact I was behind a counter when we first met. Shopgirls didn't register with him as having other ambitions, other skills. So he thinks I might prove the new broom that sweeps clean and that at the first frightening encounter with the dangers of the solitudes, I'll head back to the sound of cash-registers.'

They stared, then Stella said quickly, 'It's a wonder Mr Pengelly allowed you to carry her off, Nat.'

Nathaniel shrugged. 'Allowed? He suggested it! Oh, not to get rid of her. I don't want to put Letty down at all, even if she deserves it for a remark like that, but she'd already given in notice intending to try for a position like this. So he suggested she came to my property and, being a dutiful son, I agreed.'

Lucinda's eyes were slits of mirth. 'I'd guess that so much compliance rocked Tristan. He'd think it was out of character.'

Nathaniel grinned, conceding that, looked teasingly at his new employee and said, 'Scarcity of applicants. I snapped her up.'

Robin Adair chuckled. 'Well, if you're already on these devastating terms of candour, you'll probably do well together. Nat, in time to come, say Easter, how about working in with us on a new venture? We're thinking of starting pony-trekking and yours would be an adventurous sort of place to take them to. It wouldn't involve you in any entertaining. They'd take packed lunches, but there could be something in it for you. A basic charge. I know it's a bit far for a return trip by your mule-track—so called—both ways, but after a bit of sightseeing round your estate, say showing them a bit of dog-handling, or tailing or dagging, whatever was seasonable, they could make their way through Big Slip by your bridle-path, and from there it's not much more than a dozen miles on that road to Queenstown.'

The tawny eyes lit up, and Nathaniel dashed his hand through his hair, a mannerism Letty had noticed in the shop. Then, it was usually when faced with an irate customer. It had indicated puzzlement, she had thought. Now it denoted eagerness. 'That'd be splendid, Rob. Knowing how you organise things, I know it would be well conducted. We farmers are getting instructions all the time to diversify, but in the main that means variety of stock or crops; this is something the red-tape wallahs haven't come up with. Sure . . . in the light of changing markets and regulations, anything's welcome.'

Rob said slowly, 'To be fair to the Powers That Be, this is more to do with the Tourist Department than the Department of Agriculture. They're pretty well on their toes. Not a bad idea to combine both, like us, with Giles in charge of the farming, us with the guests. You'll do all right with the deer. I know the cost's heavy to buy them in, and put up the high fences, but I've an idea that some of the farmers nearer the coast who'd like to invest in deer might like to have you, and a few others, pasture some for them. Some of your land, further out, if fenced, could be ideal. Think about it. I know you can't afford to buy too many yourself.'

It seemed strange to Letty to hear that a son of Pengelly's couldn't afford to buy in stock. Nathaniel must have a fair hump of pride not to let his father finance him. He seemed very determined to be independent. So he was hardly likely to take his father's advice when he wanted a wife. Her moments of eavesdropping humiliation washed over her again. Because she was going to have a determined try at making him desire her. Oh, what a sweet moment it would be when she spurned him. Instantly that wretched phrase flashed into her mind . . . *meanness of motive*. Equally instantly she rejected it. It wasn't just cheap revenge she wanted. She wanted his respect as a girl who could take the high-country solitary existence, who had what was needed for isolation. There . . . a much more admirable motive!

She realised that night that the world of Drumlogie was entirely different from the world she would find at journey's end. This was so cosmopolitan. They were having one of their drawing-room evenings—these were noted for the old-time entertainments of last century. How gifted musically this family was! Robin was a fine singer with a repertoire of Scots songs, Stella accompanying him. Lucinda sat at a spinning-wheel, spinning, while Giles sang an appropriate song that Chris, Lucinda's half-brother, had set to music; Kirsty, his wife, gave some charming monologues.

Letty knew a fierce envy. What a family! All together and here she was, quite alone in New Zealand, save for her cousin at Macandrew Bay. She looked up at Nathaniel, sitting beside her on the arm of a couch. 'What a united family. They give an aura of happiness. It's enviable.'

Nathaniel spoke in a low tone, under cover of the chat that had broken out. She was amazed at his perception.

He said, 'Because your mother and the twins are thirteen thousand miles away?'

She nodded. He said, 'You'd have a lot in common with Lucinda. Her state when she came here wasn't dissimilar. Her mother and stepfather were missionaries in India. They were drowned, rescuing villagers from flood waters. She has a twin sister and brother too. They were, still are, both in England. She came here seeking a family relationship and found heartbreak instead. Until, in God's good time, all knots were unravelled. Life's got a habit of unravelling the knots, Stella said once. And Stella ought to know. She's a survivor.'

Letty experienced the strangest emotion. Could this be the man who had despised her speaking? She couldn't look up at him. She said, rather shamedly, 'We speak out of ignorance, sometimes, but thank you for telling me, Mr Nathaniel.'

There was no opportunity to say more. The evening was too full of other people. The hour grew late. Presently Letitia, when tea and cake had been served, said, 'I believe you want an early start, Mr Nathaniel. I'll away to my room. It's such a charming one, with lashings of books I'd like to be let loose amongst for a month!'

Stella, overhearing, said, 'You must take a dozen or so with you. No libraries up there! Actually, Giles's grand-father was given some of them from The Wilderness when the property was sold. I've a feeling that when Nat gets more shelves built they ought to go back. But aren't you going through the Moon-Gate first? Nat would take you. I know you'll be back, but there mightn't be a moon next time.'

Letitia said lightly, 'I'll risk that. I'm tired, and the thought of those books draws me like a magnet. Good-night, all.'

She certainly didn't want to go wandering in the gloam-ing—or moonlight—with Nathaniel. She mustn't appear too eager, and it was noticeable that he hadn't seconded the idea.

By the time she had poked around the fascinating titles she came wide awake. She put aside the ones she would

take with her and walked to the window to close the
curtains because the moon was shining in with a white
intensity almost as bright as day. There were still lights on
in the restaurant and the standard lamps in the hillside
garden added more brilliance. Kirsty had pointed out the
path that led to the white flower-garden.

She couldn't resist going. She'd changed into a white
frock for dinner, a simple crêpey summer dress with a
girdle of blue beads linked with silver chains. She picked
up a soft white woollen stole in case it was cooler outside
now. It wasn't, even among the mountains. The air was
balmy.

She went through the copsy patch where so many trees
and flowers of other countries grew that they called it *The
United Nations' Garden,* on through the larch grove where
the moonlight spilled through on to whitened stepping-
stones, then round a tiny conical hill. Must be herbs
growing here, the aromas came up to her. How idyllic! She
turned a bend and there, like a frame round a circular
picture, was the Moon-Gate, set in a stone wall that barred
the way.

She halted, loath to step through to possibly mar the
symmetry of that view. It was sheer perfection. Could it be
any lovelier through there?

A voice behind her said, 'Don't you want to go through?
It's quite safe.' Nathaniel's.

'No, it's ridiculous. It's so exquisite I felt reluctant to go
on in case it was less beautiful through there.'

'It isn't. It's beauty-plus because Angus's flowers add
something to a hillside that was just bare tussock till he
turned it into a night-garden for his Marguerite, Giles's
mother. Many are perfumed.'

It was imperative to go on then. A breeze earlier had
scattered white rose-petals on the ground. Naturally there
were white marguerites with dark centres, white petunias,
the cerastium that was called snow-in-summer, white pinks,
springing from every crevice, alyssum foaming over the
rocks, nameless little alpine flowers brought down from the
heights in Angus's haversack, and, as Nathaniel stooped

to show her, clumps of edelweiss.

But one's eyes were drawn upwards and outwards. Above the lights that sequinned a peninsula that jutted out into the dark waters were the jagged outlines of the Remarkables, and opposite Walter Peak and Cecil Peak and others unnamed to her yet. The great dog-leg lake took a sharp curve southwards here, with moon-shimmer on the waters and a thousand reflections from the lights of the little bays nestled into the contours. Such solitary roadless bays, where only boats called. The lights were from the various cottages on the estates.

They stood, not speaking, for long enough. Finally two deep breaths were drawn in, expelled. They laughed. 'Twin sighs of satisfaction,' Nathaniel said companionably.

'No words needed to express it,' said Letty.

Nathaniel's brows drew together. 'Now, where did I hear exactly that lately? Or almost? How tantalising!' He looked down on her, considering it. She looked up at him, waiting for remembrance to dawn. Then he said, 'Got it! I didn't hear it, I read it. It was Lady Barker way back in last century, in one of her books. She said it of Lake Coleridge. That silence was its most expressive language.'

Letitia said slowly, 'How strange. I've not read her books, but they look fascinating. Two of them were among those I sorted out to take with us. I think we'd better go back. I've seen the Moon-Gate.'

All of a sudden she was dimly afraid of the alchemy of this magic garden, the sleeping lake, the brooding mountains, the stars, that moon, the silences.

He said abruptly, 'Has it worked?'

'Has what worked?'

'Giles's legend. That whoever sees the moon through the Moon-Gate knows that for ever it remains the one place beloved over all.'

Her tone was light. 'Does that mean just that view . . . of Walter Peak, or this whole Lake District?'

'I don't know. And you haven't seen *my* valley yet. We have a gate too. Ellen built it from stones of the area, multi-coloured. On the hill above the valley, where she hoped a road might go some day. She called it The Gate Beautiful. Because the Maori name for the valley is Mararangi, so it means——'

She interrupted him, 'It means The Garden of Heaven?'

He nodded. Again she felt moved as she had been back in that room.

Then he said, 'Mararangi has a view too, of the lake, but not from the Gate. You've got to climb to see it. That immense landslide not only blocked the access to the lake but also the view except for a tiny wedge of blue you can see from one upstairs window above the schoolroom. But some day I'll conquer Big Slip, though it may take me most of my lifetime. I'll make that old sheep-station of my fore-bears pay enough to warrant the cost.'

Something struck Letty. 'Mr Nathaniel, if it's a valley, wouldn't it have at least a stream running through? Wouldn't that in time have forced its way through to reach the lake?'

'Good point. You aren't just a beautiful face. The slip blocked the original outlet but the same storm caused several smaller slips and neatly diverted our small river round a hill into another valley that doesn't reach the lake, and it empties into a river that eventually goes into the Shotover. No access there. But it saved the valley from being flooded at the time. I'll be glad to get home now. I hate like hell for them to be cut off by phone when I'm not there. That phone's our greatest boon and worth every bit of capital to get it through. But you're always at the mercy of wind and weather. The linesmen are out there now, camping, trying to find the fault. They use terrifically tough vehicles. The line doesn't always follow the road. It takes the shortest way possible.'

She thought his tone held deep unease. He probably felt that if breakdowns in communications occurred often, Hope Maybury might not want to stay. After all, that was his reason for engaging *her*.

She said lightly, 'This time tomorrow communication will probably be restored and I'll be there to take the two older children off Mrs Maybury's hands.'

'Yes. It's the interim that worries me. Well, no use meeting trouble head on. As Dad has always said, most of our dreads never happen.'

It was out before she thought. 'Then you do appreciate some things about your father?'

The moonlight was so bright she clearly saw his expression change. He was amazed. He swung round to face her with the vehemence of his reaction. 'What *can* you mean? Dad's a great guy. Just because his chief love in life doesn't happen to be the way I want *my* life it doesn't mean I don't love and respect him. I just want to stand on my own two feet. I like the way he runs that business, his integrity, his innate kindness. What on earth made you say that, Letitia Greenaway? Our lives have scarcely touched. We—well, even when I was in the shop—I——'

Even though she knew she shouldn't have said what she had, she was instantly on the defensive. She finished for him, 'Even in business you avoided my department like the plague.'

Surprisingly he laughed. 'I sure did. I'm now dependent upon you to help me keep Hope and Owen in my valley. Serves me right. But you haven't answered my question. What made you think Dad and I are at loggerheads?'

She said weakly, 'Sorry, I picked up the wrong impression. You so obviously hated the shop-life I imagined Mr Pengelly was disappointed both his sons weren't in the business.' It would never do to have him suspect she'd been an involuntary eavesdropper that morning.

'Dad *was* disappointed, but he was fair. Said I wasn't just *his* son but my mother's and if her ancestor's genes were the stronger then go to it. But he did think me crazy to take up the old Wilderness. He—like most fathers —wanted his son to have it easier. To farm in a less rundown, more accessible spot. He said the only way to make it viable was to pour money in. But I wouldn't risk it for him. I preferred to approach the Rural Bank and pay interest.'

'Wasn't that——?' Letitia stopped dead.

He said, 'Go on. You interest me.'

'Second thoughts are sometimes best. It's not my business.'

'But I'd very much like to know what you were going to say.'

'Why? I'm just an employee. Not my right.'

He gripped her upper arm, his fingers hurting. 'Don't be chicken. So often when you're the son of a big business tycoon people are less than candid. I can take it. I find your candour refreshing.'

'I was going to say wasn't that just stiff-necked pride? Most parents, you said, want their sons to have it easier. I heard that Tristan Pengelly himself had a rags-to-riches story. Didn't you deny him the joy of helping?'

His tone was rueful. 'You're so right, but it wasn't just pride. Dad still can't realise we're not in the boom-time of the sixties. Oh, he's well-oiled, but big businesses can have big crashes. And the sort of money to put Mararangi on its feet isn't chicken-feed. I'd never forgive myself if in developing my own dream, I gave him any financial insecurity. James could suffer too.'

'Then I've done you an injustice. That reason I can admire but——'

'But what?'

'But don't deny him *every* privilege of helping you. Some day take something from him. Oh, this sounds like hero-worship of my former boss, and it is . . . I've known of many kindnesses your father has done for his staff. I don't like to think of him being frustrated in the family circle. He's a bit of an autocrat, yes, he wouldn't have got where he is if he hadn't been, but there's a heart of butter underneath.' Then she added, 'And I so admired the way he controlled his grief when he lost your mother.'

'I didn't think you'd have known much about that. I do realise, though, that he's got a soft spot for you.'

Ah . . . he was thinking of what his father had said about if he'd been twenty years younger . . .

She said, 'You'd better understand, he wasn't aware that I hero-worshipped him. It was done from that distance between employer and employee. Except once. I'd been in the buying-room all afternoon and at closing-time realised

I'd left my rough order-list there. I was going to go over it at night as we'd a big day coming up the next day. Most of the staff had gone when I flew back for it and, because I'd a bus to catch, positively burst in. Made so much noise I couldn't retreat unnoticed.

'Your father was bowed over that big old counter we used to work on, and at that moment her name burst out of him as if he couldn't bear she was no longer with him. "Nancy . . . Oh, Nancy!" Yet all afternoon he'd been so wonderful with us and the travellers, telling jokes, making decisions, letting my second-in-charge give her opinion . . . I didn't know whether to apologise and retreat or what. Then, rather to my horror, I found myself bending over him and taking his hands. Nathaniel, they were wet with tears, and he wasn't ashamed of them. He was too big a man to be ashamed of tears. We sat and talked about your mother—little things, endearing things. I slipped along and made us some tea. I asked if he'd like a brandy, but he wouldn't, he was driving. He dropped me home and on the way he was as witty as ever. I felt he did it for my sake so I shouldn't worry about him. That's why I wondered if you knew how vulnerable he is.'

He said slowly, 'Mother and Father had strong views on grief. We knew they were ideally matched, and sometimes they talked very naturally over the fact that one of them would probably outlive the other. They said life was for getting on with, that they'd like to be missed but they'd had so much fun together that the one who was left must remember that with gratitude and not inflict their sorrow on others. Perhaps we took that idealistic view too much for granted. It was only a probability then. But maybe the reality was tougher. Letitia, I'm glad someone was there when he felt like that. But we're not at loggerheads. Now . . . for some sleep to face our day tomorrow. I think I'll sleep the better for this time . . . out in the open air. I always feel I can cope with anything when I'm actually at The Wilderness. No doubt the phone will be on tomorrow. Hope will be delighted I've actually brought a governess back with me, and Owen and I can get on with the dagging. When I'm at the helm, I don't dread so much

CHAPTER FOUR

LETTY found her pulses quickened on awakening. This was the day she would realise a dream . . . she would be teaching in the high-country. Pity that, despite that more gentle interlude last night, she felt so much animosity towards her new employer, but you couldn't have everything. Even if she'd found a place for herself instead of being chivvied into it by Tristan and his son, her employers might have been anything but kindred spirits and in isolated circumstances it was only too easy to get on each other's nerves to the point of explosion. Anyway, she'd have the occasional weekend off when she could book herself a weekend at Drumlogie even if Tristan didn't bring her car up.

Mr Nathaniel would want to be early. She showered, donned trews that were one degree more dressy than faded jeans, which she felt the redoubtable Jamesina mightn't approve of for a governess, but weren't calculated to make Hope feel she was too stylish. They were thin dark green cotton cords, and a matching checked shirt hung loosely over them because it was going to be a scorcher of a day. Already Letitia could hear splashing from the fenced-in pool.

It would have been lovely to join the swimmers, but she wasn't going to have Nathaniel remark that she wasn't on holiday and that he wanted to get to Mararangi as soon as possible. She stuffed her night things into her bag and ran down to put them in the station wagon. His stuff was still there, so it could all be transferred at once into the big four-wheel-drive ancient army truck. As she came back Nathaniel and Giles emerged from the door of the pool area, gleaming wet, in briefs. They looked the picture of health. They stopped, Nathaniel ran his eye over Letty, and said, 'Well, I could have given you the chance of an early dip after all, but Stella said you ought to be allowed to sleep.'

She said coolly, 'My impression had been that you'd want to be on the way at the crack of dawn. I'm all ready for breakfast. I'll hurry it if you've already eaten.'

Giles cocked a comical eyebrow. 'Looks as if you're going to be regimented within an inch of your life, Nat. A governess to a T. So off you go and get dried, man. Use the downstairs shower. I'll bring your things down. It's worth it to see this free-as-air bachelor toeing the line.' They all three laughed, but Letty was conscious of a petty satisfaction. She was going to impress Nathaniel within a hair's breadth of chagrin. He'd thought her *so* unsuitable. Even a disaster!

She knew a great sense of adventure as they began winding into the hills, leaving behind them the colourful, gay world of holidaymakers and tourists. They went through huge paddocks where chestnut-flanked, white-faced Herefords grazed, through others with snowy-fleeced sheep. They didn't have to open any gates because all these were served with cattle-stops over which they rattled noisily. 'Till we get beyond Drumlogie land and into mine,' said Nathaniel, 'then you'll have to hop out and do the opening. In time I'll run to stock-grids. You do know it's an unwritten law that the passenger does that?'

She chuckled. 'I'm not a greenhorn, just newly arrived in New Zealand. I've spent as much time as possible on holiday in the country, to say nothing of knowing almost every walkway across the Dunedin hills. I know enough to come in when it's raining, never to leave gates open, and to ask permission before letting farm dogs off the chain!'

To her surprise he said gently, 'Sorry, that was stupid. My very humble apologies.'

Unguardedly, she said, 'Goodness, I wouldn't have imagined——' and stopped. There were limits to candour.

'Not have imagined what?'

She couldn't dodge it. 'Have imagined you on even a speaking acquaintance with humility.'

Oddly, he didn't seem to resent that. It rather put her out. 'Oh, I've eaten quite a bit of humble pie in my day. my mother couldn't stand arrogance, especially in kids. We both had it knocked out of us.'

She couldn't think of anything to say. There was amusement in his voice then. 'I've a feeling you don't think she succeeded very well.'

She said as lightly as she could manage, 'I think I'd better just say: "No comment". You are, after all, my boss.'

He smiled. 'Technically, yes. But with governesses so hard to get, and keep, I'm rather in a cleft stick.'

Heavens, just about what she'd said to Tim!

She looked out and saw a small graveyard, tucked into a sunlit V of a tiny valley on their right, and said, 'Does that belong to Drumlogie?' Better get away from the too-personal.

'Yes. Very necessary in the days of the first Logies here, Giles's and Stella's ancestors. The winters were harsh and the snows deep and it wasn't always possible to make it to Queenstown. The clergy, who were bricks, mostly made it, on horseback, through the drifts. That is, if they got a message through. Mostly family, bar a few gold-diggers.'

She said, 'It must be rather lovely in some ways to be still within sight and sound of all you loved most on earth.'

'I think so. Then you won't find it too grim as we enter our valley that, with the sun where it will be, the first thing you will see on the hill opposite will be white tombstones standing out?'

'No, I won't find it grim, just fitting.'

When he spoke, the tone of his voice made her wonder if that had moved him. It had a controlled sound. 'Then perhaps you're right for here after all.'

Letitia grinned to herself. Good . . . it's going to be easy. A pushover. He'll soon find out I've got what it takes . . . and when I shake the dust off my feet and leave here for another station, it will wipe out for me the humiliation this man heaped on me!

None of this was betrayed in her voice. 'I suppose no one has been buried there for years? At Mararangi, I mean.'

'Not exactly. But before the land came on to the market openly, Mother and I came up here one day. I've had this track improved since then, though you'd hardly think so, but we had to come up on horses. Mother was a great rider, a show-jumper in her time. Her father ran a riding school. We brought in sleeping-bags and provisions. We got permission from the folk the land was leased to and camped in the old house for the night. I'd had experience as a farm manager in the Lake Hawea district, and Mother had a yen to see this back in the family again but said if I thought it was hopeless I wasn't to consider it.

'It was fun, and within minutes I knew I was committed. Next day we visited the Little Acre, as all these private burial-grounds are called, and it was quite well kept, as sheep had been allowed to graze it. Mother chuckled and said, "Daresay it'll be a long time yet but when I'm gone, Nathan, will you scatter my ashes over Ellen and Grigor's grave?" ' He paused, swallowed, said, 'I said I'd do more than that. I'd add her name to the stone. I did. Because Mother was gone before two years were up. And though they weren't his forebears, Dad wants the same with his ashes. I used a legacy-in-lifetime from Mother to help buy this in, had considerable savings myself and got the rest on loan. I've been pretty lucky taking it all round . . . with the loss of so many of our primary markets, high interest rates and a few other factors that have bugged farmers of late, it's much harder for some young guys who want to do nothing but farm, who have had less deposit to put down and tougher country to bring under production. I know *The Wilderness* has great drawbacks, but it's the land my pioneer forebears wrested from nothing and I don't want it passing out of the family ever again.'

Letitia looked at the narrowing road, if it could be called road, the signs of erosion on some of the hills they were heading into, hills in dire need of afforestation to check that erosion, and wondered if other stations *could* be much tougher. An unwelcome admiration began to stir in her. The road climbed, turned, twisted, dipped and climbed again. 'It really would make marvellous trekking country,' she said, 'and if they're willing to pay to come it could add to income.'

'It will have to be in the future. I can't land any more in Hope's lap, and these things snowball. We'd have to at least make them hot drinks, provide some facilities. But it's an idea.'

How strange that here there was no glimpse of the lake. It didn't seem possible that anything as huge as a lake that covered well over a hundred square miles could be on their left, hidden by what most New Zealanders called foothills, but shrugged off as mountains even though you could see on this grilling day where the snowline had been, bare and rocky. Below it in the gullies were pockets of bush and through into the cab of the truck came the matchless sound of water cascading down them, and here and there the sun struck glints of silver from leaping water. Where the track dipped down they forded shallow streams that could, she was told, cut them off in times of heavy rain or sudden thaws after snow. 'Then, if the telephone fails us, our only means of contact is to ride across and through the slip on a bridle-path to the Queenstown-Glenorchy road, and stop the first car if it's an emergency, or send a message if it's not absolutely panic-stations.' He paused. 'What am I talking like this for? We haven't had an emergency since the Mayburys have been here. Only it's always on the cards.'

'Am I right in thinking there's more bush on these hills?' asked Letitia. 'Of course they're closer together so they get more shade and I expect the more trees there are, the more rain is attracted?'

'Yes, and our valley has the most trees of all, partly because it reverted to its natural state, partly because Grigor loved trees about him and Ellen loved her garden and wanted shelter, so they kept it almost like parkland. The main grazing is on the hills beyond. Of course the sheep-yards and the woolshed and stables are all within the compass of the valley. I've done a lot of renewing there and I built a new house for the Mayburys. That was priority if ever I was going to get and keep a married couple. I spent my first years with single chaps, camping in the homestead with me. We took turns at the cooking! They came and went with monotonous regularity. Can you hear a helicopter? Common enough here. Use them for deer-recovery and shooting, and for flying in deer-stalkers and rescuing climbers. Soon you'll see Ellen's Gate. Not a moon-gate, I doubt if she'd ever heard of one, but it was something unnecessary that seemed to fulfil *some* need. Perhaps reminded her of the big estates in Scotland. Grigor put in the foundations for her. She put the stones one on the other herself, mortaring them—took her years. The stones were brought uplake from the Shotover in the whale-boat, some of them dug out of their own hillsides. And when she'd built a pillar each side, Grigor found an old gold-miner who'd been a mason, and he carved her two thistle-heads such as had been on the gate-posts of the estate in Scotland Ellen's father had worked on, and he had them set there for her birthday. A nice touch.'

They swung round to the left, with nearly twenty miles of the track behind them, and as they turned the corner, there was the gateway, really a short wall each side of the road, in all the beauty of the greatly varied stone, grey, with specks of mica that sparkled in the sun, rose-coloured, lilac, green, slate-coloured, beautifully split for ornamental work. A labour of love, and crowning it on the pillars, the Scots thistles. Nathaniel drew in before entering so Letitia could have her first glimpse of the valley below it and she saw that here he must have had set his first stock-grid, because the iron rails were still gleaming silverly.

Suddenly Letty was aware that this moment held no enmity on her part. She could appreciate a man being very proud of this inheritance of his that he'd rescued from neglect and ruin. They each stood with a hand on a pillar. The stone was sun-warm. All about them were the green and ochre of the hills, pasture and tussock, and a sky above that was cobalt this burning hot January day, of the Southern Hemisphere, but framed in between the pillars was a more endearing view, intimate, impressing one immediately that here was a valley loved and enhanced by those who sought to get their living from this land.

These were solitudes, yes, but on a fair day like this there was no hint of the hazards of smothering drifts and roaring torrents that could loosen great boulders and undermine hillsides.

Below them the track, smoother now, wound like a ribbon to the valley floor below that was sweet with Douglas firs and quick-growing *pinus radiata*, great oaks and sycamores, native beeches with tiny leaves, limes, liquidambars, aspen poplars and lombardy poplars . . . an ancient woolshed, restored with bright red paint and a new tin roof, splashed colour among the greens, and the tombstones gleamed whitely on the hillside opposite. Letitia couldn't see any old homestead but in a wide clearing, in the sunniest place of all, was the new house. Their employer hadn't spared any pains to delight his working couple. Some would have been content with the plainest of buildings, built on utility lines, but this had been planned to retain existing trees in its garden area and was stepped in a winged effect to get maximum sun in winter. It was built of green Summerhill bricks, faced with natural stone, wide-windowed and with patios enclosed with glass to keep out the bitter winds that at times, despite its sheltered look today, must whistle through the valley. Glorious places for children to play.

Suddenly Letitia could hear Grayson Moore saying, when they visited a lovely estate in Canterbury, 'I like a man who houses his staff as well as himself.' But this man beside her, although he was working under financial restraints, was housing his married couple in what must be better conditions than his own.

'You can't see the homestead from here,' Nathaniel told her. 'Grigor had to put his first hut up in the most sheltered place he could find so it's tucked away round the shoulder of the hill. He set it to face *north* so it could get sun most of the day, but it also gets the first rays in the east. Hello, hello . . . what on earth does that chopper think he's doing? He's coming down. Now why? Back into the truck! I think we're having trouble. I do hope Owen's not done himself any harm, or one of the kids. No, wait. Hand me those binoculars, Letitia.'

The helicopter dropped to a perfect landing and then three figures got out. Nathaniel was adjusting the glasses. There were two men, one woman. Nathaniel groaned. 'That's the Doc and a district nurse, I'd say. Get in!'

They wasted no time, yet he took no risks. No use compounding disaster. The road was narrow and had a drop on the right. They saw two children rush out of the new house. 'Not them, thank God,' said Nathaniel. Letty understood how he was feeling. She felt sick herself.

'Devilish country,' he groaned. 'Why can't I be content with somewhere more accessible? Things can happen here that would never happen in town.'

But as it turned out this could have happened anywhere in suburbia. They ran when the truck stopped and were into the house in a flash. Two patients, Jamesina and Hope, and Hope definitely the more seriously injured one, because Jamesina was protesting snortingly, 'Of course I'm not going to hospital! I've had sprains before and not gone to hospital. There's got to be a woman here. It's Hope you'd better be worrying about. A broken leg!'

The doctor was already attending to the leg and the nurse said with crisp authority, 'Mrs Forbes, you had a nasty crack on the head. Owen told me you were out to it for quite some time and we'll want it X-rayed. Otherwise Doctor's reputation would suffer. Yes, Doctor, I'm coming.'

When Hope saw Nathaniel and Letitia she blushed furiously over her pallor. 'It's all my fault, Nat. I was just plain crazy. Only the poor little thing was scared stiff and Owen was away up the yards. It was one of the kittens—it was stranded on the roof. I tried to be careful. Jamesina insisted on holding the ladder steady and she did. I got the kitten okay, but coming down it bit my ear and I slewed sideways and fell on Jamesina and the ladder fell on us both. I'm terribly sorry—this is so disrupting. And what about the new governess? When is she——'

Letitia stepped forward. 'That's me, but not to worry. I'll be here with the children. Don't talk any more. Save your strength.'

The doctor, a youngish man, grunted. 'Most sensible thing I've yet heard. You women! Think you can't be done without, but someone always steps into the breach. Even husbands and employers rise to the occasion. Like young Roberta here . . . acted like a veteran. Said to her father she'd rather ride over Big Slip than stay with the injured and was off on her pony before he could stop her. It was fortunate a car came along as soon as she reached the road and when he contacted me, I was free to come and so was the chopper.'

Nathaniel gasped, which was most gratifying to Roberta. 'Rode right through Big Slip? Good for you, Roberta! But does that mean the phone's still off? Oh hell! That's all we need. I was sure they'd have found the fault by now.'

To prove his point the phone rang stridently, making them jump. Nathaniel grabbed it, said, 'Yes? Oh, you're testing? Praise be. Yes, getting you loud and clear, and for God's sake keep it that way. It's Pengelly here. I've just arrived, five minutes after the chopper you probably heard landed here to take Hope Maybury and Mrs Forbes to hospital. They fell off a ladder. Broken leg for Hope, damaged ankle and concussion for my housekeeper. Could have been worse. But at all costs keep this line open, so we can stay in touch with the hospital. What was the trouble? Likely to recur? Oh, good show, thanks very much.'

He turned to them. 'Not likely to fault again. A big gull. Must have come over from the West Coast. Went bang into the wires. Its body was lying beneath the break.'

Letitia said to the doctor, 'Would you like me to take them a hot sweet drink? Tea? When you've immobilised that leg?'

He nodded. 'We'll all have one, then be off. I'll give these two something to steady them.'

Suddenly Mrs Forbes said, 'Miss Greenaway, turn your head towards me, would you?'

Mystified, she did, and Jamesina said in a satisfied tone, 'I thought so. Though I didn't recognise you at first with your hair short and less make-up. You're Letitia from

Pengelly's, aren't you? Rememember me?'

Letitia blinked. 'Oh, yes, you're a customer. But I never knew your name. And of course you wouldn't know my surname.'

Nathaniel said, 'Well, I'm darned! Who'd have thought you'd have known our *Letitia for*——' He stopped short because Letty had trodden on his foot.

Jamesina Forbes looked at him. 'I don't think I altogether appreciate that! Why wouldn't *I* go for a bit of camouflage? I need it more than most. I'm so sick and tired of my daughters insisting I was past things. This one here helped me no end—gave me some very natural-looking rinses. Well, dyes if you like. If she's as good at governessing as she is at serving customers, she'll do us. But what in the world came over your father to let her go?'

Nathaniel's cheeks creased in a grin. 'Let her go? Why, he practically threw her at me! I told her it was a place of great hazards, so this proves my point. But I'm sure Letty Greenaway can cope with anything.'

Letty could have hit him. She marched out to the kitchen, filled the kettle, switched it on.

Hope Maybury was asking the doctor something. He shook his head. 'Sorry, Hope, they're not fully staffed as it is. If she was three months old and spending most of her time in a bassinet you could take her to hospital. In fact if you were still feeding her you'd have to, but a crawling baby is out of the question. You haven't anyone in Queenstown who could take her, I suppose. Nurse, do you know of——'

Letitia said crisply, 'What's wrong with me looking after her? School's not started yet and you could be back home by the time it is, Mrs Maybury. Roberta and Damien will know all her little fads and fancies. I won't let her out of my sight, I promise you. And I'll be careful about the pots and pans on the stove. My cousin has a year-old baby at the crawling stage.'

'Josselyn's only nine months, but she was born with an itch to be up and doing. Oh, if you could! I'd hate her to go to strange surroundings with someone she'd never seen before. But it's a lot of work.'

'That doesn't matter in an emergency. Roberta will put me wise to things. What sort of mixture does she take in her bottle?'

'She's on dried milk because our supplies of fresh are irregular here. Roberta knows all the rest, so does Owen. Be sure to run cold water in the bath first, in case she suddenly stands up and tips in. And never leave her in the bath unattended. Oh, that tea is going to be good. Oh, I don't feel half so bad now I've met you.'

By the time Hope had the tea the injection was taking effect and she was less inclined to worry. The doctor grinned, said to Jamesina, 'And if you stop protesting, I'll feel better. If you don't you'll get one of the same. Things have changed since you were at Glenorchy and there you stuck things out and hoped for the best. I'll make sure you've no injury to your head, strap up that ankle, rest you for a few days and then you can return.'

They brought in the stretchers. Hope struggled to open her eyes. 'Owen, you aren't to worry about me—I'll be okay. It was so foolish of me. But I'm sure there's just the break.'

Nathaniel's voice held authority. 'He won't worry about you, Hope, because he's going to be right on the spot. He'll go down with you. Miss Mattie'll put you up, Owen, and probably lend you her car to go visiting your wife. With a bit of luck they won't be away too long, but if they are and you feel you must get back, hitch a ride up the road and I'll meet you there with a spare horse to ride back through the Slip. How about that? If Letty and I can't manage the family between us, we oughtn't to be here. What say you, Letty?'

'Of course . . . but tell me, where is the baby in all this?'

Owen, though protesting, was thanking Nathaniel and turned and said, 'Having her morning nap which extends into early afternoon. You won't wake her by peeping in on her. She sleeps like the dead and isn't shy, takes to everyone. Well, I'll pack a bag. Bags!'

Roberta went flying over to the homestead for Mrs Forbes's things, and Letty helped Owen. The pilot took

Damien off to see inside the helicopter. Soon they were standing back against the house, the chopper rose and became a whirring silver speck in the blue dome of the sky. Within minutes, incredible though it seemed, the two injured women would be in comfort at the hospital nearer the foot of the lake, past Queenstown.

'They specialise in broken legs,' said Nathaniel, almost callously, 'once the skiing season starts. Both doctors are flat out then and plaster from head to foot. Well, it's a great start to your apprenticeship here, Miss Greenaway.'

'I think I'll last the course,' she informed him. 'I was after a less tame life. I think I've got it.'

He turned to Roberta. 'You've got what it takes for the high-country, Roberta. Good for you!'

The little girl flushed. She had a calm and beautiful face, with huge luminous hazel eyes. 'Thanks, Nat, but wait till you hear what Damien did, and him only eight. He thought I might rush it and get thrown, so he sneaked behind me on Paul Revere. I never heard him. And he had to saddle up, too. I didn't. Jigger was already saddled. He caught up a bit but kept behind on the bends so I shouldn't hear him. Didn't come up with me till I was tying Jigger to the fence. And it's the first time he'd been on the bridle-path.'

Nathaniel clapped the small boy on the shoulder. 'Well done, mate. You'll make a real high-country man. I'm proud of you. Can't regard you as a small boy now, you've earned your spurs. We'll put you on the payroll.'

Letty added praise, then said, 'And now we'll put the oven on and heat up those sausage rolls they gave us at Drumlogie. There's some coleslaw too, and fresh tomatoes. What will Josselyn have later?'

'She could just have tinned vegetables today and chicken out of a tin. I'll get it ready to heat in case she wakes early.'

Roberta set the table in the kitchen beautifully, put out sliced bread, butter, honey, jam, and home-made orange cake. Suddenly they were all hungry.

Letitia suddenly had an instant flashback to that furiously humiliating moment when Nathaniel had said his great-great-grandmother would turn in her grave if he took anyone like Letitia up to The Wilderness. ' . . . She wouldn't know B from a bull's foot,' he'd declared. 'I'd want someone who wouldn't turn a hair if she had to help with the tailing in an emergency . . . not go round smothered in make-up, looking like something out of a sheikh's harem . . . ' Later he'd compared her with an icicle! Well, for better or for worse, she was going to make him realise he'd be absolutely helpless without her . . . a man alone in a wilderness, with three children, one of them at the worst stage of all, crawling! Pity tailing-time was long past. At this moment, remembering the scorn in his voice, Letitia was quite sure that if need be, she could tie this crawling infant to a fence with one hand, and tail lambs with the other . . . whatever it involved!

High-and-mighty Pengelly was going to eat his words some day. He was going to be lost in wonder, love and praise, as the hymn had it. For one exalted second she felt as if she could cope with anything. Then a loud cry from Josselyn's room stopped the train of her thoughts. Oh, those rash words she'd uttered to Hope . . . on the strength of having looked after her cousin's baby for one afternoon! Yes, she could cope with most things, but a crawling nine-month-old baby, never in her life before, and she was twenty or thirty hideously rough miles from Stella and Lucinda who might have helped her out!

CHAPTER FIVE

LETITIA took Roberta into the bedroom with her. Better not to front the baby with a stranger. They got a surprise. Hope's guess that she might soon be pulling herself up by the edge of the bath was true. Josselyn was standing hanging on to the rails of her cot, obviously wet-tailed. She was exactly like a kewpie doll with an absurd and endearing quiff of brown hair standing on top of her head. Roberta gave a squeal of delight. 'Look at that! Who's the clever girl, then? Letty, do you think that means she'll walk early?'

'I should think so. Babies vary greatly. My cousin's baby isn't standing yet, though she's a year. But a friend of mine had a walking wonder at ten months, though she said she hoped never to have an early one again. They can't see the dangers and don't recognise steps for what they are, and step blithely into space.'

Roberta said sturdily, 'I'll be glad if she walks early. We've got cousins whose baby brother had his first tooth at four months and Josselyn hadn't one at seven months. You've no idea how uppity they were. I'll write and tell them tonight.'

'What do you do about mail?'

'We're sort of on rural mail. Dad, or Nat rides through Big Slip twice a week. We've got a big stand and mailbox on the Glenorchy Road and we can post things in it too, of course, but it isn't exactly express delivery. Up, you come, Joss.'

In the kitchen Roberta spread a blanket out on the table, brought napkins, baby powder and oil, and said, 'I'm always glad Mum folds them ready to put on.'

'So'm I!' said Letty fervently. 'Mother once said that in her day it was easier. They were all put on triangular-wise,

72

but now there are half a dozen ways, some for boys, some for girls, and every mother thinks her own way is best. Oh, good, I know this way. And I like using two pins.' She looked up to catch Nathaniel grinning. She said drily, 'It may not seem important to you, but babies hate change. And there's nothing amusing about——'

'Oh, but there is. To me, anyway. The first time I ever saw you in that glamorous get-up behind that counter I couldn't have imagined you on even speaking terms with babies' nappies.'

'No doubt, it all adds up to a male characteristic.'

'Which is?'

'Men are greatly given, poor creatures, to preconceived ideas. And part with them hardly. And not all, or even many, cosmeticians are lilies of the field.' Letitia scooped up the discarded naps and whisked them out to the very well-equipped laundry.

She came back to hear Nathaniel saying: 'Well, Damien and I must be off to the yards. Roberta, when you've spooned that stuff into Josselyn, you'd better come up and help. Damien does the button-pushing, of course,' he added to Letty, 'and I'll do the dagging, but I need someone to keep them coming along the race. We sure miss Hope for that.'

Letty said crisply, '*I'll* feed Joss. Roberta can go with you now.'

'Don't push your luck too far. Sometimes she jibs.' But Roberta was all for getting up to the yards right away. 'I'll dish it out for her, Miss Greenaway, and put her bottle ready . . . I say, I know I called you Letty before, but perhaps when school starts we'll have to make it Miss. Eh?'

Letty considered it. 'Not in these circumstances. You'll find I'm a disciplinarian even if you do call me by my given name. But I appreciate your asking.'

Roberta said honestly, 'Well, Mum said we mustn't take it for granted when Nat said he was getting you,' and she whisked off.

Letty looked up to find Nathaniel surveying her with a quizzical expression and she could have choked him for the derision in his voice. 'You sure landed yourself in it, didn't you, when you got all starry-eyed about the great open spaces. In town there's always a neighbour at hand. Someone the baby's used to. You're faced with life in the raw immediately . . . '

She replied just as sarcastically. 'Well, observe me in a flap. I don't think I'll wring my hands or press the panic button. I'm here, in this emergency. In sole charge. So what?'

'So it'll rub some of the glamour off. It's not all scenery and peace, is it? You may change your mind about this being a miniature Garden of Eden.'

She pursed her lips, then said, 'Oh, I don't know. I didn't expect it to be without a serpent. And at the moment, that's you, croaking like Cassandra. You're tempting me to say, "Oh get to hell out of here on your own job and leave me to get on with mine".'

Maddeningly he chuckled and departed. She'd show him!

She rather wished he'd been there to observe the docile way Josselyn mopped up the chicken and vegetables, and the puréed apricots her mother had had ready in the fridge. Nothing to it, a piece of cake.

Roberta came running back. 'Nat told me off, said we didn't want any more washing than necessary, that I was to put on really old denims. Thought I was saving time so I'd have got away with it. He's very observant for a man. Gosh, is she finished already? One up to you.'

Letitia grinned and from that moment they were allies. 'Roberta, I'm mystified. What on earth did Nathaniel mean when he said Damien could push the button? Was he trying to take the mickey out of me? You're dagging, aren't you? I used to go for my holidays to a small farm on the Mani-ototo, but I haven't for years. Dagging's just taking dirty wool off their hindquarters, isn't it? But nobody pushed any buttons. It makes me feel a greenhorn. I'll kill Nathaniel if he's trying to take a rise out of me.'

Roberta's giggle held real mirth. 'Well, if he had been he didn't get it, did he? But he isn't. It's a marvellous contraption called "Easy-Crutch". You'll have seen sheep being shoved along narrow races to go through mister dips and so on? You have? Just like that, only with this they step on to a platform at the end and up comes a sort of cradle to fit firmly round the animal's ribs. It's padded and plastic and it's held that way while Nat shears its backside with electric shears. It's worked by pressure, and that's where Damien comes in: he pushes the button. He's good at it and judges exactly when to do it and when to release it. Then I urge the next one on. The lambs are worst. They're absolutely obstreperous—clean mad.'

Letitia felt a rush of gratitude towards this composed child. Roberta reappeared, zipping up her overalls as she came. 'Letty, have you got some really old duds in your cases? If not, hunt out some of Mum's. I reckon we could do with you at the other end of the race. Mum takes Joss to the yards. Keeps her away from the dust, of course, but just opposite, under the big rowan tree, Dad built her a little pen. It's grassed in and Mum dumps her in with this basket of things here.' She dived into the laundry and came out with it, full of blocks and a string of cotton-reels and a few small cars. 'You could bring her down in the stroller, strapped in. I'll tell Nat I asked you to come.' She flashed the governess a conspiratorial twinkle and disappeared.

And why not? It didn't take Letty long to find a pair of brown denim overalls she'd used for gardening. Another step away from the cosmetic image! They had patched knees and braces over the shoulders. It was hot enough for jandals on bare feet, but that would make her feet too dirty, and recalcitrant hooves could scratch badly. She fished out her shabbiest pair of sneakers. She'd nearly not brought them. She'd gone fishing with Tim in these. She took a meat pie out of the freezer. Hope had suggested that. Good for her. She popped the baby into the push-chair, and was glad she was firmly fastened in when the concrete path gave way to a very rough track, though Josselyn took it well, crowing with delight as they bumped over the stones. Letty's spirits began to lift.

She didn't think Nathaniel looked overjoyed at her appearance. She ignored that, lifted Josselyn over the rough pickets of her pen, threw in the basket contents and strolled across. They were working at a furiously fast pace.

No wonder. She looked at the covered yards and when she saw the number of bleating mobs, deduced that Owen had expected them to be working here most of the day. Hours had been lost already. In any case, no doubt the farm work was behind schedule with Mr Nathaniel working at the shop in his brother's absence. She knew now that it must have been quite a sacrifice, and wondered whether it had been sheer affection for old Tristan, or the fact that a few weeks' salary had helped the situation here.

She recognised immediately that Damien was indeed good at this . . . every inch a farmer. His face was filthy and sweat had made rivulets down the grime. He and Nathaniel were working as one. Roberta was having a tough time keeping the stock coming fast enough. Well, Letty had helped many a sheep along during those early holidays. She walked purposefully towards the far end of the race. At that moment a plump lamb evaded Roberta's lunge to shove it on, did a somersault and leaped nimbly over the side. Instinctively Letitia pounced, almost hurling herself at it, fastening her fingers in the wool.

Nathaniel gave an exclamation, switched off his shears, began to rush towards her, 'Don't let go!' he yelled. Before he reached her, Letty, with a super-human effort that surprised even herself, yanked the lamb off its feet, strode towards the race with the kicking scrambling animal and dropped it in, fortunately facing the right way, smacked its rump and it wasted no time heading towards Damien in turn.

'Well, I'll be damned,' said Nathaniel, 'couldn't have done better myself.' He rushed back to his post. 'Where'd you summon up the strength for that?'

Her eyes disappeared into green slits of sheer mirth, 'Oh, you develop muscles you'd not dream of applying eye-shadow to recalcitrant customers . . . reluctant lambs are nothing in my young life!'

It was beyond Damien, but Roberta had already summed up, to a slight degree, the situation between the two adults. She said, 'I think we can notch one up to Miss Greenaway, don't you, Nat?'

Letty had to hand it to him, he bore her no malice. He was still laughing as he switched the shears on again. He began to finish the lamb still in the clamp. 'I rather think it's one up to my father. But if a ewe gets away, Letty, leave her to me, or *you'll* be off in a chopper too, with a slipped disc.'

She relented. 'I mightn't be as lucky another time. It was luck, and automatic reaction. If Josselyn stays contented, may I assist?'

'Too right you can. It'd be unthinkable to let any of them back into the paddocks again. Especially if Owen doesn't get back for a few days.'

It had been a long, hot summer; the January sky was brassily blue without a single cloud and smothering dust rose up from the dry floors of the covered yards. The sheep were hot, the wool greasy with lanolin, the atmosphere smelly with the dags, but the speed was amazing. It was much faster with two bringing the sheep along. Nathaniel decreed that Letty should work nearest him and Damien, urging them on into the 'Easy-Crutch' without pause, while Roberta brought them from the yards into the race. It was unbelievable how stubborn and toey some were. Letty pushed her ash-blonde slanting fringe back from her hot forehead with her forearm, her hands were so filthy, but it still left a black streak across it. 'To see a flock of sheep in a paddock you'd think they were like peas in a pod, but they're so grittily different and wicked it's an eye-opener. I'd forgotten how individual they can be. Get along, you!'

Nathaniel cast an uneasy eye towards Josselyn. 'We're going to have to take our break soon. Can you see what I see? She's thrown about nine hundred and ninety-nine of her thousand-and-one blocks over the fence, and that's the signal for her to yell her head off till we start throwing them back. We'll all head back for smoko—we need a break anyway. Then we'll bring her reins back and loop her to the fence and given a bit of luck she'll throw them all back in again. Now she's standing she can aim better.'

Letty said anxiously, 'Would you rather I went back and brought the tea up, then took her back to the house. I don't want to let her be a nuisance.'

'No fear. *We* can use you. Anyway, I'm dry. I'm soft after all those weeks shop-walking. You'll find out a few muscles you never suspected you had, Letitia. We'll work twice as fast after a spell. Wash your hands under the pump before you pick the child up. All right, poppet, that's your last block. You've had your fun, you tyrant. Back you go in the pushchair.'

Hope must have made an early start before the rescue of the kitten, because on the laundry bench was a batch of date scones ready to be buttered and a double-size caramel cake to be cut into squares, under an organdie throw-over. 'The scones that are over can go in the deep-freeze,' said Nathaniel, 'and the cake in the tins.' The children had grapefruit juice topped up with fizzy lemonade, but Nathaniel made them a huge pot of tea.

Letty said, 'You said "smoko" . . . do you smoke?'

'No, it's just a time-honoured term. When the shearing gangs come some smoke, but neither Owen nor I do. Nor does Hope. Do you? Feel free.'

'No, never started it, thank goodness. I just wondered. Tell me, do the shearing gangs live in? They'd have to here, wouldn't they? Though I know most come by the day nowadays, and bring their own food.'

He nodded. 'Yes. Down-country it's mostly that now, but we still put them up. The shearing-quarters were kept in better trim than the old house. The chap who leased this still used the woolshed. And he kept a couple of shepherds up here—found the stock weathered the winter better if shepherds were on hand close by. There's a good cook-house too, thank goodness. I've been lucky, in that most of the gangs have brought a cook. Didn't want Jamesina to overdo it. Oddly enough, she rather resents not having to do it. Think she liked to boast to family and friends that she was still capable of coping,'

Letty smiled sweetly as she bit into a square of caramel cake. 'Or it just could be, of course, that you're in the habit of under-estimating women. Psychological, I suppose. In spite of being grateful for unexpected help in emergency, Mr Nathaniel, you cling rather to the role of the dominant

male, don't you? To say nothing of judging by appear-
ances. Perhaps you should drop being protective and
counting us not capable of doing what we *want* to do. But
we know what we *can* do.'

The children had run outside. He took another long
draught of tea, surveyed her, said sardonically, 'With a
tongue like yours, Miss Greenaway, you're in no need of
protection. You're so keen to show me I was way out
about your suitability for here, you'll probably burn yourself out in a week. Don't be afraid to admit it, if you do.
Up here is no place for bravado and foolishness. We need
someone with the sense to maintain a steady pace. If you
work on till you drop out of sheer cussedness, I'll be in a
worse spot than ever and if you're laid up, I'll be forced
to take the children to Queenstown and throw myself on
the mercy of Miss Mattie.'

This time he scored. Letitia bit her lip. She'd overplayed
her hand. She rallied. 'Perhaps I over-reacted. But that's
your own fault, mostly. But I think that in an emergency
anyone would throw themselves into doing what must be
done. Like finishing the sheep in the yards without wasting
all the time spent rounding them up, or letting them lose
condition from being penned up. I'm really a very sensible
and staid person. I'm not trying to score off you. How
about if I say I'll take it more slowly tomorrow?'

'That's better. You can't show me you're a perfect high-
country woman in twenty-four hours. If you stop doing
that we'll get on famously. We'll call a truce. I was beginning to feel as if I'd been cast up on a desert island with
an incompatible spirit.'

All she could trust herself to say was, 'How odd that we
both felt that. Then let's get at it. If I don't feel my motives
are suspect, I'm sure the work won't exhaust me so much.'

She hastily removed the remains of a large jammy scone
from Joss's face, picked up a face-cloth, wiped her mouth,
removed her feeder, and said, 'Hope told me to heat up a
meat pie for the evening meal and that it had lashings of
vegetables in it, so I think I'll scrub some potatoes now
and pop them in the oven in their jackets, in the slow oven.

That way they'd be ready when we get in. And there are
jellies and fruit in the fridge for dessert. Okay?'

'Sure. And I dare say when I take you over to the homestead tomorrow, you'll find everything well stocked up
there, so we should manage fine till Jamesina gets back.'

'Well, even if she does have to spend longer in hospital,
I'll be able to rustle up some reasonable meals . . . that's
a good storeroom . . . without depleting the deep-freeze
too much.'

'All this and a cook too,' he mocked, going out of the
door. 'How lucky can a man get?'

'I'm not up to Cordon Bleu standard, of course, but you
won't go hungry. I wouldn't dare to put on a Ritzy meal
or you'd think I was out to impress you. It's just that
Mother and I had to share the cooking because she had
to take a job after Dad died.'

He waved the child harness at her as he departed. 'See
you back at the sheds, Man Friday. But do take your time.'

So she didn't hurry. She let Josselyn have an unham-
pered kick while she scrubbed the potatoes, whipped
cream, changed the child into a cooler-looking pair of
rompers because the sun would be on the enclosure by
now, tied a cute-looking yellow sunbonnet over the brown
curls. She left the darling feet bare. What a blessing the
baby was so docile!

The break had revived them, they tackled the sheep
almost enthusiastically, heartened by the fact that the
hordes in the yards were diminishing. Letty gave Nathaniel
full marks for saying to that small heroic figure, covered
with dust, doggedly pushing the button, 'You've got to tell
me when you've had enough, Damien, you've worked like
a Trojan.'

He didn't look set back when Damien scowled and said,
with a jerk of his dusty head towards his sister, 'When *she*
quits, *I'll* quit.'

'Right. I think you've enough sense to know when you're
whacked, mate.' It was a wonderful moment when at five-
thirty Roberta announced, 'Twelve to go!' It was also the
best sight of all to see every animal back in the paddocks,

nibbling madly, and lambs gambolling as they had weeks ago when younger.

They looked at each other and burst out laughing. They all had huge black circles under their eyes. 'Let's sluice off under the pump here,' said Nathaniel. 'I've plenty of old towels piled up. I don't fancy even the veranda getting clogged up with all this dirt. But first fluff your hair out and shake your heads.'

Even aching as they were, and with parched throats, it began to feel like fun and they had a greater sense of achievement because they'd triumphed over a disastrous day. They slapped at their clothing to disperse great clouds of dust.

Josselyn had discovered another pastime, pulling up tufts of grass and throwing them into her enclosure. What a brown berry of a child she was! As Letty turned from the pump, Nathaniel stopped her, a hand on her shoulder. She turned a look of enquiry on him.

To her surprise he took her chin between damp cool fingers, and gazed into her eyes. 'Good grief, they *are* real!' he exclaimed.

'What are, for goodness' sake?'

'Your eyelashes.'

'She was astounded. 'Mr Nathaniel! You really aren't dumb enough to think I'd wear false lashes in a sheep-yard?'

He burst out laughing. 'I didn't mean the lashes, I meant the colour. I thought that had to be artificial. Never dreamed that anyone with hair that fair could have such dark lashes.'

She heaved a sigh. 'I've never known anyone so mad! Look at Damien.' Damien was bending over Josselyn and turned round then. 'His lashes are darker than mine and look at *his* hair!' Then she added, 'But perhaps you think I bleach my hair. I can assure you——'

He held up a hand, pretending to dodge a blow. 'Pax! Pax! You wild woman. No, I don't. It's every bit as ash-blonde at the roots . . . even I can see that. And now you've washed the dust off even the down on your arms is pale gold.'

She glanced down, then up, and met a very intent look, a strange look. For quite a moment both looks held, wavered, looked away. She moistened her lips, felt she must say something . . . why on earth was she blushing? That was crazy. She said, 'Poor Mr Nathaniel, I've never known anyone part with his preconceived ideas so reluctantly. You were so determined to find me artificial, you can't believe any of me is for real. There are a few shocks ahead of you, believe me.'

She was amazed at how fiercely she wanted him to look put down. Instead the craggy face with its thatch of tussocky hair above it creased into . . . into what? Not laughter. Something that almost looked like tenderness. Just how absurd could one get? But he slipped an arm about her shoulders and hugged her. 'And I hope every shock ahead of me is as pleasant as I've had today . . . finding you *can* take it.'

He kept his arm about her shoulders. 'Now, home, mate. The job's done and a thousand thanks.'

Unseen, Letitia permitted herself a smirk. It was going to be quite easy to bring this tawny high-countryman to heel.

Damien was allowed first shower so he could watch his favourite motorbike serial. Roberta took next turn and offered to put Josselyn in her bath. 'Mum always says it refreshes her if she can play there while we get tea, but I have to stay with her. Okay?'

'Too right.' Letitia popped the pie in. The potatoes were ready. Nathaniel was showering in the laundry and came out looking a different person. How different from the shopwalker . . . this was his rightful element beyond a doubt. Glowing, confident, a man of the outdoors. 'I'll use that shower too,' said Letitia. 'There's so much dirt in my hair I wouldn't dare use the bathroom one.'

It felt marvellous. What a blessing she'd had it cut short. She just rubbed it dry and brushed it out: how heavenly to feel cool. She slipped into bra and panties, wriggled into a yellow cotton dress, flipped a tortoiseshell bracelet on one slender wrist and slid her feet into white thonged sandals.

She appeared unconscious of Nathaniel's admiring gaze. She was glad he didn't know she ached in every muscle, every bone, and would have loved to have sunk into an easy chair and complete oblivion.

He helped her dish up. Damien's programme finished, Josselyn sat in a high chair, gnawing a rusk, Damien bent his head and said in one breath, 'For every cup and plateful, Lord make us truly grateful, gosh you wouldn't believe how starving I am,' and fell to. Nathaniel picked up his plate, put it in the oven, said, 'I'm going to ring the hospital. They said it was no use when I rang earlier, but they'll be fairly sure now. You all go on eating.'

He spoke to the matron first, in the small hospital, then to Owen. They could tell the news was reasonably good, but he explained when he resumed his meal, 'It's a very clean break and, as it wasn't to the shin bone, it won't take as long as it might have. Jamesina's wasn't just a sprain, it was a small bone in her foot, broken. Your dad was thrilled, not to say surprised, that we've finished the dagging, and you heard me telling him to stay on a while. We won't take on anything but necessary jobs the next few days. He's staying at Miss Mattie's, and what he'll pass on from what I told him will make both women feel easier in their minds. Especially Hope.' He glanced at Letty, whose face was pink from the praise he'd given over the phone. He sat down and began demolishing his wedge of pie and the floury potatoes in their crisp brown skins, swimming with butter. Josselyn loved the potatoes too, opening her mouth like a hungry nestling as Letitia spooned in alternate mouthfuls with chopped up soft-boiled egg.

'Thank heaven she's a good feeder,' said Letty. 'Give me a greedy child every time. Timmy's mother had twins and one was an absolute monster to feed. Talk about taking a horse to water and not being able to make it drink . . . it was nothing to small Kit. But he was all right as soon as he could feed himself.' She began to laugh. 'His mother was so sick of it, she once sieved vegetables into an ice-cream cone and let him eat it like that. Now does she have a bottle and off to bed?'

Roberta nodded. 'Yes, she has it in bed, but Mum always holds it. She doesn't always finish it, she falls asleep.'

Fortunately Letitia found it worked, and tiptoed out to find Damien in bed reading and Roberta and Nathaniel finishing the dishes. She flopped with a huge sigh into an easy chair and accepted the cup of coffee he brought her. He said, 'I take it you'll sleep in the double room that the baby's room opens off, so you'll be near?'

She nodded. 'Roberta tells me she sleeps right through till about six-thirty as a rule. What a blessing! But I'd like to be near. I'll change the sheets when I've revived. Do you want to go to the homestead? We'll be all right.'

'No, I'm staying here, in the spare room, just in case of emergencies. Not that I anticipate any, but I'm not leaving you on your own.'

She sat bolt upright. 'What makes you think I wouldn't be able to handle them if there were emergencies?'

He waved her down. 'Calm down! The responsibility is mine. Kids can be sick in the night or run temperatures. And I've an idea you're so determined to show me you can take this life, you wouldn't call me.'

She looked at him with unfriendly eyes. 'Mr Nathaniel, I'm not so pig-headed that I'd put the children at risk to score one off you.'

He lifted a sardonic eyebrow. 'Wouldn't you? Maybe you wouldn't but I don't know you well enough to be sure of that. *I stay*. Now don't argue about it. Roberta will be back in a moment. She's looking through those books Dad sent up for the kids. You needn't have any qualms. I'm not a womaniser. None of these doors have locks, very few modern doors have. Interesting, that. But you can drop off to chaste slumbers as untroubled as Josselyn did.'

She looked at him witheringly. 'You flatter yourself! The thought hadn't crossed my mind. I haven't reached twenty-six without learning how to call the tune. And in any case, you don't need to stay here. I'm sure we'll all be flat out to it till tomorrow after the day we've had.'

In which she was quite, quite wrong.

CHAPTER SIX

LETITIA surfaced from fathomless depths of sleep to darkness and an unfamiliar sound, and to a bewildering sense of not knowing where she was. Then the events of yesterday rushed back on her in a dismaying flood. That was a baby crying! Josselyn, the placid infant who never, they'd said, woke before six-thirty! The baby who now was going to be confronted by a stranger. The luminous alarm clock said two o'clock.

The years at Pengelly's had given Letitia selfconfidence to a remarkable degree, but she felt it ooze out of her there and then. She pulled herself together. She didn't want the whole household wakened, so she sprang out of bed, snapped on a light, went into the little room. Poor mite, she was probably just wet, and a dry tail and perhaps half a bottle would work wonders.

She spoke soothingly as she went, 'It's all right, darling . . . here's Letty.' She switched on a light that had a dimmer. She felt remorseful when she saw the child. She was sitting up and her face was so red and blotched it was evident she'd been crying for some time. Letitia had been so tired her level of unconsciousness had been shockingly deep.

To her alarm the baby turned from her and screamed even louder. Letty picked her up, held her firmly, put her hand at the back of the downy head, pressed the little face into her . . . perhaps the feel of a comforting shoulder would be less strange than a face and voice she didn't know. She uttered hushing noises, 'There, there . . . my wee lambkin . . . sssh . . . ' over and over again. Yes, she was wet and a change might benefit immensely. Roberta had left some of the folded nappies ready for the morning, praise be, so Letty carried the baby into the big room, laid her on the bed, slipped the wet ones off, almost praying that Josselyn would cease this ghastly yelling. It would be so humiliating to have to waken Roberta to try to pacify her. She didn't think this crying indicated pain, just sheer upset and real paddy. Josselyn had two teeth at the top and two at the bottom and she positively gritted them together.

Her little legs were going as if she were cycling and it was quite evident that if she'd been standing she'd have stamped her feet. Her world was all wrong! Letty thought she'd never get the dry ones on, but at last it was done and the flannel one pinned on top, all without piercing the child, although it was by no means the secure job Roberta had made of it. They'd get kicked off any moment.

The kitchen was more distant from the other bedrooms, so she made for it. Letty would hate his high-and-mightiness Nathaniel Pengelly to arrive out to find her at a loss. Roberta had left the mixture ready for that six-thirty feed, and the bottle was sitting in a steel pannikin on one of the electric elements. She padded out, in her bare feet and flimsy nightgown, gratefully glad of the cool feel of the vinyl under her feet this stiflingly hot January night. Oh, that was an idea . . . the baby might be too hot.

She managed to get a finger under the chin and it came away moist and hot. The baby clothes were kept in a press in the kitchen, so she took a clean face-cloth from a pile, held it under the cold tap with one hand, squeezed it out well, managed to hold the baby away from her long enough to get it under the chin, wiped well round the neck and across the back of the brown curls, which were damp too. Josselyn actually desisted for a relieved moment in her yelling, but when Letitia wiped the little face she realised it for a mistake immediately, because all babies object to face-washing . . . Josselyn fairly let the cries rip then!

The bottle was warm enough . . . she tried a drop on her wrist . . . better to have it too cool than too hot, and she went into the living-room and sank on to the couch. Josselyn fought madly against all her efforts to get the teat into her mouth, it was just no go. Letitia felt her ears were

ringing . . . impossible to believe that two tiny lungs
could hold all that sound . . . also impossible that three
people in that house were sleeping the sleep of the dead,
lucky things! Letitia stood up, put the bottle down and
began to pace the floor, wiping the tears away. What a
reservoir those tear-ducts must hold! She stopped at each
picture on the wall, making idiotic remarks, hoping the
child's interest might be caught long enough to stop a
scream in mid-performance.

Letty found herself thinking wrathfully, I wanted to be
a governess, not a nursemaid and rouseabout and housekeeper and all! Then she felt ashamed, she who was so sure
she could show Nathaniel Pengelly she had what it took
for the high-country. Here was this poor scrap, deprived
suddenly of mother and father and all that was dear and
familiar . . . she'd better return the bottle to the hot
water meanwhile.

She came back into the living-room. Josselyn's breathing
was distressed, naturally, she was all stuffed up, a sorry
sight, and now the sobs were developing into hiccups. This
could go on for hours yet.

At that the door opened and Nathaniel stood there,
bare-chested, shortie pyjama pants on, hair tousled, sleepy-
eyed. 'Heavens, what a noise! How long's this been going
on?'

'Only about an hour,' said Letitia tartly, 'I envy you
your quality of sleep.'

'Good grief, you mean she's been yelling at that pitch
for all that time, or was it just a whimper at first?'

'It was no whimper, it was bellows at top, unless I too
was forty fathoms deep when she started. Believe me, it was
much louder than this when I first picked her up. Talk
about lungs! I've changed her, patted her, tried to bottle
her, wiped a cool flannel all round her neck and head . . .
Hush, darling, hush. I've crooned *Rockabye Baby* to her,
all to no avail. She's not ill, I'm sure of that, just missing
her mother.'

Nathaniel came across, attempted to take the child . . .
and that really did it. The little face screwed itself up into
a paroxysm of rage and the tiny hands beat against Leti-

tia's chest. For one unworthy moment Letty was glad. If
Josselyn had held out her hands to Nathaniel and subsided
into silence it would have been galling, but the next
moment she knew it would have been heaven to have even
momentary cessation of the racket. Nathaniel contented
himself with patting the protesting back. 'She can't keep
it up for ever,' he said feebly.

Letitia's tone was bitter. 'I wish I could be sure of that!'
Suddenly she giggled. 'If only she'd stop for a second I
might be able to see the funny side of this. My nightgown
is absolutely soaked!'

For the first time Nathaniel looked at her properly. He
said, rather roughly, 'You ought to have more than that
on.'

Letitia could have stamped her foot. 'All I could think
of was trying to stop her disturbing the whole household.
It's far too hot to think about the decencies.'

Nathaniel, over the roaring, sounded a real chuckle.
'Don't be absurd, any man would appreciate that delectable if skimpy garment! But when you said your
nightgown was wet, I thought it would feel most uncomfortable. Here, I'll get something.'

He strode off, came back with a pale blue housecoat. 'I
suppose this is Hope's, didn't like to dive into your case.
Now, that child can damned well come to me . . . she
can't yell much louder . . . and you can get into this.'

He yanked Josselyn away from her. 'Help, *you are wet*
. . . I say, can that really be just tears or has she——'

'No, she hasn't. Her tail's quite dry.' She slipped into
the housecoat, then took Josselyn, still crying, back.
Josselyn stopped in mid-yell, a relieved smile lit the little
face, and she held out her arms most joyously to Letitia
and buried her face against the soft blue gown.

Over her head two pairs of eyes met, the green and the
tawny. 'Well, I'll be damned! That's done it. Her mother's
dressing-gown! Letitia, sit down, keep on patting her just
like that. You must be exhausted. I'm terribly sorry I didn't
wake earlier.'

'I'm not sitting down yet. As long as she stays quiet, I'll
stay upright, just walking about slowly. I was terrified she'd

do herself some harm. Mr Nathaniel, would you get me a clean handkerchief? I used up several mopping her up. I put a pile of them on my dressing-table.'

He came back with a towelling robe on, and her slippers in his hand. Gently she dried the little face, talking foolish baby-talk such as women have used for generations. The sobs gradually ceased, an occasional hiccup persisted. Nathaniel steered Letitia to the couch and she sat down slowly. Josselyn snuggled into her, a little hand came up, pushed aside the lace-trimmed frills of the nightgown, nuzzled into its dampness. Nathaniel stared, then couldn't stop a chuckle. 'Well, look at that! Didn't Hope say she'd weaned her just a month ago? It beats all. What a memory!'

Letitia said quickly, 'Not memory, instinct, I suppose,' and to her annoyance, blushed.

He said instantly, 'Sorry, Letty. Forgive a crude farmer, but I was astounded and intrigued. I'm also intrigued that you should blush. I thought it was a dying art. I'd put you down—in the shop—as definitely hard-boiled. I'm finding out some surprising things about you.'

She said sarcastically, even though keeping her voice low, 'And you have more surprises ahead of you, believe me. I'm not hard-boiled, Nathaniel Pengelly, and I'm not a prude. That blush surprised me too. Now, if you would get that bottle out of the pannikin, she may just take it, and when I put her down, I'm going to take one blanket off. She had two on. I'm sure she was too hot.'

He padded out, came back. Two little hands reached up eagerly, clutched it, guided the teat between the rosebud lips. It was hard to believe this tranquil infant had ever been capable of those lusty roars, those gushing tears. She made no objection when the drink was interrupted and Letitia sat her up, and rubbed her back. She merely obliged with a resounding burp and returned to the bottle. Nathaniel took it out to the kitchen and returned to sit beside them. Letty said, 'You could go off to bed now, she's almost off. I'll let her get pretty sound before I put her down.'

He shook his head. 'No, it wouldn't be fair. I'm not going till she's down and you're back in bed. Otherwise you'll be dead on your feet tomorrow. Then I'll doss down here so I'm bound to hear her if she wakes again.'

Josselyn cuddled down, one little hand came up to push itself inside the housecoat again and remained, like a little starfish, just under Letitia's throat. A feeling she'd never known before swept over Letty. Purely maternal, she supposed, and felt stirred strangely.

Then another feeling took its place . . . it was quite incredible, this. It was three-thirty on a summer's night, in a remote inland valley, and she was sitting here, a baby on her lap, with Mr Nathaniel Pengelly, who'd called her a human iceberg, who'd never come near her in the shop if he could help it . . . his shoulder was against hers, his hand was still automatically patting the sleeping child. It was a very comfortable couch . . . she mustn't stir yet though . . . it would be too dreadful if she had to go through it all again . . . the patting was very soothing. Good for Mr Nathaniel . . . very soothing . . .

Suddenly she woke. Her face was against something rough . . . like a towel . . . her eyes tried to focus . . . blue towelling . . . and there was something warm under it, and something else warm on her lap and a soft head under her chin. She came fully awake. Her head, heaven help her, was against Mr Nathaniel's shoulder, Josselyn was fast asleep. He was no longer patting but his left arm was across the baby holding her safe, lest Letitia relax too much. His hand was clamping her right elbow to keep the baby firm. He must have stayed awake.

She stirred, looked up. His chin was very near. Yes, he was awake, he looked down on her and grinned. 'At least you've had half-an-hour. I was just going to wake you. I thought it might look a bit odd if we were still here by morning. Roberta's a very outspoken child—she'd probably tell her father on the phone. I'll take Josselyn and you can yank that blanket off the cot and with a bit of luck we'll get three or four hours in by morning.'

She didn't stir till Roberta came in with a cup of tea at eight o'clock. 'Nat mentioned you'd had a bad night with Josselyn. She's flat out to it still. He's cooking breakfast.' Neither of the children seemed in the least curious about

Josselyn's performance. Like most children Letty supposed they were themselves the hub of their own little world. Letitia was a substitute mother and wakeful nights were parents' concern, not children's. It was better that way. This was a slightly tricky situation, even for these days.

There was more relaxation about today. The crutching was over and although no doubt there'd be plenty other farm chores, Nathaniel wouldn't be looking for them. He hoped to stay fairly near the houses. 'I'll take you over to the homestead when Josselyn wakes. At the moment I'm all in favour of letting sleeping dogs lie. You'll want to see the old schoolroom and your own quarters.'

'Quarters? That sounds extensive for a bedroom at the schoolroom end.'

He grinned. 'It's decidedly extensive. Might tie in with your idea of keeping out from under Jamesina's feet. In its day there was quite a staff carried here, after the first few frugal years. There were plenty of women of a type, who came in the wake of the miners . . . dance-hall girls, camp-followers, but gradually others came, those who had accompanied their men into the wilderness, wives of early farmers. There was the occasional tragedy, due to the tough terrain, and when it was the bread-winner who lost his life, the widow couldn't always return to the towns. She had to earn her keep and the children's. In time, here, there were two or three cottages for farm workers and families. My great-great-grandmother had educated her own family, but she couldn't cope with the others, so she had an annexe built on, at the far end. One of the upper rooms gives a glimpse of the lake, despite Big Slip.'

'The first real governess was a woman whose husband was drowned swimming his sheep over the Kawarau, and she had two children to support. Gran-Ellen, as she was called in her later years by my grandfather, whom I remember quite well, built a good schoolroom, and the annexe had a sitting-room, kitchen, and four bedrooms eventually. Gran-Ellen added to it when this governess married Joseph, Ellen and Grigor's eldest son, and it became their home because Ellen didn't believe in young couples sharing a parents' home. Kitty had a third child, called Nicol Nathaniel, and he sired my mother.

'Grigor kept a whale-boat at our cove for supplies and quick access to Queenstown. There was a jolly good wagon trail down to the cove—they shipped their wool out that way of course, and supplied mutton to the miners too. There were stables and horse-yards and paddocks there just up from the jetty. The slip obliterated them completely, and it was a miracle not an animal was lost. There was a big party on here for Joseph and Kitty's silver wedding, so the wagons and horses were all up at the homestead stables because they'd brought the guests who'd come by boat. The storm broke, it's remembered yet by the few surviving old-timers in the district, it lasted three days and on the third night the hillsides caved in. The lake banked up too, there was a terrific flood. That, and the rabbit menace, finished Mararangi.'

'Till now,' Letty found herself saying. She looked up and in that instant as he echoed her words, Nathaniel lifted his chin in a gesture of pride that had come to him from a long-dead ancestor and she realised how much the valley meant to him.

Roberta said wistfully, 'I expect Miss Greenaway will want to get the schoolroom all set up for when Mum gets back. Wouldn't it be a good idea to stay over there, all of us, so we could get on with it? I love fixing things up and I dare say,' she added maturely, 'like all men, you'd rather be in your own bed, Nat.'

He grinned. 'The wisdom of the serpent! All women have a bit of it. They twist things for their own ends. It wouldn't have anything to do with the fact that you and Damien like the old house for hide-and-seek?'

Roberta said composedly, 'Well, there's that too,' and spoilt it by giggling.

Nathaniel said, 'I'm not sure. This house is infinitely easier to manage, for Miss Greenaway, and we don't want to upset Josselyn.'

Roberta was nothing if not persistent. 'But if you had such a bad night with her last night, you'd have blamed that if we'd gone to the homestead then, wouldn't you?

Besides, if she slept so little then she'll go off like a lamb tonight.'

'I make no promises. We'll wash up, make the beds, feed the dogs and hens and go over home. It's over to Miss Greenaway.'

The stables, built on the old English style, with a clock tower centred on the roof, were between the two houses, and the valley, as Damien said, turned a corner before they could get a glimpse of chimneys between the very fine old English trees that clustered about it, so the entire setting was revealed to Letty like looking at a finished canvas.

It was long and wide, built against the natural contours of the hill that curved back here, the ideal place for a pioneer dwelling in a once treeless valley that could be devastated by the winds that had swept across Lake Wakatipu, especially before Big Slip blocked the lake access. It somehow, in one comprehensive look, revealed its past history . . . the humble little cottage at this end, the dormer-windowed and very fine, if shabby, structure in the middle, the rather higgledy-piggledy annexe at the lakeward end.

More than that, in the improvements already begun, Letty read its future. It was a startling recognition that came to her . . . in that although it could take years, she felt in her very bones that here was a homestead destined to become one of the most beautiful show-places of the Lake Country. So she stopped in her tracks, drinking it in.

Roberta was pushing Josselyn in the stroller and she and Damien ran on ahead, but Nathaniel stopped with Letty, not speaking. He'd kept silent instinctively, brought to it by her very stillness.

He saw her lift her lashes and sweep her look from side to side, her gaze drop to the low terraces on which it stood, no doubt built there in case the valley floor ever flooded, then take in the far from perfect gardens, weedy but colourful, the blaze of geraniums against the uneven patio of lake-stones, coral and scarlet, blush-pink and magenta, the nasturtiums tumbling down the old steps, each cup among their circular green leaves a bit of sunset gold, and everywhere for relief from the brightness of their hues, the purples and blues of aubrietia, michaelmas daisies, campanulas. It looked as if someone had come out among the surviving remnants of Ellen's and Kitty's garden and scattered with a prodigal hand the contents of scores of seed-packets, anything to restore the glory that had once been this Garden of Heaven.

Finally, Nathaniel demanded, 'Well?'

She mustn't gush. He'd hate that. There was still so much to be done and most of Nathaniel's time must be spent on tractors, on horseback, in the woolshed, out on these mountainsides when the harsh winters clothed them in treacherous, stifling snow . . . She said simply, 'It is good, Nathaniel. It would be a crime not to restore this.' For once she had left the 'Mr' off.

He released a deep breath. 'Thank you. I think so. You aren't like someone else I brought here. She called it God-forsaken.'

A protest was wrung from her. 'Oh, no, *never* forsaken by God. It's just waiting to come back into its own.'

He said nothing, then she couldn't help herself. 'Was that someone Portia Latimer? Because if so, I wouldn't let it matter if I were you. In my years at Pengelly's there were very few customers I actively detested. She was one. She reduced one of my assistants to tears one day. She was shallow and artificial and rude. Her judgment of a thing of beauty like this needn't matter. That's blunt, but I make no apologies.'

He didn't answer immediately. Then, 'No, it wasn't Portia. That was only a flash-in-the-pan. This was someone who mattered a great deal—then.'

There was nothing to reply to that. She mustn't betray curiosity. She said crisply. 'The children are getting too far ahead. I like the way you've enlarged the windows without destroying the—oh, how can I put it?—without making it look like a modern out-of-place improvement. And I take it you've deepened the entrance to make it a spot for enjoying the out-of-doors?'

They quickened their steps. 'Yes, it was rather clever of you to pick that. I'd heard Gran-Ellen would have loved pillars each side, but their finance just wouldn't run to it. There were always greater priorities. Grandfather told me. She said once that she hoped a descendant of hers and Grigor's might some day be wealthy enough to do it. It was crazy, I know, but I had it done in my first year up here, otherwise I felt I'd be like Grigor, never quite able to afford it. I was lucky. An old district hall was being demolished down the foot of the lake. I got them dirt cheap, so was able to put my money into the haulage. *That* did nearly break the bank.'

'How satisfying. It makes me think of that proverb . . . it's a Chinese one, I think. I'm not sure. "If you have two loaves of bread, sell one and buy a lily." ' Their eyes met and Letitia had the strangest sensation. Could this possibly be the man who'd been so scathing about her, who'd only brought her here because governesses were nearly extinct? And what a strange thing that for all of ten minutes she had completely forgotten that. Forgotten her avowed goal . . . to make him eat his words. She realised something else . . . *she was in dire danger of admiring him!*

Because of the stroller they didn't go up the old-fashioned steps that were flanked by grey stone urns that some day would have flowers spilling out of them again, but went round by a side-path, giving Josselyn a 'Rocky road to Dublin,' over the lake-stones.

'Isn't it funny—and nice—not to have to lock one's door?' said Letitia. 'Time was, in our suburb, Mother said, when they never had to bother. It's so different now in the cities.'

Damien turned the brass door-knob and they stepped in. The staircase was *kauri* so must have come by coastal steamer from the North Island to Invercargill, brought by bullock wagon to the foot of the lake, and rafted up here or brought on one of the paddle-steamers that plied their trade so constantly in earlier years, she supposed.

Nathaniel nodded. 'Probably. I don't think I ever heard. But it must have been one of the few extravagances they allowed themselves.'

'No wonder you dreamed of restoring this. When I was a child, it would have enchanted me to have something like this in the family, but ours was very much a working-class background, both the English and the Dutch side. You seem to have done quite a bit already to the inside. I wasn't prepared for that. Not when you so desperately needed to bring the land back into full production and at a bad time in farming economy.'

He said, without emotion, 'Mother began to worry lest she'd landed too much on my plate. She put up some of the original capital needed, then when she saw the fluctuating markets, down-trends in many traditional ones, and high interest rates, she slightly panicked. She thought she'd hung a millstone round my neck to satisfy her own dreams. So I used some of my own money to bring the pillars here and have them erected. It couldn't be a do-it-yourself job as it had to be done by experts in construction. I got it done as a surprise for her, brought the whole family up when it was finished: Mother, Dad, James, and Maddie, my sister. You've served her, I suppose? Yes, well, we came round the bend with a flourish in the jeep.

'I'll never forget Mother's face. She ran up the steps like a young girl, and patted each pillar. She said, "Now I know you'll make a go of it, Nathaniel." She was quite well then. She had no idea, neither had we, that she would be gone within the year. That made it all the more satisfying . . . that she'd seen it. Not just a promise to create what Ellen had wanted, but seeing it accomplished.' He stopped, said, 'I'd better get on with showing you round and start being practical or you'll think me a sentimental twit.'

'No, never that. Those pillars and what prompted you to erect them are a poem in stone. The Correspondence School likes to have the pupils do projects on their backgrounds. Or at least where they're living. These children are fortunate in having a setting like this. They could produce something that would be worth preserving in the national archives.'

Some of the rooms needed much decorating, but the kitchen, the women's workshop, was all a kitchen should be, yet with a homely touch in the retention of the old black coal-range that Jamesina had restored to ebony glossiness. But all the labour-saving devices were there. Letitia approved of that. In some farmhouses, kitchen improvements came last, but she had an idea that in these days men knew that convenience in the kitchen was a necessity. Of course, it also freed the women to lend a hand outside . . . she hoped that wasn't too cynical. However, she needn't impute that to Nathaniel; he'd done this to provide first-class conditions for a housekeeper, not a wife. Jamesina would hardly be expected to lend a hand dipping, tailing, lambing, driving the fork-lift! But he was lucky to have Jamesina up here.

The big drawing-room, as it had been called originally, was entirely bare, but the sitting-room off the kitchen was reasonably sized and comfortable. The carpet, wall-to-wall, was one of the superb New Zealand woollen ones, in soft greens; heavy, lined curtains repeated that colour and there was no need to provide window nets for privacy here. The fireplace was fashioned of the Wakatipu stone in all its beautiful colours, pearly, rose, and sage-green, grey and mauve. No more beautiful stone existed. A blackened iron kettle sat on one of the wide hobs, and there was a trivet on the grate to be swung over.

Jamesina's mending-basket stood beside one of the chintzy chairs that looked so comfortable, and her knitting lay on an ancient round table. A bowl of dark red roses stood on it too, so fresh they must have been picked just yesterday when she had been preparing for the master's return and his newly acquired governess. How different the situation now. The bookcases in the alcoves each side of the fireplace were crammed. She went across to them and ran her eye over the titles. She turned, said, 'These, at least most of them, belonged to the early days here, didn't they? Were they left here when Kitty and Joseph left?'

He nodded. 'They took a lot, but these just had old sheets tacked over the shelves. Some are hopelessly outdated but a lot of them we revelled in when we used to camp here in school holidays. We used to rent it from the man who used the land for rough grazing. Even Dad loved it. It took him right away from business. Beyond reach of a phone then, of course.'

Her eye lit on a row of books . . . 'Oh, Anthony Trollope! How lovely to see early editions, not just paperbacks of the TV series.'

He nodded, 'You can see some of those in quite a few old houses around Queenstown. No doubt his trip here generated local interest.'

The green eyes lit up, widened. 'Do you mean he was actually here? Surely not. Did he ever come to New Zealand? When?'

He thought for a moment. 'Must have been in the eighteen-seventies, because I remember reading his account of bathing in the pools in the pink and white terraces at Rotorua, so it must have been before the eruption of Mount Tarawera that destroyed them. He'd ridden down from Auckland. It was winter when he was here. He came up from the foot of the lake by steamer, in drenching rain. Mrs Trollope, Rose, was with him. They travelled through the gorges in heavy snow, got stuck at Lawrence, had to get out and help the horses drag the coach through the drifts, and were glad to reach Milton for dry clothes and warm hospitality.'

'You've made my day,' said Letitia. 'Isn't it marvellous? Life, I mean. Always new exciting things to find out.'

Nathaniel said slowly, 'I think you'll do as a governess after all. If you've that attitude you'll infect the kids with a desire to learn.'

Her eyes sparked. 'I don't like that *after all*. It's horribly patronising. You're still going on the wholly superficial impression you had of me as *Letitia for Loveliness,* which was a false one in any case, brought about by our financial needs and your father's kink. Oh dear, I can hear the children coming. We mustn't appear to be quarrelling. It undermines authority.'

His mouth twitched. 'Were we quarrelling? I thought it took two.'

It reduced her heated remarks to unimportance. He added, 'To me it was more in the way of finding out things, just as you found out about Anthony Trollope just now.

If you want to continue that search, you can dig into that bookcase over there. The new one. It contains my books from home. Hennessy's biography of Anthony is among them. It's superb. What I liked about Trollope was that he was so disciplined in his writing. Even on board ship, on British Postal business, when he wrote *End* to one book, he started another next morning. It applies to most ways of earning one's crust. Yes, kids?'

'There are slots on the staircase,' said Roberta excitedly. You know what you said when you were trying to put us off coming over here? That Josselyn would probably crawl safely up, then tumble down; well, there are these grooves just like one our grannie has in her house. You've got lots of core-board. You'd just have to saw it to size and slip it in.'

Damien got in, 'It would be best to do two, then if she's upstairs with us, we could put it at the top. Save carrying it up.'

Letty expected him to squash them with the legitimate excuse that he had better things to do, but he said good-humouredly, 'Okay, kids, but we'll try Joss down for her midday nap first over here and if she settles we'll move in. I'm not having your governess's sleep disturbed again tonight.'

As they rushed out again he said to Letitia, 'Perhaps I'm soft, but they stayed home most of the holidays and living in another house for a few days might seem like a vacation. That stove here is the same as the one over there and you managed that okay. The freezer here is well filled.'

'Oh, I'll try not to use too much of that. It's not as if I'm teaching yet. It'd be daunting to any housekeeper to find her emergency stores depleted. There'll be plenty of home-killed lamb and mutton?'

'Sure is, and land-locked salmon and our own beef and venison.'

'Oh, yes, you mentioned running some deer.'

'Yes, like most farmers these days, I'm diversifying. You can't see them from here because their enclosures are in one or two smaller valleys leading out of this one. I'll extend them when I can spare more capital for the fencing.

We'll take you to see them some time when Hope is back. Do you happen to ride?'

'I suppose you could call it riding. I had two or three holidays on a Maniototo farm and they taught me to ride a slow old thing, aptly called Tortoise. Why?'

'You don't forget the knack and we've a very placid mare. You can try her out and when you feel confident enough we'll take you to see the deer valleys.'

The door to the schoolroom annexe was down a long passage that opened into a tiny sitting-room still with its original furniture, but it was spotlessly kept. Evidently Jamesina had given it a good clean-up. There were dahlias in glowing yellows and tangerines on a gate-legged table in the middle, some shabby easy chairs and a bookcase. The schoolroom led off it and as they went in something stirred in Letitia. It wasn't the sort of classroom she'd envisaged teaching in years ago, but here was the atmosphere of what she'd longed to do in life. A big old table, at which, presumably, generations of farm children had done their lessons, was now given to drawing requisites and—in a good light—made her itch to sketch. Near the end windows were two new desks. Evidently Nathaniel wouldn't economise on the welfare of the station children. There was an old map, belonging to the days when there was a false pride in the fact that 'the sun never sets on the British Empire' because their possessions were splashed all over it in red, but there were also splendid up-dated maps, neatly pinned up, a brand-new globe, and the huge blackboard that ran the length of one wall had been freshly painted. Vinyl covered the floor and there were thick sheepskins for cold feet to rest upon under the desks, including Letitia's own.

Nathaniel's priorities were ones Letitia had to approve. Again she had a curious, lost sort of tremor run over her as if she felt her deep resentment and strong purpose about this man seemed to be slipping away from her. But no doubt it would return in some solitary hour when what he'd said about her to his father would sting again in a whiplash that made her very spirit writhe.

There was a reasonably large bedroom downstairs, with a tiny one off it, ideal for Josselyn's cot. 'But where on earth is the staircase, children?' she demanded.

They shouted with laughter. 'We thought you'd never ask! Off the sitting-room. Bet you thought it was a cupboard. We call it the Secret Stair. That's why we like it.'

No wonder she'd thought it a cupboard. It was twin to one the other side of the fireplace, the leaded panels in it just the same. When they led the way up she was surprised to find the walls were brick, hand-made ones, of the local clay, baked in a kiln on the estate. 'Kitty was afraid of wooden walls in so narrow a stairway, in case of fire, so Grigor and Joseph made these,' Nathaniel added. 'And there's a good fire-escape, iron-ladder type, from the landing up top too.'

There were two narrow beds in each room, not the now valuable old brass ones, but iron ones, black, with white honeycomb-fringed quilts on each. But it was the view from one that took Letitia's fancy. It looked out high above the trees through a gap in the hills of Big Slip, to the lake and the mountains on its far side. And there, ideally, in that triangle of startlingly blue water, perfectly centred, was the graceful *SS Earnslaw*, making its way with a load of tourists up-lake.

Letty said slowly, 'I suppose the Slip has been hated ever since it happened, it must have changed life so disastrously for Joseph and Kitty, but many an artist would feel that gap is a perfect frame for the view. Gives a perspective that the wider view could never have had. What am I looking at over there?'

'At Mount Nicholas Station and the mountains that reach behind it right to Lake Te Anau and the road to Milford Sound. And if you climbed to the top of the first hill of Big Slip, you could look back along Wakatipu to Queenstown and up the other way to Glenorchy and Paradise.'

She said slowly, '*This* Garden of Eden will do me.' She hadn't meant to say it.

They began arranging the schoolroom. Letty felt that at last she was settling in, that this was more normal. The lessons to start the first term of the year at the beginning of February were already there in their large packages and she decided she would work on these at night. She'd need to keep a hop, step, and jump ahead of the children.

To their great surprise Josselyn went down like a lamb, so they moved quietly upstairs and made up the beds there. Roberta and Damien brought over what toys and books they couldn't live without, and with the last lot Letitia said, 'Mr Nathaniel, you don't need to stay to help, surely I can manage this?'

'Oh, you got stuck into the sheep yesterday, it's up to me to get you settled in here. We'll have lunch in a moment now Josselyn's off, then I'll take the other two away with me. I've some work to do on culverts and they love that. To them it's like the age-old fascination of building dams in streams, only in reverse: we clear the blockages. You could have a lie-down if you want to, while Josselyn sleeps.'

She turned a scornful look on him. 'Not likely! In theory that's what mothers are supposed to do. In practice it's the time they scoot round the housework like hell. And just as relaxing, to know they've coped with the chores. How about eggs and chips for lunch?'

It was going to be heavenly when he departed and she had some thinking-time to herself. Her hands could be busy but her mind could roam uninhibitedly. Nevertheless, as their voices faded in the distance, she flopped down and let the blessed silence roll over her. She'd come up here in such a blaze of hostility that now she needed to analyse some very contradictory feelings. She had been determined to be the stiff and starchy governess, cool and distant yet capable of being confined in an almost inaccessible area. She'd imagined everyone attending to their own duties. Instead she'd been pitchforked into the most intimate of domestic chores with the man who had so despised her. Even though some of the things she'd managed had surprised him—and delighted him, she knew—he was still extremely doubtful of this cosmetician his father had practically forced upon him. Not to say wondering if this was the new broom merely sweeping clean!

A little smile touched her lips. Well, it was a wonderful opportunity really to impress upon him her other qualities, her other image. The true Letty. A girl who genuinely loved the high-country. Who could, in an emergency, turn not only cook-and-bottle-washer, but minder of babies, hustler along of recalcitrant lambs, everything a high-country wife ought to be. She'd notched up several scores to her tally already. She would build on that . . . set him up nicely. With a few feminine wiles thrown in, she didn't doubt she could bring him to the proposing point.

CHAPTER SEVEN

LETITIA'S thoughts flew as she prepared vegetables, peeled apples for a pie, gave the leg of lamb extra cooking time because it hadn't quite defrosted. She decided to serve redcurrant jelly with it when she discovered some in the jam cupboard, but she'd make mint sauce too, in case Nathaniel didn't like the jelly. She'd noticed mint clustering round the back steps. She grinned to herself, knowing she was thinking that the best way to a man's heart was through his stomach! She hardly recognised herself in this scheming female who had taken over. She pushed the recurring jab from her conscience about meanness of motive to the back of her mind.

She must get as much as possible done before Josselyn woke. It would be maddening to fail to impress a man just because one got distracted by one small crawling baby. She had to admit to herself that she found the baby-care more daunting than anything else. It would be so awful to get so disorganised that she burnt the pastry, reduced the lovely waxy new potatoes to mush . . . perhaps she should put some of the larger ones to roast round the meat just in case . . . because you couldn't leave a baby in the middle of changing her or feeding her. Thank heaven, though, that she'd behaved like an angel today. And bless Nathaniel, in spite of everything, for taking the others off her hands.

She even managed to get out to pick some flowers. The perfume of roses was heavy on the air. Of course these were probably descendants of long-ago roses when the accent wasn't so heavy on colour but rather on sweetness. It was lovely to be able to savour this untidy old garden to the full. That trellis would probably have fallen down but for the gnarled and ancient honeysuckle about it, and that arch

over there had evidently been strengthened not long ago.
What old-fashioned blooms! They were clusters of half-
open white roses with creamy centres. What had Grannie
Greenaway called them? Seven-sister roses. And there was
a very pale yellow. She'd read recently that the deep yellow
roses had just been perfected this century, that till then they
had been very pale. The newer ones were more beautiful,
granted, but oh, the fragrance of these! She cut them
lavishly. They'd perfume her own little sitting-room. Her
own? Go easy, Letitia Greenaway. Don't get too fond of
it. You're here only for a time and for a purpose. She broke
off a few stalks of lavender, and some gypsophila for her
bedroom.

As she went in she looked down on her floury jeans
distastefully. She'd change. Josselyn slept on. Letitia
splashed water on her face, opened her wardrobe, ran her
eye along. Yes, green was the coolest colour of all. A sun-
dress. It was loose, a shift dress, and with just straps, it left
her shoulders bare. She would set the table in the living-
room away from the cooking smells and the heat of the
kitchen. She slipped her feet into thonged green sandals
and caught back the short hair each side with two old-
fashioned, but coming back into popularity again, green
bone clasps. Nothing new under the sun. She decided
against the matching earrings, it might look too dressed
up.

They all exclaimed with pleasure when they came in.
Josselyn had been changed, fed, and was playing contentedly in her play-pen. There was a white cloth on the round
table, with a border of green. A delectably cool-looking
glass jug stood on it, with a sort of fruit punch Letty had
concocted from grapefruit juice, pineapple juice, and dry
ginger ale, and slivers of lemon and cucumber floated on
its surface. The mint sauce and redcurrant jelly made
splashes of colour. She took pleasure in their approval,
went out to the kitchen, took the leg of lamb out of the
warming drawer and began to carve it.

She looked at Nathaniel. 'I dare say, like most men, you
dodge the carving except when you have visitors?'

'Sure do. About three hundred and sixty times a year. I like my dinner all put out for me on my plate. Stays hotter.'

She nodded. 'I thought so, but I've got extra vegies in dishes in the warming drawer because I'm not sure how much everyone likes.'

'I think,' said Damien solemnly, 'I won't need to be told to eat up tonight. I feel as if my stomach's the size of an elephant's and very empty.'

They washed quickly and sat down. As Nathaniel finished his second helping of pie he groaned. 'I shouldn't have. That was sheer greed!' Then he laughed as if irresistibly. 'I still feel slightly stunned. Never in my wildest dreams could I have imagined ten days ago that I'd be sitting here, with *Letitia for*—with Letitia the cosmetician, eating her pie and knowing she's not just my governess but the woman at the helm in an emergency.'

Roberta looked up from scooping up her last spoonful, 'What? You were a cosmetician? You mean you were at the cosmetics counter? Oh, beauty, Miss Greenaway! You'd be able to tell Mum how soon girls wear nail polish and have their ears pierced these days, wouldn't you?'

That was a trap for young players. Nathaniel couldn't have looked more askance had he been Roberta's father. Letitia said, 'That's entirely over to your mother. If you're anything like I was at your age, and till I was about fourteen, I was such a tomboy I utterly despised such things. Then suddenly I changed. It's nicer really not to have to bother about such things till you're older. It's a frightful bore having to be careful not to chip your colour off.'

Roberta completely disregarded this. 'What changed you, then?'

Letty conceded her the right to ask. She chuckled. 'I fell in love. He was all of eighteen. I thought in my despair he'd never look at a schoolgirl, so I went the whole hog—blusher, lipstick, eyeshadow, nail varnish. I was most gratified when he asked me to a party—over the phone. He hadn't seen the new me. So I put everything on even more heavily. And what happened?'

'He kissed you when he said goodnight?' hazarded Roberta, eyes astar. Damien made an indisputably male sound of scorn.

Letty said drily, 'When he called for me and I swam out in all my glory, he took one horrified look and said, "You'd better wash that muck off your face. You look awful! Who do you think you are?" '

She grinned reminiscently. 'My father looked most gratified. He'd been surprised Mother was even allowing me to date at that age, but it reconciled him to this boy, anyway. Mother was wonderful, came into the bedroom with her crestfallen daughter and said soothing things like: "Aren't men conservative, even at that age?" and said, like a pal instead of a parent, "I think, though, that you should have *some* make-up on, darling; look, let me do it for you, very subdued, but prettily, so neither he nor your father will notice but you won't feel naked." That's why, behind my counter, I've always enjoyed introducing young girls to their first make-up.'

'I hope my mum will be like that when I start,' said Roberta. 'Dad's reactions will be quite predictable, I know.'

'Never mind, if he's typically male, he'll still get a thrill out of the sight of his daughter in her first evening dress for the School Ball. You'll go to High School in Queenstown, I suppose?'

'Yes, I'm going to board with Miss Mattie. It's all arranged.'

It must be gratifying to Nathaniel to know his married couple looked ahead as much as that. Letty hoped the accident hadn't put Hope off. She changed the subject. 'Nathaniel, when I was cooking the meal, I was most grateful in this heat that I didn't have to light the range. In the old days that'd be all they had. But it must have cost you the earth to have it brought in right from Drumlogie.'

'Oh, no. We may have Big Slip as a barrier for access, but that's nothing to electrical engineers. It just came in from the road to Glenorchy.'

She looked taken aback. 'Oh, of course. How stupid of me.' Then she thought of something. 'Then why didn't the phone come in that way too? But that break was away from the mule-track, wasn't it?'

He looked slightly embarrassed, said to the children, 'You may leave the table now, and play outside for a bit.' They scampered off, and he said, 'Well . . . way back in the valleys beyond a small lake up there, are a couple of chaps trying to make a go of things in very isolated surroundings. They had very little capital at the back of them. Wanted to get away from the cities. They're making out, too. If there were two properties to share the cost of the longer way in, it halved the installation costs. It makes us a party line, so that cuts down on rental too.'

Something else to admire about the man she'd started out hating. She said swiftly, 'I like that, Nathaniel. I like it very much.'

He said rather brusquely, 'Don't hand *me* the bouquet. I wanted to do it, but I couldn't run to it. Dad paid for it.'

She gave him a steady, considering look then smiled, the first really candid smile she'd ever given him. 'Then I like that even more, Nathaniel. It went against the grain, didn't it, when you were so keen about being independent? But you sank your pride for your friends' sake.' She twinkled. 'Now I've embarrassed you. You were amazed before to find yourself with *me* for a governess . . . I'm equally amazed to find the high-and-mighty Nathaniel Pengelly bashful! But again, I rather like it.'

To her surprise he caught her hand as she rose to clear the table. 'Letitia . . . did I strike you like that? You mean in the shop?'

She didn't reply immediately. She knew she'd gone too far. He said, 'Letitia, look at me.'

She looked and he saw her colour rise. 'Sorry, girl, but I'd like to know.'

She was reluctant. 'Nathaniel, I shouldn't have said that. Perhaps I was too sensitive. I felt you despised the shop and even all of us. But perhaps I misjudged you. It could have been that I knew that against all my inclination I was tied to a setting I didn't love, and you were lucky enough, as the boss's son, I *thought,* to have the capital to buy your way in to a big property. I didn't know the odds you were facing, or the fact that you wouldn't let your father risk too much in backing you. So I'm sorry.'

That slow smile of his did something to her, something she didn't welcome. He said, 'I'm sorry I appeared like that. And I think it was true. It's damned snooty to think there's only one way of life. I'm not proud of myself if I made anyone else feel like that also.' He stood up, reached out for some dishes, then, as he passed her chair, stopped, so that she looked up, surprised. Still smiling, he dropped a light kiss on her forehead, 'You're a nice kid, Letty. I don't know what I've done to deserve you.'

She decided to take no notice of it, so she stood up, and went on clearing the table. She'd have to watch herself. She found she liked being called a kid. And she was twenty-six!

The children were so eager to try their new rooms out they were soon off to bed with their books, and surprisingly Josselyn began to droop. 'Despite her long nap this afternoon, she's catching up on last night, as Roberta predicted,' said Letty. 'Mr Nathaniel, when she goes down, I'll go into my sitting-room. This room's too far from her. I'll skip TV tonight.'

She'd been most surprised they had it, but it was beamed in for several homesteads, although reception was often poor among these mountains.

'I'll just watch the news and come through too if that's all right by you. Even when I'm just reading I like company. I miss Jamesina. What are you laughing at?'

'Who laughed? Not me.'

'Your lips twitched. You were subduing an inward chuckle.'

'Fancy yourself as a mind-reader, do you, Sir Omniscience?'

'You're side-tracking. What was funny about that?'

'I wouldn't know.' She got up and went across to one of the bookcases. She'd suddenly thought that could take away any glamour—being a substitute for Jamesina. She must change the subject.

'Here's *Riders of the Purple Sage* by Zane Grey. My grandfather used to read him. They lived at Sumner near Christchurch so we had beach holidays with them. I read all his books because I was such a fast reader they got tired of taking me to the library. Strange, I thought of Zane Grey yesterday when we came to *The Gate Beautiful* and looked down on your valley. There was another book of his where the hero and heroine were pursued on horseback and they escaped to this secret valley where the ingress was guarded by a balancing stone that could be rolled to seal the valley in. I can't remember the name. I looked across to Big Slip and thought it was similar, sealing it off from the lake.'

'I don't remember that book,' said Nathaniel. 'Evidently the old people had several of his here. What a sombre setting! A valley that was a prison. But no one need ever look on this valley as a prison, there's always been a way out. And now of course, we can drop in from the sky. Now no one could call it God-forsaken, even in emergencies.' Once more the two pairs of eyes met. There was almost a challenge in his. Was it because it still rankled? That someone had once called it that? And was that someone still important to Nathaniel Pengelly?

She was glad there was an extension phone in her sitting-room. 'It's so long a passage,' he said, 'I felt it necessary to save Jamesina's legs. Not that she's here much, but even without a governess, it needed cleaning once in a while.'

'Of course. But now Jamesina needn't worry about doing in here any more. I'll keep my own little domain right, Mr Nathaniel.'

'I'd like to say don't bother, but in fact I'd be grateful. That foot may take some healing.' At that moment the phone rang.

He picked it up, 'Oh, hello, Owen. I was going to ring you soon. How are things? Oh, good show, coming home tomorrow? Man, that'd be good, but how? After all, you went down by chopper . . . Oh, that's splendid. Sheer good luck. Yes, looks as if the weather's holding. How are the patients? Good, but on no account let Jamesina have any ideas about coming back with you. What? Miss Mattie's coming? That's great. Isn't she a sport? By the way, we've got the children over here. Miss Greenaway has shifted into the quarters and the kids were dying to sleep upstairs, think it's as good as a holiday and Miss G. has Josselyn in the wee room off hers. No, Josselyn's given no trouble at all,' his eye flickered whimsically to Letitia's as he lied, 'we got some work done on the culverts today while she cooked the dinner. We've fallen on our feet with our new staff member, I can tell you. Nevertheless, it'll set Hope's mind at rest if she knows Miss Mattie is up here. No, Owen, I think not. Miss Mattie can sleep here too; if you take the kids back right away they'll be disappointed. You can come up for your meals. Would Fiona have room for some fencing wire? The firm were getting it in today. Just if she has.'

He put the phone down and said to Letitia's surprised look, 'Fiona is the pilot—a first-class one. Fiona Campbell of Belleknowes Station on Lake Wanaka. They haven't a Slip like ours but they haven't a road either. Their only other access is by water, so they have a helicopter. It's a great help to them if they're short of staff—they can use it for mustering from the air. She and Edward, her husband, both have licences. Stroke of luck for us as they're not often in Queenstown, but her youngsters have been holidaying there and she's picking them up. She went to the hospital to see a friend and bumped into Owen. Hope wanted him home because she's worried the extra responsibility will scare you off. Would it, had it been prolonged?'

'No; if it had gone on too long I might have got crotchety because of tiredness, but I wouldn't have dropped my bundle. I hope you don't think today's effort and yesterday's were just the new broom sweeping clean!'

His eyes held hers. 'I wouldn't dream of hinting such a thing. After all, it's in my interests not to offend you, isn't it?' He insisted on making their last snack, brought in strips of toast piled with melted cheese and snippets of bacon, and a pot of tea. Then he said, 'Goodnight, Letitia, and don't forget my bedroom's down this end of the house and if Josselyn repeats last night's performance, and I don't appear to hear her, don't hesitate to call me.'

'Thanks, I don't think she will. By the way, keep it to Letty like you did earlier. Every time you say Letitia I expect you to tack on that ridiculous commercial title and it makes my hackles rise.'

Oddly enough, instead of just accepting that, he appeared to consider it. 'I dare say I'll make it Letty at times, but I like Letitia best. It smacks of lavender and old lace, doesn't it? Delightfully Victorian for someone who, at first glance, behind that over-perfumed counter, I regarded as being as trendy as tomorrow.'

She shruged. 'It *is* Victorian. It belonged to my great-grandmother, who was born in the eighteen-forties. Dad had always liked the sound of his grandmother, though he never knew her. She died before he was born, in fact shortly before his parents emigrated from London.'

'Any relation to the famous Kate Greenaway? Wasn't she born in London? Some of her books are in one of the schoolroom cupboards.'

'I think there was some distant connection. We were brought up on Kate and Beatrix Potter and Allison Uttley. Are those books old or oldish editions? They could be quite valuable. Oh, I'm being stupid. They wouldn't have been left up here all that time.'

'They were, actually. Mother heard about them and had them taken down to Dunedin, then gave them to me to put back here. She thought it was fitting. Said my grand-children could treasure them. Oh, I do wish Mother had known that a far distant connection of Kate's was governessing here. I'd like her to have known you.'

Letitia dimpled. 'A back-handed compliment, if you like . . . only because of a distinguished forebear and the connection is so slight!' In a trice the cool cosmetician had disappeared and she was a mischievous and tantalising girl. Nathaniel stared, then chuckled. '*Touché,* sorry about that.'

She added, 'In fact, I knew your mother fairly well. I always served her. We—the girls at the counter—thought it quite endearing that the boss's wife, who could have had her pick of any French perfume, always took Devon Violet in those little wicker bottles. She said once your father couldn't stand her changing her perfume. Said it was like sleeping with a strange woman. We thought that was sweet.'

The tawny eyes widened. 'That's something I didn't know. Oh, I knew she never used anything else, but not why. You seem to reveal Dad to me. I can tell you it was an eye-opener to me when he was so poetical about you kissing him.'

'Poetical?'

'Don't you remember? He mentioned a poem by Leigh Hunt. Don't tell me you didn't look it up. Haven't you any curiosity?'

'Don't *you* remember my reaction . . . that I caught on after a moment? It was a roundel we learned at school, so short it was easy to remember. Did you not know it yourself?'

'Not till then. There's a Palgrave over there, though I looked it up in Dunedin. That same night.' He took the book out, slapped it to expel the dust on the top edge, looked at the index, found it, read it out. 'I'll take a liberty and substitute Letty for Jenny. How convenient it has the same number of syllables:

' "Letty kissed me when we met,
    Jumping from the chair she sat in;
Time, you thief, who love to get
    Sweets into your list, put that in:
Say I'm weary, say I'm sad,
    Say that health and wealth have missed me,
Say I'm growing old, but add,
    Letty kissed me." '

Nathaniel grinned at her. 'It knocked me for six when Dad suddenly said what he did about that poem . . . after you'd kissed him. At the time——' He paused.

Mischief again lit the green eyes almost on a level with his. She had risen to go to bed, and was resting her hands on the table between them. 'Go on,' she dared him. 'At the time . . . you were astounded he could be saying it to *me*. Go on, admit it.'

He looked rueful. 'Yes, I was, but not now. I've seen you in a different light and a different setting.'

Letty permitted herself an inward smirk. It *was* going to be a pushover.

'And of course I'd not known Dad knew you so well and had even——' He stopped again.

She said sweetly, 'And had even said had he been twenty years younger he might have fancied me himself,' and she too stopped dead too late to recall those rash words. But she'd been so sure he was going to say just that, she'd blundered on. Now, oh, how hideous. He'd know she'd overheard them. Colour flamed from her neckline right into her cheeks.

Nathaniel looked staggered. 'But—but how did you know? I mean, he did tell me that, but you weren't there. I——'

Letty recovered herself, she hoped. It was a desperate attempt and might not come off, but something had to be said. She attempted a grin. 'Nathaniel, knowing your blunt father I could bet my bottom dollar he did when he recommended me to you as a governess. If you reacted unfavourably, as I'm sure you did, he wouldn't be able to resist saying that to you to give you a better image of me. Isn't that true?'

She was intrigued to notice that his own neck had reddened. He snorted, said, 'True. But how you leapt to it I'll never know. You must be very—um—what's the word I want?'

She was so relieved, inspiration came, 'I think you must mean perspicacious.'

'That's it, exactly. The sort of word you read but never use. What a governess you'll make! Miss Mattie will certainly approve of you.'

She heaved a sigh of relief . . . he'd never guess she'd eavesdropped. But he was looking at her with that weighing-up look again. 'Not only perspicacious, I'd say, but also devious. To come out pat with that I think Dad must have told you at some time how he felt about you.'

Tricky. She pursed up her lips, then said impishly, 'Let's say I treasure those words.'

'I think I've underestimated my father. Well,' he picked up the book he'd been reading, 'I'll say goodnight. By the way, you'll see the door into the connecting passage has a key. I won't be offended if you turn it. I would if I were a girl in these circumstances.'

She blinked, then looked him straight in the eye. 'Mr Nathaniel, I can only think you've been watching too many TV episodes where they hop into bed with each other at the drop of a hat. As if lovemaking—so-called—were as basic as food and drink. I wouldn't do you the injustice of even entertaining such a thought. Or insult you by turning that key.'

In her earnestness she'd come across to him. She was surprised at the change that came over his face. The craggy lines disappeared, the crowsfeet of laughter at the corners of his eyes deepened. 'You'll do Mararangi all right. We're all woefully outspoken. We don't wrap things up.' To her immense surprise he brought the back of his hand up, rubbed it against her cheek for a fleeting instant, said, 'Goodnight, Letty,' and the next moment had closed the door between them.

She stood there, staring at the door; that had been unexpectedly sweet. Without knowing she did she brought her right hand up, touched her fingers to her left cheek where he had made that brief caress. He was like his father, after all, the occasional touch of sentimentality breaking through a crusty exterior.

They woke to another shimmeringly hot day. The tourists who would be thronging the streets of Queenstown must be loving this. Letitia had Josselyn on her hip when the children upstairs called, 'Miss Greenaway, come up and see the lake!' She went up with the baby. Damien was perched on Roberta's bed and both children were gazing out past Big Slip. Had there ever been a lovelier morning? In November there had been a phenomenally late snowfall and streaks of it still lay in the folds of the opposite peaks, but below them the lake was glinting in its Mediterranean blue and even as they watched, a speedboat they couldn't hear sliced the blue with a foaming white wake and shot out of sight.

Letty had a turbulent moment of rebellion that that great mass of rocks and soil knitted together by tussock and scrub and trees should bar them from all except this one glimpse. Imagine if Mararangi still had water transport and water-sports! But what a cost to bulldoze a way through. How far it extended she couldn't guess. Shoulder after shoulder of hills nudged each other. The bridle-path showed like an uneven scar winding and climbing and disappearing. Quite pathetic.

'Now, bathroom first, Roberta, no skimping of neck and ears . . . same to you, Damien. I'll go and start the breakfast, but I want Roberta to feed Josselyn in her high chair while I'm getting it.'

Nathaniel had beaten her to it. The porridge pot was on, a pan of bacon started. 'Oh, how lovely, I'll be able to start Josselyn myself.' She sat her in her high-chair, cooled some porridge, sprinkled brown sugar on, and milk. The children arrived at the kitchen in what seemed like the speed of light, which didn't augur well for the thoroughness of their ablutions, and Nathaniel told them their dad was being flown in but they could still stay here. There was great excitement at the thought that the Campbell youngsters would be here today, though they were warned it mightn't be for long. 'Letitia, how many eggs for you?'

She looked horrified, 'After a porridge ration like that I think I'll just have toast and tea.'

'Rubbish, you're bound to eat more in this mountain air, and you need it too for the extra energy you'll expend cooking for us, looking after the baby, getting lessons ready.'

She was amazed to find she could tackle an egg, but slid half the rashers back. The phone rang. One of the stock firms to say a truck would be in in two days for the lambs for the freezing works. 'Thank heaven Owen will be back and that we got them dagged.'

'I suppose it costs the earth for freight right from here?' said Letty.

'Yes, unfortunately. It would cut costs by more than a third if we had access to the lake. In the old days the steamers would take them out, but once they got that road put through to Glenorchy, it was more maddening still. Not much more than twelve miles to Queenstown from there. Well, no good kicking against the pricks, but I'd like to think that by the time my son takes over, if I'm lucky enough to have a son *and* he wants to farm, and doesn't take after James and Dad and prefer the rag trade, that they'll force a way through.'

She said, 'You wouldn't try to influence him if his heart wasn't in it?'

'No, I've always felt ancestors play a large part in our make-up. I've never wanted to do anything but farm. So I'm more a Wildernesse and a Nathaniel than a Pengelly. I'll hand it to Dad that while we had to work behind a counter in our young days, or in the reserves . . . before your day, of course . . . once he was sure what I wanted he brought no pressure to bear, just sent me off to Lincoln College to gain all the agricultural know-how. Good thing James wanted nothing but the shop. I still feel, though, that if Dad needs me, like this last month when James was spending Christmas in Canada with his wife's people, I must do my stint. Damien, I can do with you down at the yards once you've fed the dogs, and Roberta, when you've fed the hens you can help Miss Greenaway. We almost always get into lunch about twelve-thirty, Letty, but if you need us send Roberta, or in an emergency, beat the gong.'

Roberta and Letty put two loads of washing through the automatic machine, then one of nappies alone, swept floors, made beds, and Letty decided to put a batch of scones in. They'd brought fresh cream with them, and there was a vast amount of raspberry and strawberry jam in the storeroom. If Fiona and her children had time, they could do them proud with a Devonshire cream snack. Roberta said, 'I suppose we should put Miss Mattie in the spare room next to Jamesina's, would you say? It's smaller, but then we wouldn't need to disturb Jamesina's things.'

'Good thinking. And Miss Mattie might stay on after Jamesina gets back.' Letty was rather apprehensive about

Miss Mattie's arrival; she might be formidable. And though
she realised that she herself might know more than some
wives about supervising lessons, she *had* been away from
educational circles a long time.

Roberta and Damien thought the time dragged till the
sound of the chopper was heard, but then it was an event
when a couple of playmates dropped in from the sky. It
settled incredibly quickly and the occupants piled out.
Fiona Campbell had the trace of a Scots accent in her
voice. She held out two hands to Letitia. 'Join the union.
I came to the high-country as a governess too . . . from
Scotland. As you can see, these two savages are Robert and
Elspeth. Elspeth, do you *have* to demonstrate you can now
stand on your head without the support of a wall the very
moment you arrive? And if I'd known you were going to,
I'd have insisted you wear shorts, not a skirt.' Elspeth came
right way up and formally presented a hand to Miss
Greenaway, who had succumbed to laughter.

Owen was still helping Miss Mattie out. Letitia was glad
Nathaniel had told her that Miss Mattie was what she
preferred to be called, because it would have been a strain
to have uttered 'Miss Clutterbone' soberly.

Miss Mattie, she felt, presented a more usual type of
governess, a spare, wiry-looking figure with a no-nonsense
look, hair done up in a not unbecoming topknot, and a
brisk bird-like way with her, but after the first exchanges
she said to Letty, 'Don't have any qualms at the thought
of a retired governess being wished on to you. I'm here
solely as a friend of Hope's mother, to help with meals and
look after Josselyn while you reign supreme in the schoolroom.' Letty's heart warmed to her.

'That'll be great. I'm so terrified of something happening
to Josselyn if I turn my back for a moment. Mind you, it
could be I'll need a few pointers . . . you have years of
experience behind you and though I've enjoyed it so far,
it was a bit daunting to be so suddenly the only woman
on the sheep-station. Mrs Campbell, any chance of you
having time for afternoon tea and to let your two see the
schoolroom? Roberta and Damien have had a busy time
helping me fix it up and it would be great if they had

someone to ooh and aah. Last term, which was their first here, they just did their lessons at their place, and they're enchanted with being here.'

The children melted away and Nathaniel went to help Owen unload the fencing wire and some supplies Owen had brought in. The three women went into the house. Fiona looked about her appreciatively. 'Jamesina will be pleased. You're keeping up to her standards. Though what she was most scared of was whether or not having to cope with everything might put you off your job. Though she said she'd met you before and felt you were a sensible kind of body. That, from Jamesina, was high praise.' Letty wished Nathaniel might have heard that.

Fiona continued, 'But that fear was really why Miss Mattie offered to come up. I can understand the children wanting to stay here. The other house has everything that opens and shuts in the way of labour-saving devices, but this has charm. I came over here a few years ago before Nat took over and it really hurt me to see the lovely lines of the old place, yet know if it was left much longer it would rot away and the trees and weeds would gradually smother it. Nat's got a tough job ahead of him. Pity it hadn't been in the days of the high wool and meat prices, but if anyone'll succeed it will be Nathaniel Pengelly. If only that accursed Slip would disintegrate! The secret of our success at the head of Lake Wanaka was that we had access by water. It's maddening to think that this has even a road just through there.'

The hour sped, then reluctantly Fiona and the children took off again to whirr their way to Lake Wanaka. 'Sorry Edward wasn't with us, but he was called for consultation over some roading project—for ski-field access to Mount Aspiring National Park. They sent another chopper for him.' To Letitia she added, 'Edward was an engineer but took over his brother's estate when he was killed. Now Edward thinks he has the best of both worlds with these consultations.'

When Letty went to bed that night she had the comfortable feeling she and Miss Mattie were going to get on well together. She'd told Letitia, as they sat out on the terrace steps in the long southern twilight, some of the trials that had beset her when she'd been a raw young girl attempting to teach children on remote stations. She could laugh now at some of her high-flown ideas about children and recount a few adventurous happenings, paint a picture of historical local events before her time. They finished with supper in Letitia's sitting-room.

Nathaniel had taken advantage of her being there, evidently, and Letty no longer needing moral support and company, to spend the entire evening in the farm office, knee-deep, he said, in paperwork sadly neglected when he'd been at the shop.

Yes, an uneventful, pleasant evening. Letitia opened her window that looked out over that end of the terraced garden towards the dark bulk of Big Slip and the perfumes of the roses and the catmint rose up to her . . . but why, oh, why, did she suddenly feel flat? It had been much less strain to spend the evening with Miss Mattie . . . to know someone would take over the chore of looking after Josselyn. Naturally Nathaniel would be relieved he no longer had to bear her company. It was very stupid to feel like this. You ought to be ashamed of yourself, Letitia Greenaway . . . finding a certain piquancy in being alone in these solitudes with Nathaniel Pengelly!

CHAPTER EIGHT

LETITIA had longed for the days of January to pass so she could get into the schoolroom and justify her wages, but the hours had flown because there was so much else to do on a property like this, and the day Owen returned from his ride over the bridle-path to that isolated mailbox with the last of the lessons from the Correspondence School, she felt another cog slipped into place. The lessons were fascinating. While the children assisted with the yarding of the sheep to go to the works, she spent hours studying them, working out a timetable, checking the times the School would be on the air and other recommended items. At night she got the children covering their exercise-books and studybooks with plastic. 'You know that town children have to cover their books as soon as they got them—well, you can be one step ahead and have them ready for the very first morning.'

Nathaniel was insistent on her not spending all her time on the preparation. 'There are other things to governessing up here. It's essential you brush up your riding. You may feel nervous if you haven't ridden for years, but we won't bustle you and you never really forget the art anyway.'

She said coolly, 'I'm not in the least nervous. When you want me, just let me know. I'll put preparation aside then and take up that duty. After all, you're the boss; you pay the piper and call the tune. What day would suit you best, Mr Nathaniel?'

'Today,' said Mr Nathaniel, watching her closely. Why? She thought he might be needling her a little, perhaps thought she was nervous, after all, and would try to postpone it.

'Right. I'll change into trews.' She was wearing a green linen skirt and a white shirt blouse with a green linen tie loosely knotted.

'I've got the quiet mare all saddled up. We'll take a turn or two in the long narrow paddock past the stables first. Then you won't have the feeling she might get away with you.'

He'd certainly been determined she would have her first try-out today. She was down very shortly in dun-coloured drill slacks. She'd already, by way of apples and carrots and wisps of hay, made friends with Betsy. She'd asked the children on the quiet which mount it was likely to be.

The children appeared, all enthusiasm. 'We'd like to see the fun,' said Damien, those grey eyes gleaming wickedly.

'It's not a circus,' said Nathaniel squashingly. 'She's not going to be bucked off or sail through the air to the other side of the fence. She's ridden before, but not for some time. Your father wants you at the wool-shed, so scram!'

Betsy came quite eagerly and Letty put her hand in her pocket and brought it out with her hand flat and a lump of sugar on the palm. What a lovely feel the velvety muzzle had. How daintily she took it.

'I can see you've put in some preliminary public relationship work,' said the astute Mr Nathaniel. 'I'll help you up,' and the next moment she was in the saddle. He led her up and down the paddock, talking to the little mare, giving Letty instructions about her hands, her knees, lengthened the stirrups the tiniest bit. 'I can tell you aren't starting from scratch; most novices complain that one stirrup's longer than the other.'

She was loving the feel of a horse under her again. This beat driving hollow. It was a long time since those Maniototo holidays when her father was alive and since then she'd not felt justified in spending money on a city riding school, though she had longed to. At a guess she'd think Nathaniel had taught a good few youngsters to ride. Perhaps on those farms where he'd gained his experience. He was very patient. She gathered her reins in one hand, leaned forward to pat the warm chestnut neck.

'Don't be too confident yet, though Betsy's so docile. Never been known to rear or roll her eyes.' The lesson proceeded and he seemed well pleased, even surprised. 'Want to walk her up and down the centre of the paddock by yourself quietly? Just walk, mind.'

She hid a little smile, knowing she was far from the novice class, but did as she was bid. When she'd accomplished it several times he nodded, 'Now go just half the length this time and coming back to me you can let her trot a little bit, but don't forget to rise in your stirrups with her movement. Don't let her jig you round like a sack of potatoes.' What a flattering simile! 'If you rise she'll know you're in command. You've obviously got a feeling for riding.'

She managed the gentle trot, stopped Betsy at the right time. He got her to increase the pace, then, 'By the way you're shaping you'll be okay till I get Shiraz. He's saddled and waiting through the far gate. Keep walking her, trot a little if you like, but on no account gallop. Needs a bigger paddock for that.'

He strode off, and Letty followed his instructions to the letter. He probably thought it better to be astride himself before he increased the pace. Suddenly, in the far paddock, the pony that had been Betsy's last foal trotted up to the fence. Betsy turned and brought herself up to him very sedately. A charming picture they made, rubbing their heads together. This was the pony Damien had ridden, following Roberta, through Big Gap. Courageous youngster, that. Letitia had seen only the beginning of the bridle-path, but it was very rough, though not as steep as further on, evidently. She wondered how long before Nathaniel would let her attempt it. How marvellous it would be to climb Big Slip, collect mail and stores, see the lake in all its beauty, close to, walk to the edge and dabble one's fingers in the water, fresh from the pure snows.

Paul Revere—a fine name for the pony—scampered along the fence line. Betsy followed suit on her side, increasing her pace to keep up with her son. It was delightful. Letty turned her head. Nathaniel was coming but leading Shiraz, probably because his pace might tempt

Betsy to quicken hers before he considered Letty proficient. Then it happened. The mare squealed, jerked, stumbled, gave a sound of real terror, pain and fright, and up went her front legs.

The sound and the jerk had alerted Letty and she acted instinctively and as the mare reared, she gripped with her knees, waiting for the downward crash of hooves, and stayed on. She realised Nathaniel had let Shiraz go and was running towards her but not yelling. The grass near the fence was longer, but as the right hoof rose again sunlight flashed on something and Letty realised that barbed wire was caught round it. Dear God! Panic lasted only a moment, she knew she must control the lashing mare. She spoke soothingly, didn't pull her head back, but exercised firm control of the reins. She knew a second of real alarm when Betsy tried to free her foot and she saw the other end of the strand was attached to a fence-post. She rapped out a word of command and miraculously the mare stood still.

Nathaniel reached them, took an iron grip close to the bit, held her head down, said 'Good girl!' and Letitia didn't know which of them he meant. The animal was impatiently trying to shake her leg free. She'd do herself harm if she persisted.

Nathaniel said, 'Get down, Letty. I can't risk you being thrown. Come down behind me and get away from her smartly.'

She said coolly, 'I think I've got better control up here. I'll hold her till she stops thrashing about. I think the wire's attached to the fence. If she pulls away when she loses my weight she might rip her leg badly. I'm all right.'

Surprisingly he accepted that. 'Right, but next time I say "get down" you *must*. Quiet now, lass. Stand still . . . we'll soon get this away. That's it. Good . . . quiet.'

Letty said softly, 'Mind she doesn't kick you.'

'I'll be very careful. It's not as bad as a hind hoof. When you're off if you come round in front of me—after you've stepped away first, mind—I'll get you to hold her head. But if you're nervous, I'll continue holding her and you can go for Owen.'

'I'm not nervous and he's too far away.'

The trembling ceased, Betsy stood still. She seemed to sense it was better that way. Letty came down very steadily, moved back two paces, but the horse didn't budge. She came round in front of Nathaniel and grasped the bit from him. He stepped back, surveyed the tangle. 'I'll have to do it very slowly. It's in two coils and very springy. If she lashes out, which she may do if I catch the other leg with the wire, let her go and get back. Don't be a heroine. Watch out for her swinging her hindquarters round if that happens.'

Letty kept on speaking reassuringly to Betsy. The mare, to her amazement, put her muzzle down on Letty's shoulder, slobbering down the white shirt. She was looking for a tasty morsel. Letty was afraid for the man when he squatted down, but he got a good grip of the free end and twisted it back between the two forelegs, then paused. 'Keep talking to her, the second loop is tighter.'

Then, 'Aaah . . . whoa, lass . . . gently does it . . . whoa . . . right, oh, you beauty!' And he pressed the strand down into the rough turf. Unfortunately it was still between the forelegs and the hindlegs.

'She'll have to step over it, but I'll have to hold it down. The damned thing is so springy. Can you take her forward? But let go if she lunges.'

No fear she wouldn't, with Nathaniel's head so near those hooves! The mare, in response to Letty's gentle pressure and her voice, stepped quite daintily over it and she was free and unharmed save for trickles of blood running down towards her hoof.

Nathaniel rose from his squatting position, said, 'Let her go now. No more lesson.'

Only disappointment coloured Letitia's tones. 'Oh, do I have to? Won't we just take her to the stables to put something on those rips? And I've a reward for her.' Her free hand fished in her trouser pocket and brought out a lump of sugar that Betsy gratefully accepted.

'Anti-climax!' said Nathaniel. 'Right, let me have her then,' and in silence they walked back to the stables. 'I'll leave her in the yard here till she gets over it. These wooden rails will restore confidence.' Then he leaned on the gate he was shutting and said, 'You don't appear to need *your* confidence restored, but you must be feeling pretty shattered.'

She grinned the gamine grin that always made him wonder if this could be the artificial-looking creature behind that toiletry counter and said, 'I was surprised at myself. But in a way that's a natural reaction; I suppose because I knew I was the only one who could bring her down. It would have been much worse to have been bucked off. So I did the only common-sense thing, and stayed on.'

He straightened up, said brusquely, 'You did much more than that. You brought her completely under control. Oh, my God, I died about a thousand deaths . . . I could see you describing an arc and landing on that fence or on one of the rocks on the other side. And this flaming place is so hellishly isolated. The lake road is so near yet so far. That Slip!'

Oddly Letitia felt resentment sweep over her. 'Don't you dare call it a flaming place! That's as bad as God-forsaken, and it isn't. It's Mararangi, the Garden of Heaven.'

He stared and the next instant she saw the blood leave his face. This weather-beaten giant, broad-shouldered, well fleshed, was normally so ruddy, so tough, he almost looked a stranger. She grabbed at his shoulder, said, 'Nathaniel, don't you dare flake out on me, you stupid thing. Here, sit down!' There was a stile right beside the gate to save a lot of opening and shutting and she pushed him down on the lower step, shoving his head down.

Not for long. The colour flooded back almost immediately. She was still standing over him. She thought he'd be annoyed at this display of weakness and sat beside him. 'It's all right, tough guy. It's always worse being the onlooker than the participant. Think nothing of it. It upsets your equilibrium.'

To her surprise he gave a weak laugh. 'Oh, Letty, you're a born governess. The big words you use, even in moments like this! You've got Miss Mattie licked to a frazzle.' They both chuckled and felt more normal.

They went into the stables to get something for Betsy's scratches. Letitia leaned back against a counter-like shelf. 'Nathaniel, that accident to Hope and Jamesina shook you, didn't it? And you thought there was going to be another. That could have happened on any farm close to a town. And you do have that helicopter service. I think you're letting Big Slip become a real bogey. A bug-a-boo, as my grannie used to call it. Don't. We'll cope, come what may. Even in pioneering days when there was open land right to the little cove, they didn't have a road to go the twelve miles to Queenstown then. They had to go, if injured, to Queenstown by whale-boat, and it's much further round the headlands. Think of it, in all sorts of weather, and rowing! And there were no miracle drugs then.'

He seemed to be waiting for her to continue. So she did. 'You met with too much opposition in opening up this sequestered valley again. Everyone told you that you could have it easier in another locale, that you were crazy. I think it would have been a crime to let this moulder away, just used for grazing. Farming's in a low just now, but there have always been lows and highs in farming. Because of that, you can't imagine that Slip being bulldozed through for access in the foreseeable future. You're too proud to let your father do it for you. But you've still got that track leading out to Drumlogie. Don't let that Slip eat into you. Don't be turned from your purpose just because there were a couple of casualties lately and one was averted this afternoon. You're developing a guilt complex!'

He put the medication down, then straightened up to his full height. 'Oh, was that what made me almost flake out? A guilt complex? Now I'd thought it was a very natural reaction that a man might have when he thought that because of his ruling passion for a place like this, you might have been lying hideously injured internally or paralysed. A lovely creature like you, always tiptoe with expectancy, one moment full of grace, the next . . . ' He broke off, took her by the shoulders, closed the gap between them by pulling her roughly to him, bent his head, smiling in that way that softened the craggy face, and put his mouth on hers.

She couldn't have told, afterwards, how long it had lasted. It seemed as if time was suspended. She couldn't move, it seemed, didn't want to. She'd never experienced a kiss like this before. No, that wasn't right. She'd never experienced this sort of *response* to a kiss. Almost, she thought, dazedly, a surrendering, a *wanting* to surrender.

They drew apart, Letitia shaken with the force of her feelings, so she instinctively turned away from him and put her hands on the dusty bench. He stepped up behind her, very close, suffocatingly close, put his arms about her, clasping them in front of her, brought his head against her head so that his rough cheek was against hers. He said nothing for what seemed quite a long time, then, with a hint of amusement in his voice, 'A kiss . . . like that kiss . . . was almost worth the fright!'

She couldn't answer, but just stood. He meant the way she had shared . . . returned the kiss. It hadn't been a snatched one. He chuckled. 'I believe you're embarrassed! Well, who'd have thought it? Behind that counter of yours I could never have imagined it. All icy perfection, you were.'

That broke the spell. She said, turning, 'It could merely be that I was pretty shaken by the incident after all. Glad not to be thrown and trampled. Think nothing of it.'

He should have looked squashed. He didn't. He chuckled again in the most maddening way and said, 'Oh, a man would have to be a robot not to dwell on a moment like that. Right, since that seems to be the way you want it, let's get on with the mundane task of dabbing this on Betsy's wounds. Though thanks to you they're just minor.'

Miss Mattie had an appetising meal ready for them. Nathaniel said, twinkling, 'It *was* a circus after all, Damien. You really did miss something. Betsy rearing all over the place and screaming her head off. Nothing more blood-curdling than a horse-scream. She'd caught her left front leg in a coil of barbed wire and couldn't shake it off as the other end was still stapled to the post. She stood clean on her hind legs. I died about a thousand deaths . . . and our Miss Greenaway, to the manner born, brought her down, stayed on, and managed to calm her. Wouldn't dismount when ordered to because she thought she could control her better in the saddle. Then after I managed to get it unwound, she walked her over it. I reckon our governess ought to enter for the Wanaka Rodeo.'

Damien sighed. 'Wouldn't it make a fella mad to miss a show like that, and I'd wanted to stay!'

Owen realised it hadn't been fun. 'But it scared hell out of you?'

'It did. I made a perfect fool of myself when we got back to the yard. She had to shove my head between my knees. On the stile. Then she accused me of making a bogey out of Big Slip. No sympathy for me.'

Owen said, 'You mean you had a reaction, thinking what might have happened?' He added, 'With no easy exit.'

'Exactly, and two accidents close together.'

Owen said slowly, 'Oddly enough with this accident to the two women a fortnight ago, I thought it might have put Hope off a bit, but it hasn't. The fact of, despite the phone being off, Damien and Roberta's reaction to an emergency and the quick drop-in of the chopper once they were alerted has given her a different feeling about here. Plus the fact, of course, that Letitia is here now, another woman and a young one.'

'Good Lord! I've worried ever since that you and Hope might feel you could get a place as manager of another property much closer and with the school bus coming to the door. You mean that?'

'I sure do. She loves this valley—much to her surprise. So no more bogeys, Nat.'

'No more bug-a-boos,' he said. 'Letitia's name for them.'

Letitia surprised an aware look on Miss Mattie's face as she glanced quickly from Nathaniel to Letitia. Letty looked away swiftly. Miss Mattie was very astute and Nathaniel's tone had been affectionate.

February splashed colour all over the rocks of the garden. Flowers that had been planted generations ago and had seeded year after year sprang up as if remembering that once again tender care was taking the place of neglect, and every day brought a new surprise. There were seas of candytuft in white, pink and mauve, Russell lupins in rainbow spires lighting up dark corners, golden rod and dahlias, lavender and mignonette giving off waves of fragrance as busy feet crushed their uncontrolled rioting over the paths, daisy bushes of every conceivable colour, balsam with crinkly pungent leaves and scarlet blossoms, and forget-me-nots that seeded so abundantly they would never be eradicated, and wallflowers and pansies thick under the roses.

After school when the children went off on pursuits of their own, Letty and Miss Mattie joined forces in an onslaught on weeds and some sort of organised restoration. Nathaniel heard gales of laughter from them one afternoon and found Letitia engulfed in a tangle of honeysuckle, with only her head poking through, not even her feet visible, while Miss Mattie, inefficiently for such a competent person, was trying to control her mirth so she could summon up enough strength to take the weight of it and push back to some sort of anchorage the rotting trellis it had adorned.

He bounded up the terrace steps and added his weight, pushing his arms into each side, trying to grasp some of the heavier boughs and hold it upright. 'Got it,' he said finally. 'Now, Miss Mattie, go for your life, get me a hammer and the longest nails you can find that aren't too hefty—I don't want to reduce this to timber-dust. If I can drive three or four into the big posts till we can prune it down, it could save the situation.'

Miss Mattie sped off. Letty said, gasping, 'I was holding it up against the trellis so Miss Mattie could chop away the lower branches and she got too enthusiastic. We were trying to save the top boughs because they're covered with blossom and it just collapsed and enveloped me. Good job honeysuckle doesn't have thorns, though it's still prickly. Briar roses would have been a disaster. But I wish these bees would keep away!'

Nathaniel waved the bees off and moved upwards gingerly. Now his eyes were on a level with hers. She added,

'Imagine if I was stung on the nose by a bee and it swelled. What a hideous thought!'

'I can save you from hideousness anyway,' he said. 'The thing is not to give the bee any room.' Her eyes widened as his dancing eyes gave away his intention. She couldn't move. He said, 'Isn't there an old song about "you are the honeysuckle, I am the bee . . . I'd like to sip the honey sweet from those red lips I see . . . "?'

She said, twisting furiously, in a futile attempt to dodge his kiss, 'Of all the mawkish, treacly songs . . . Mr Nathaniel, stop it this moment! Talk about public . . . Miss Mattie's coming . . . '

'You lie, madam,' he said, 'she'll hardly have reached the shed yet. I can time it . . . besides, who knows, she might get a kick out of witnessing a kiss like this!'

She jerked her head to the other side, said, 'Oh, please? The children could come and I'm their governess. Oh, Nathaniel . . . ' Then she couldn't say another thing. He lifted his head briefly and said, 'No wonder I prefer this to drapery. Nothing like the opportunities there! Isn't this fun?'

Letitia twisted again, her mouth going right across his cheek because his grip was so close, so hard. She burst out into muffled speech, 'In the shop, you fiend, you avoided me like the plague!'

His chuckle was unrepentant. 'I know. *How* the mighty are fallen. It serves me right. Pity we haven't an artist on the spot—what a picture this would make. You know those top strands of your hair that the sun has bleached? They're almost the colour of the honeysuckle.'

'Stop being so idiotic.' A pause, then, 'Nathaniel, *stop kissing me.* It's caddish when I can't get away from you.' She gave a violent, desperate wriggle and the whole mass slid to the ground, pulling away the rotten slats. She made a terrific leap over the tangled vines, and Nathaniel lost his balance and he sprawled backwards!

She actually stamped her foot at him in temper. 'Now look what you've done! It serves you damned well right. It'll take you hours to fix this. And all that lovely scented honeysuckle will have to be chopped away.' He lay there.

laughing helplessly, gazing up at her. 'It was well worth it. What chap wouldn't think so? But if you really care what Miss Mattie thinks, you'd better do those two top buttons up.'

She looked and yelped. 'Why didn't you tell me?'

He was getting up. 'How could I? I couldn't see till now. You were shrouded to your neck in twigs and flowers . . . possibly even spiders.'

She gave a shout of revulsion, began shaking herself, turned her back, undid the rest of her blouse buttons, shook herself again, buttoned up, then turned back.

'Spoilsport,' said Nathaniel.

Miss Mattie came round the corner of the house, looked down with horror and said, 'Oh, what a calamity, couldn't the two of you hold it till I got back? Sorry I was so long.'

'It didn't matter how long you'd taken, dear Miss Mattie,' said Nathaniel generously, 'it would still have fallen. It was completely Letty's fault. She started thinking about creepy-crawlies and shook herself so vigorously, it collapsed and knocked me over.'

Letty glared at him. Miss Mattie looked sharply from one to the other, said, mock-severely, 'Now, children, no tale-telling.' Then her eyes twinkled and she said, 'Nat, give me your handkerchief.'

He looked surprised. 'Haven't you got one of your own?'

She answered drily as he handed it to her, 'Yes, but lipstick is so hard to wash off and I'd rather use yours. Stand still,' and she calmly scrubbed at his cheek. 'No finesse, Nathaniel. Surely you could find better places for this sort of thing. There's a time and a place for every-thing.'

He pinched her cheek. 'You sound just like that chapter in *Ecclesiastes* . . . you know, "a time to love and a time to hate . . . a time to be born and a time to die . . ." '

Letty said smartly, 'Don't leave out a very important verse . . . "a time to embrace and a time to refrain from embracing . . . " Don't just pick out the verses that suit you, smart Alec!'

Unabashed, he said, 'Miss Mattie, aren't you sorry for me? The lady hath a waspish tongue, methinks. Do you agree?'

Miss Mattie looked him straight in the eye. 'You'd do well to cultivate a more gracious speech yourself, if you want to go a-wooing, Nathaniel Pengelly.'

Letty stared. Could this be Miss Mattie? At first sight she'd looked so prim! Nathaniel gave a great shout of appreciation. 'Letty, if only you could see your own face! There's far more to our Miss Mattie than you realise.' He leaned forward and dropped a kiss on Miss Mattie's cheek and was delighted to see a faint rose colour rise in her face. There was a little silence, then he said savagely, 'Only that hellish war put paid to it. Mother told me.'

Letty felt a traitorous rush of tears to her eyes. Miss Mattie lifted her chin a little and gazed unseeingly into the rhododendron bushes. No tears, but a tender light in her eyes. Then she said, 'Thank you, Nathaniel, for just remembering. Nice that someone of your generation does. I shouldn't like Sholto to be quite forgotten. And it's most gratifying of all that someone who never knew him should think of him.' She looked at Letty. 'And thank you, too, for those tears. Sholto died in the Pacific area of the war. It was the anniversary of his death yesterday. But I've been so lucky. I've taught so many other dear children. Especially the ones up at the Mount Olivet, near Glenorchy. And the next generation of them still comes to my little Queenstown house when they need board. Now, what shall we do with this mess? We'll have to be ruthless.'

'We'll preserve a few strands,' said Nathaniel. 'It's such a glorious colour. I wonder if Ellen Nathaniel planted it. Or wouldn't it last that long? Perhaps someone else grew it from a slip of the original. What would you girls think if I put up a hefty standard and attached it to one of those old trolley wheels? It could look just like the supports they sell for weeping roses. By next year, you'll see, it will be a mass of gold again.'

Next year? It sounded so permanent. But also unreal. Meanwhile, there was work to do. At the end of two hours' hard work, a new garden feature added its own beauty to what Ellen had lovingly created in the wilderness.

As Nathaniel went to trundle off the last barrowload, Miss Mattie said, 'And talking of time, dear boy, I hope you realise that Letty hasn't had as much as an afternoon off since she came here.'

Letty said, 'Miss Mattie, I'm not going off this place until Jamesina and Hope are both back. This is an emergency. Later on Tristan Pengelly is going to bring my car up. He said, and if you don't think it an imposition, that he could leave it at your place, and when I want a weekend off in Queenstown I can have my own transport.'

'He certainly can. But I told him on the phone the other night not to bring it till I'm back home. I wasn't thinking of that, but that all your bathes in the river pool even have been spent with the children. An extension of school hours, teaching them new strokes. And it's quite a ride to reach it. Nat said the other night that he'd take you off exploring soon, up towards where those two enterprising young men are working long hours to raise capital for a farm of their own some day. There are the most delightful pockets of bush up there.'

Letty said nothing. She felt dismayed. 'Good idea,' said Nathaniel,'I'm all for keeping my staff contented. Thanks for reminding me.' He trundled off, to the accompaniment of agonising squeals from the wheelbarrow, rusty from long disuse.

Letty said, 'I'll go and get the oilcan, I can't stand that noise. I'll see you at the dump, Nat.'

See him she did. She said, waving the oilcan in indignation, 'Mr Nathaniel, don't encourage Miss Mattie. Sometimes you fair get the devil in you!'

'Encourage her in what, Letty?' His tone was far too innocent.

'As if you didn't know. In matchmaking. People her age can't help themselves. It's most embarrassing.'

'You *are* a spoilsport. She's enjoying a little romance vicariously. Why spoil her fun? She's having a whale of a time up here.'

Letty couldn't think what to say. Instead she seized on another topic. 'You didn't tell me your father had rung. I presume he spoke to you first.'

'Should I have told you? As a matter of fact he's rung twice and once I rang him.'

She said, a little forlornly, 'I'd like to have spoken to him myself. Didn't he want to find out from me, myself, how I like it up here?'

Nathaniel grinned in that infuriating way of his. 'He did ask, but I told him I'd rather he didn't yet.'

'You what? Now that's really going too far!'

'Yes, I know, but I couldn't risk Dad——'

'You couldn't risk him doing *what*?'

His tone was solemn. 'Risk him unsettling my valuable governess. Might have made you nostalgic for the shop and the city.'

Her tone was scornful. 'You're lying. You didn't think that at all. Tell me the truth.'

'All right. Because I didn't want him putting his big foot in it, in anything at all.'

It puzzled her. 'Such as what?'

His laugh was frustrating. 'Not all things are good for you to know. I've told Dad not to come up at present, not even without your car.'

She said, challengingly, 'I could ring him myself when you aren't in.'

'I can't forbid you to, but I would rather you didn't, Letty. Please?'

She said, 'If you hadn't added that please, I'd have gone and rung him right here and now.'

His lips twitched. 'Then it's just as well I said it. I'll say it again for something else. Letty, will you please let me take you up and out of the valley tomorrow for a day on our own? I promise not to take advantage of it as I did with the honeysuckle . . . I know you'd enjoy it.' He looked at her a little strangely, she thought, though why would that be? He continued, 'It's a great place for bell-birds . . . a pocket of native bush, and a tiny rock-strewn pass.'

She said, 'Goodness, you're taking Miss Mattie's words to heart. You sound quite poetical.'

His eyes seemed a little intent. 'So I should. I was practically quoting.'

'Oh, what from? I thought it sounded familiar.' Then, 'What's so funny about that?'

His voice was drawling. 'I'll tell you some day. But it's nice to have you guessing for once. You almost give me an inferiority complex the way you reel off sources of quotations, not just for the children, but when you and Miss Mattie are doing crosswords.'

She said, uncertainly, 'You're in a strange mood. All right, I'll come with you. I'd love to explore beyond this one valley.'

Letitia lay awake a long time that night. She was all confused. Yes, she had come up here with the avowed intention of bringing this man to the proposal point, for the sheer satisfaction of turning him down, but for sure she didn't want it to happen too quickly, and Miss Mattie was a danger point, a complication she'd not bargained for. Because when that day came, she was going to turn him down, and intimate that although she wouldn't leave the children at any critical point in their school year, she would not be staying. That was what she wanted, *wasn't* it?

She wished she could be more objective about it. As sure that that was what she wanted as she had been in her first stinging resentment when she had overheard Nathaniel's scathing comments upon her. She hadn't even needed to lead him on much. Why? There must be some subtle alchemy in this wilderness, a blend of the timeless affections that had blossomed here, the beauty of it, the lasting reminders in the flowers that seeded year after year, the poignancy of trellises that collapsed with age, the shabby wallpaper in that bare drawing-room, that funny little iron cot in the small room off the unfurnished master bedroom . . . most of all the ever-present reminder of the death knell of colonial hopes represented by the solid mass of Big Slip, that with the plague of rabbits had swept this property away from this family for so many years.

Swept away something else too . . . or threatened to sweep it away . . . the pettiness of the feminine revenge she'd planned . . . that *meanness of motive*. Had she still the courage—or the spite?—to lead him on, and turn him down?

For a revealing instant she hated herself. He'd deserved her reaction at the time of overhearing, but now? Now her admiration for the way he worked, his caring concern about everyone . . . the way he loved Miss Mattie . . . she sat up in bed, thumped her pillow yet again, turned it over, said to herself, 'Stop it, Letitia Greenaway, you're getting things out of proportion. Okay, so you no longer feel vindictive towards him? *That's all it is*. And you're just the sort of governess he wanted and, man-like, he just can't resist a bit of . . . well, what? In another day and age it would have been called flirtation. Something that passed the time and relieved the monotony. You're the only female his age around! So go to sleep, or you'll be crabby at breakfast.' Having reduced, she thought, her problem to the level of commonsense, she fell straight into dreamless slumber.

Nathaniel was surprised to find her in a skirt and shirt at breakfast. 'We're going straight off, Letty. Not even washing a dish. The kids are to help Miss Mattie.'

At her surprised look Damien said matter-of-factly, 'He bribed us. We can have two chocolate bars out of the storeroom and a ride on the gondolas up to the Chalet next time we're in Queenstown.'

Roberta added, 'But we've got to do the lunch dishes too, and look after Josselyn if Miss Mattie needs a break.'

'Next time,' said Nathaniel, scowling, 'the bribe will include keeping dumb about it. If you aren't careful your governess will develop a conscience and refuse to leave the valley at all. And she deserves a day off. Miss Mattie ordered it, didn't you, Mattie?'

'I did,' she said placidly. 'So stop making such a stramash about it and be off with you. I made the sandwiches last night. They're in the fridge. And I'll fill the flasks while you're getting into riding gear, Letitia. Nat can carry them. He has a knack of arriving home with them still intact, even riding.'

Just before Letty swung up into the saddle, she said, 'Nathaniel?'

'Yes, what, Letitia? By the way, at last you seem to be leaving off the "Mr". Keep it up. You nearly always seem to be shocked at me when you use it.'

'Not always. It's merely from habit. It had to be Mr James and Mr Nathaniel in the shop, you know that. And if you don't want me to sound shocked, you could try behaving yourself. That was what I was starting to say. I'm the only female around, and men just can't resist flirting, to use an old-fashioned word. And I haven't got much use for it.'

'Oh, haven't you? Now I could have sworn you quite enjoyed it yesterday.'

She heaved a sigh. 'That's sheer vanity, and you're lucky I've come out with you today. Only I couldn't face saying to Miss Mattie why I didn't want to go.'

He laughed. Was there no way of getting under his skin? 'You really mean you didn't want to disappoint her.' She didn't know what to say. She just stood, against Betsy. He came across to her, took one hand and said gently, 'All right. You want just a good-comradely day, don't you? A picnic, a bathe, a little exploration. And you deserve it. Right, I'll stop teasing. Let's go to it, pal.'

There had never been a lovelier day. Letty was very accustomed to the saddle now, and the pace Nathaniel made easy, although now and again as they left their own valley their way widened out through miniature river-flats where streams meandered. She'd seen the deer enclosures close at hand, of course, but further on there were just sheep, and because December had had a lot of rainfall, as a contrast to January and February when it had been drier and hotter than was desirable, the lower slopes of the hills were green and lush and the sheep were lying down contentedly instead of on the move, foraging.

He led her through fords that were shallow because of this, following narrow tracks; it was so enchanting to think

that here was still an almost untouched wilderness where
no roads snaked their way, no dust rose beneath hot tyres,
no fumes of fuel hung on the air. That very air was like a
caress against one's cheeks, and the fragrance was of
crushed turf, hot tussock, clover.

Even when the solitudes seemed to owe so little to man,
one was suddenly reminded that these hills and gullies had
known the taming hand of the Nathaniels for well over a
century, because here were the European deciduous trees
that had brought the beauty of autumn to enhance this
bewitching evergreen land. Nathaniel turned to her; Betsy
was a little to the rear of Shiraz. 'We're coming near the
border of my land now. The rest belongs to the Beaumont
boys. Beyond that ridgy hill there. In a moment we'll see
the river that was diverted in its course the night Big Slip
occurred. It always came through where we're going to
have our dip, but where we are riding at the moment was
once its bed. That's why it's still so stony. The pool, the
best for swimming round here, is still on our land. And
apart from the weeping willows Ellen planted, from the
trees they first put in round the homestead, the trees are
natives. So it's always cool and green. Ah . . . listen, the
first bellbird.'

Magic feathered over the pulses in Letty's wrists as,
above the cascading water-song of the river, rose the crystal
clear bell-like notes, adding a descant to the silver sound
of waters running over the rocks of the miniature gorge.
The sun shone on the seemingly enamelled leaves that
characterised the New Zealand bush, so that it always
seemed sprayed with dew. 'Oh, Nathaniel,' she cried, as the
song ended, 'those must have been planted . . . the red-
hot pokers. Would you know who planted those? Are they
for the bellbirds and *tuis*, the honey-eaters?'

'Yes. My mother's father did. Evidently they paid a visit
here. He kept a riding-school, you know. They came in
from another station further up the road to Glenorchy. He
came up to see a rodeo. He was a marvellous gardener.
Lived at Alexandra. Also a bird-watcher. He knew these
kowhais brought the honey-eaters here, but thought they
needed summer provisions too. Plenty of flax-flowers for

them, of course, look, but the red-hot pokers are loved by
the wax-eyes too. I believe they brought so many they had
to bring a pack-horse and camped out here in a tent for
several nights.'

She said, 'How fortunate you are to have such conti-
nuity, such strong links with the past. It would have been
a crime not to restore this estate. I'm glad your genes
weren't the same as Mr James's genes, much and all as I
like and admire him.'

Nathaniel said slowly, 'You couldn't have said anything
to please me more. Thank you, Letitia. Well, here's where
we dismount. We'll tether the horses over there. We'll have
a swim before we eat. But I'll take a good look over the
pool first, it changes from time to time, and I must take
care that no snags have been brought down when we had
the heavy rains.'

She had earlier decided against a bikini, but the black
one-piece was brief enough and flung into relief her extreme
fairness. He said so, 'Now I can realise you have Dutch
ancestors. Oh, you know when the children did that essay
on Waitangi Day? Well, did you give them a little talk on
special days in other lands, like the Lazybones' and Eavesdroppers' Days in Holland? I always meant to look those
up in an encyclopaedia. Dad's got a fine set, better than
that rather skimpy set up here. I might ask him if I can
bring it up, for the schoolroom.'

She slightly froze, then managed, 'Oh, they're such trivial
days, Nathaniel. Just fun days, not important and signif-
icant ones.'

'I wouldn't have thought Eavesdroppers' Day would
have been a fun day. Sounds very menacing, really. Could
imagine it celebrating something like Guy Fawkes' . . .
after all, *that* at the time was a grim reality, trying to blow
up Parliament.'

She said lightly enough, 'Yes, but it's turned into a fun
day now, if you can call a day fun that has brought so
much tragedy in its celebration, by mishaps with fingers
and eyes. Nathaniel, is the water always cold up here? I
mean it'll be snow-fed like the lake, won't it?'

'Partly, but it comes such a distance and is shallow in many parts so it's sun-warmed on a day like this by the time it reaches here. Dive shallowly, Letty, for safety.'

It was glorious . . . a shelf of rocks at the west end made a miniature waterfall and deepened the pool, and the sun struck golden lights from the wet brown rocks. The willows were weeping-willows and trailed green fingers in the water, fan-tails flitted in and out of the branches, a *tui* alighted on a tall stick of flax-flowers, dipping its beak into an open flower in search of the nectar it loved. There was a full chorus of bellbirds.

'No wonder Captain Cook was enchanted with their dawn-song, hundreds of them, in one of the Sounds, two centuries and more ago,' Nathaniel said, clambering up on to a long rectangular rock that jutted out from the side, to dive in again. Letty turned on her back, looking up at the circle of the sky, framed by the notched green of the trees.

He swam to her, took one of the hands she was moving a little to keep her head away from the bank. She didn't mind that. It was good-comradely, matched the name he'd called her . . . pal. She liked that. It reminded her of her mother and father's relationship of long ago. You never doubted that they were lovers still, but such pals. She was suddenly hit by a wave of nostalgia for the father who'd been gone for eight years. She blinked her tears back. Dad's hands had felt like this because he was a great gardener . . . big hands with callouses at the root of every finger. They floated, fingers linked, for a few minutes, then hunger drove them to the bank.

It was all so perfect, the musical jingle of the bridles as the horses cropped the short, sweet grass, the hum of insects, the sound of shallow waters, further down, dropping with silver sound over tumbled rocks . . . the bellbirds singing, singing. What did it remind her of? Oh, that poem she had written once, that had appeared in a magazine. What was that line? . . . something about birdsong in the rock-strewn pass. Yes, that was it. And all the winds of heaven whistling through. At that moment a little breeze sprang up, heavenly cool, and lifted the hair back from her temples. Hadn't Nathaniel said something

about a rock-strewn pass the other day? And said it was
a quotation. How strange that someone else must have
used the very words she'd used, so long ago, to ease her
rebellion against that cosmetic counter. She must ask him
some time if he could recall what poem it was from. But
not now. This was a dreamy day, not a schoolroom day.
The day off that Nathaniel—and Miss Mattie—had
devised for her.

They came home in the long twilight, a little sunburnt,
a little saddle-weary, but supremely content. Letty was
surprised how wonderful it was to see the homestead valley,
the Garden of Heaven, dear Mararangi, spread out before
and below them. 'Thank you, Nathaniel,' she said. 'My
grandfather used to talk about the cathedral woods of
England. This has been a wonderful Sunday. Hills and
trees and water and birdsong. Instead of hymns.'

He nodded and leaned forward to pat the magnificent
column of Shiraz's neck. 'Dear Miss Mattie,' he said. 'She
knows the value of days like this. I hope she has a store
of them to remember.'

But Miss Mattie was no saintly soul. She was always
making Letty laugh. She'd been saying one day that she
thought she'd stay on for a few weeks when Jamesina came
back. 'Otherwise she'll overdo it. We get on very well
together. This job suits her; the family made her retire
much too soon, and this lad needs her here as much as she
needed the job. I'd like fine to see him make a go of it.'
She looked in the direction of the lake they couldn't see,
and said with venom, 'I'd like to drop a bomb on that mass
of rocks and earth! There'd be some sense in bombs if they
could be utilised like that. One day in Queenstown I found
myself singing an old hymn with the greatest gusto.
Unchristian-like, possibly. Never meant to be applied to
Big Slip, of course. In those far-off days Isaac Watts would
never think it would ever be sung in a land at the bottom
of the world . . . he died long before Captain Cook
discovered New Zealand. I found myself wishing fiercely
that it could come true right here. It was that verse that
begins, "Let mountains from their seats be hurled, down

to the deeps and buried there . . . convulsions shake the
solid world, our faith shall never yield to fear!" And I had
to take myself to task because it was like wishing for an
earthquake to hurl Big Slip into the lake!'

Letty's laughter rang out. 'Oh, Miss Mattie, you're
priceless! Most of the time you're so saintly—the rest,
sheerly human. I understand. It's so tantalising to think
there's that road there, barred by the Slip. If there was a
way through, the big articulated trucks for the sheep
wouldn't have to come all those indescribable miles from
Drumlogie and the cost would be just a fraction. Now if
only the Tourist Department would suddenly want access
to some new ski-field far back, and compensate Nathaniel
for the right to go through it, by some huge engineering
feat, it would be like a fairy-tale. But that's just wishful
thinking.'

'You never know,' said Miss Mattie, 'the age of mira-
cles might not yet be past. I must go down and take that
ironing to the other house for Owen. I'll bring the other
two children back with me. It's good of Owen to take
Josselyn down to sleep there every night. He's a very good
husband and father. He'll be glad when Hope gets back.
Are you going back into the schoolroom again to prepare
lessons for tomorrow? Don't work too late tonight, my
dear. And I wish Nathaniel would stop going over his
books. He's a glutton for work.'

But presently he came into the schoolroom. She was
bending over the globe. Globes were so fascinating. It
would be so easy for these two children, pent as they were
in this inland valley, in a small world of their own, to lose
sight of the immensity of the world outside them. It was
hard for children these days to realise the size of it, the
leagues of ocean that had brought the pioneers of New
Zealand out to the southern hemisphere, when every night
on TV they could see politicians and other celebrities
arriving to and from New Zealand, in little more than
twenty-four hours of daylight and darkness. She must get
them to take in the months at sea, in shocking conditions,
that Ellen and Grigor had experienced under sail . . .

Nathaniel said, 'Just had a phone call from Jamesina. She has a walking plaster on now, but the problem of finding transport that won't make it an endurance test is holding her up, and now she knows Mattie is here she doesn't mind waiting till Hope can come too. But it so happens Edward and Fiona will be in Queenstown next week and they'll bring them in. With Miss Mattie willing to stay on, that will give you a bit of a break. All the more to share the responsibility. You've been a brick the way you've pitched in. No job too dirty for our Miss Greenaway, governess extraordinaire! How could I ever have dreamed that *Letitia for Loveliness* would one day help me with the dagging? Chanel No 5 and sheep-droppings just didn't seem to be compatible!'

She dropped her eyes before the admiration in his, said hurriedly, 'Nathaniel, you make too much of it. Governesses who fancy the high-country life are prepared to lend a hand in an emergency, surely. Nathaniel, isn't a globe a marvellous thing? Look . . . the airlines are marked on this. Imagine . . . it takes less time to fly to Australia from New Zealand than for us to get to Queenstown via Drumlogie!'

'Uh-huh! And it'll be years before I can afford to buy and maintain a helicopter to allow us to be in Queenstown in minutes!'

'Yes, it's maddening, I know. If Big Slip wasn't there, we'd have just a dozen miles to go, around the shores of one of the most beautiful lakes in the world. Nathaniel, after that long ride the other day I'll be proficient enough on horseback to take the bridle path to the road any time, won't I?'

Nathaniel's finger was still tracing the airlines on the globe. 'Yes, but never alone. It has its danger spots. It still gives me nightmares to think of Damien and Roberta doing it.' He looked up. 'Why, Letitia? Does it get to you at times, wanting to escape from the narrow confines here?'

She found herself saying vehemently, 'No, no, never that. It's so beautifully sequestered from the rest of the world. But access would mean so much to you!' She looked up to find his eyes on her.

Her fingers tightened on the globe and it tottered from side to side. Both his hands and hers came to steady it. Nathaniel said, 'Watch it, lass. You're rocking our world on its axis!'

She managed a laugh, but felt inwardly shaken by something that really *had* rocked her. Her own private world had surely tilted over on its axis. A blinding moment of revelation. It wasn't just admiration she was finding in herself for him, not just a mellowing towards this man whom, in a moment of extreme humiliation, she had sworn to spurn when she'd brought him to heel . . . this man *was* the axis of her world.

It was as simple as that, and as devastating. She loved him.

CHAPTER NINE

LESS than a week later Letitia was saying to Miss Mattie, 'Has Nathaniel got something on, that the weather would ruin? He seems to be listening most intently to the broadcasts. Last night too.'

Miss Mattie's lips twitched. 'It's not work he's thinking of. He plans to take you over Big Slip in the long twilight. I'm to have midday dinner and a light, early tea. Ah, here's Nathaniel now.'

Letty, eyes astar, said, 'Nathaniel, you think I'm proficient enough? Oh, how lovely! I've been dying to——'

He looked puzzled, then, 'Oh, you mean riding? No, we're going on foot. It's a splendid hike, and with this hour of daylight-saving, perfect. It just isn't fair to coop you up by this loveliest of lakes and you never able to see more than a tiny triangle. I want you to see the view that enchanted Ellen and Grigor when they first took up land here. Mararangi as it ought to be.'

Letty clasped her hands together, delight in every inch of her. 'Oh, Nathaniel, what a marvellous idea! Tell me what I should wear. It's hot now, but I know the breeze off-lake can be cool later. That much of it we do get. Perhaps I should take a wind-cheater for the return trip?'

She caught a flicker in Miss Mattie's eye as if she hastily averted her gaze from Nathaniel's. But she said, sensibly, 'Of course. Nat will take a haversack, with jackets in. You'd be best in those green cotton cords and a loose shirt. Definitely not open-toed shoes. Make it those canvas shoes with the ribbed soles. Heavy brogues are too hot.'

Letitia heard Josselyn cry and went to pick her up. She put her into a delectable-looking frock of pink cotton, pin-dotted with white, and left the little feet bare. What a pity she got so grubby crawling on these ancient floors. Carrying her, she walked out to where Mattie was tatting and stood Josselyn down, steadying her a little. She'd been pulling herself up by chairs and couches for a week or two. She turned her round so Miss Mattie could admire the smocking on the wee frock.

Miss Mattie looked across, said, 'Hello, darling. Clever girl.' Josselyn, who'd not managed as much as a Dad-Dad yet, said distinctly, 'Mattie . . . Mattie . . . ' gave a crow of delight and took half a dozen steps at a rush towards her. Mattie rose, held out her hands, caught them and said unsteadily, 'Never once, in all the years, has one of the children I looked after taken first steps towards *me!*'

Letty said, 'It's a double-banger, Miss Mattie. Don't you realise, it's the first name she's ever spoken. Oh, won't Hope be pleased?'

They finished the drenching at the yards and by the time Nathaniel came up to shower, they all decided to join in the hiking pair's early tea, small bacon and egg pies that Miss Mattie declared would be more digestible than pizzas to tramp on, delicious cold lamb sandwiches, sponge-drops as light as only Miss Mattie could make them, shortbread, piping hot tea.

Nathaniel appeared immaculate in thin khaki drill shorts, a silk short-sleeved shirt in the same shade, with epaulettes buttoned in brown, oatmeal-coloured walk-socks, three-quarter length, brown canvas shoes. The ends of his hair were wet still. His eyes approved the thin green cotton shirt Letty wore over bra and trews. She'd looked longingly at shorts too, but Nathaniel had said earlier that she was so fair in the skin, he didn't think it was wise even if she'd toughened up a lot since coming to The Wilderness. They'd have the westering sun on them for a considerable time.

Miss Mattie must have packed the windcheaters already, but Letty gasped, 'That's not a haversack, that's a back-pack! Are you expecting the weather to change? I believe you've packed a pup tent in case we are benighted! Or stuck in winter clothing. Nathaniel, if you'd put it in two light haversacks, I'd have carried one.'

'I had my reasons,' he said. 'Come on, woman, don't waste time, or we'll be late.'

'You mean darkness might catch up on us coming back?'

'Something like that.' Again she caught the flicker of an eyelid, but his this time But why should he wink at Miss Mattie?

There was the faintest of zephyrs to fan their cheeks as they set out. Owen took them to the foot of Big Slip in the Land Rover. The first mile was comparatively easy, threading through the lower slopes where the Slip had petered out, but soon it began to climb. Just a bridle-track, no more, for horses in single file. At times it widened a little and they walked side by side. Nathaniel didn't push the pace and made sure they rested on rocks from time to time. Letitia was glad of his hand-clasp now and then, took pleasure when it was single file, in resting her eyes on his figure ahead of her, the sun glinting on the tawny hairs of his sinewy forearms and sturdy thighs, muscles rippling under his skin. All about them were the scents of the tussock land, the earthy, dry tang, a whiff of sheep from the merinos grazing here, and from the pockets of bush in the gullies the moist pungency of a New Zealand forest floor. Here and there were alpine flowers, pale, dainty.

She'd not thought the Slip would be so extensive, so massive, but they climbed, dipped, wound roundabout, crossed the gully streams, splashing through in their shoes, stepping from boulder to boulder where they ran more deeply, turned corners to find the track going off at right angles into steeper hills. They rested longer on a slab of rock beautifully situated by the track. 'They called it "Kitty's Picnic Table," ' said Nathaniel. He pulled two apples out of his pocket. They bit into them with relish to slake their thirst. 'Now for the steep pinch, but it's rewarded with the first glimpse of the Trough-of-the-Water-Swallower. You'll know the old legend of how he was killed down in the hollow and how the waters, melting from the snows, then rushed in to fill it? They say his heart beats still under the waters and at times you can see the lake rise and fall with his breathing.'

She nodded. 'I've seen it do just that, sitting about the shore on holiday. And in that programme on the Forty-fifth Parallel, it cropped up and was put down—rather beautifully I thought—to "the pull of the moon and the push of the wind." '

He stood up and held out a hand to her. They gained the summit shortly and stopped dead in their tracks. It was a true sapphire blue in this light, at this hour, and the sun, dropping a little, caught a thousand facets from its waters as they rippled. This view looked towards Mount Nicholas homestead on the far shore, and here, below them, the water curved gracefully in, but they couldn't see the shore-line yet. It gave the illusion of dropping down from these heights with never any hint of a road between them and the lake. All about them the poplars thrust greeny-gold candles skyward to frame that view and the hills overlake had a lavender touch of distance. The sky was clear of clouds and they could look downlake towards Walter Peak and Cecil Peak and beyond to the jagged skyline of the Remarkables.

Instinctively Nathaniel had reached for her hand, linking her fingers in his, and she turned to find his gaze upon her, assessing the impact it had upon her. He said, 'There really aren't any words, are there? Not a moment to gush, just to share. Odd how kindred silence can be. Very satisfying.' He slipped an arm about her shoulders. She was glad he didn't kiss her.

She drew in a deep breath, then said, 'I think I feel like Cortez when he gazed upon the Pacific for the first time. You know . . . as Keats said, "Silent, upon a peak in Darien." '

She could tell by his voice that he was moved. 'It's always been the custom here to name features . . . the Picnic Rock for Kitty, the Gate Beautiful for Ellen. So we'll name this one, here and now. It shall be known as Letty's Peak in Darien.'

It was a moment of sheer magic to Letty. Almost a moment of baptism.

When they went on, the going was easier. They were
descending now, even though when they reached the lake
level, they would still be more than a thousand feet above
sea-level. Quite suddenly, they were through on to a green
triangle, a sort of mini-valley where big poplars of the kind,
he told her, Americans called cotton-woods, were aquiver
in the breeze off the lake, and the ground was covered with
kapok-like fluff. Nathaniel picked up a nest blown from
one. 'One of last year's, thanks be, but look, Letty, see how
birds adapt to what is supplied by the environment . . .
see how cunningly it's lined with that fluff. Just like the
pioneers coming, building first out of the sod, the very
earth itself, then quarrying stone from these hillsides till
they could raft timber from the head of the lake for their
dwellings.'
He threw it away, linked fingers with her again. She said,
'It's all as it should be, isn't it? No false note anywhere.'
There were buttercups and scarlet pimpernels in the grass,
and foxgloves, and against the far side of the triangle a
patch of the lupins that grew wild all over Central Otago,
shading from palest pink right through to deepest purple.
They bore right a little and here were rough-barked rail-
ings looking like corrals in a Western film and a rustic sort
of shelter open one side, away from the weather.
'Nathaniel, I thought you said the Slip demolished the
yards here—oh, these are newer, aren't they?'
'Yes, there's always the chance that whoever rides down
for the mail might get caught in a thunderstorm, even
snow, so we built this. And once in a blue moon we turn
our horses loose here and hitch ourselves a ride to Queenstown and back. Not often. It could also provide shelter for
some lone hiker caught out by sudden storm on the road.
Now, we go through these trees and there's the road and
our mailbox.'
It was like stepping straight into civilisation again. Apart
from the beauty of the lake and shore beyond that road,
it looked so ordinary. A link with the rest of the world.
Twelve or fourteen miles away would be those high-rise
buildings thronged with tourists from every corner of the
globe, a cosmopolitan crowd. Unbelievable!

There was a stile by the mailbox. Nathaniel helped her over it, then stood his pack against the post. 'Let's cross the road. You must be dying to actually sit on the lake-beach, under that tree.'

Strange to be crossing a road, looking for traffic coming round the corner. The water came to within a few feet of the road verge, and a few feet below it, with a rough path leading down. A stilt rose with a harsh warning cry to its young, winged out across the lake. Some ducks, unworried, brought their heads out from under their wings, tucked them in again. Two oyster-catchers, handsome birds, continued foraging among the pebbles in the curve of the bay. There was a shelf of rock, water-worn, under the gnarled weeping-willow. They sat, listening to the soothing lap-lap of waters against the boulders. Letitia pushed her trews up, pulled off her shoes and cotton socks. 'I can't resist that water. Coming, Nathaniel?'

'In a moment. I'll just watch you first. Quite idyllic.'

He had a good turn of phrase. So, of course, had his father and James. Possibly they were all book-lovers. He laughed as she flinched when her feet plunged in. 'Odd, isn't it? The temperature doesn't vary much summer or winter. Of course it's snow-fed and practically unfathomable. I'll come in now. We'll soon get used to it.'

They did and splashed about, not caring how wet they got. Nathaniel pointed out wavy markings that showed where differing lake-levels had been, and they picked up coloured stones. It was a rock-hound's paradise. He looked at his watch. Clouds across-lake were being feathered with rose and gold and the sky between them a clear celadon green. Letitia said, regretfully, 'Yes, I suppose we mustn't linger. Some of that track would be tricky if there wasn't a moon. And it won't rise early tonight, will it?'

He laughed, looked mischievous, said, 'We aren't taking the track back—at least not tonight. We're taking it late tomorrow afternoon. We're going dining and dancing tonight.'

Her lips parted in amazement. 'We're what? Have you got a touch of the sun or something?'

He grinned. 'Oh, come, what an unromantic thing to greet my surprise for you. Miss Mattie knows. She, like me, thinks you deserve a change from The Wilderness. Governesses must at times be in touch with civilisation. Keeps them contented, she says, and she ought to know.'

'But—but how—?'

'We're being picked up. I was talking to Gideon and Annabel Darroch on the phone and they're going down tonight from Olivet. Remember I told you they had a guest-house there. They're celebrating something—forget what. They'll be staying at Miss Mattie's too in case you have qualms.'

Letty said, 'Nathaniel, you idiot! You said dine and dance. Queenstown may cater for casually dressed tourists, but how could anyone dance in canvas shoes with ribbed soles?'

'I'm not expecting you to. Surely you didn't think I wouldn't know that, you daft thing! Miss Mattie sorted out a black skirt and a quite glam top, and everything to go with it, tights, undies, shoes, the lot. She guaranteed what she picked was uncrushable too. We'll change at Miss Mattie's. So will Gideon and Annabel. Better get our shoes and socks back on, they'll be along any moment.'

She sat down on the rock and before she could do anything, Nathaniel was kneeling. He took out a large clean handkerchief, lifted one foot against him, drying it carefully. He looked up, his face near hers. She caught the flash of white teeth against that tanned face. 'I feel like Robin Hood drying Maid Marian's feet.' She didn't answer. She couldn't. She wanted to put a hand out, touch that springing tussocky hair. Then she found her tongue, laughed, and said, 'Wasn't there a New Zealand book, or was it a play . . . ? Called *The Boy with the Snowgrass Hair?* You'd be *The Man with Tussocky Hair*. I used to think that in the shop. When you were so aloof. So despising.'

His eyes smiled into hers. 'But not any more, believe me.'

A car stopped, a horn hooted. 'The Darrochs.' He carefully dried her other foot. She said, 'I'll put my socks on myself, thanks. Better get your own dried, though that hanky's sodden.'

A laughing girl piled out of the car, a large man followed her. 'How idyllic,' said Gideon Darroch.

'That's what I told Letitia,' said Nathaniel, 'then the next moment the unromantic wench cried out reproachfully that the water was icy. No soul.'

Annabel looked from one to the other and a slow, meaningful smile began to widen. 'Well, it's good to see you like this, Nathaniel; you've been so devoted to that tough valley scheme of yours, we've despaired of ever winkling you out of it. I nearly died when Gideon said you'd suggested a foursome for dining and dancing. It made my day. It looks as if you're about to start behaving like a normal man.'

Gideon looked alarmed. 'Take no notice of her. She's given to rash speech. My love, you could not only embarrass Nathaniel who, after all, has known you a long time, but Miss Greenaway, to whom we've not even been introduced.'

'Soon rectify that. And none of this Miss Greenaway, she's Letitia, mostly Letty.'

Annabel nodded. 'Oh, I know. Stella and Lucinda have already told me all about you. I feel I know you. Isn't this gorgeous? Our Frances and Luke the Less are with my stepmother tonight, so I'm really off the chain. We can shop tomorrow and pop up to the hospital to see Hope and Jamesina before coming home. Nathaniel, you didn't forget her glad rags and make-up, did you?'

He gestured towards to backpack, crossed the road to it, and they got into the station-wagon. 'This is unbelievable!' said Letty. 'How could I have dreamed, when I woke this morning, where I'd spend tonight?'

Miss Mattie's house was in a side street and set against a hill so that the stairs to the living quarters ran straight up from the front path. It was delightfully consistent with Miss Mattie's personality, and very much a second home to the Darrochs. They said so. Letitia looked puzzled. 'But you're obviously English, Annabel.'

Gideon nodded. 'But she had a New Zealand father, who married my stepmother . . . so now she's Annabel's stepmother too. It's quite a story.'

Letty clutched her head. 'It must be. Sounds a knotted relationship.'

'It was, long before Miriam married Johnny, Annabel's papa . . . we absolutely hated each other's guts to start with and now look at us.' The look he exchanged with his wife was one of sheer love.

Nathaniel chuckled. 'Must be the rarefied atmosphere of the mountains—Letty and I got off on the wrong foot too. I couldn't stand her. She was the cosmetician at the shop. Never in my wildest dreams did I imagine that one day she'd be helping me with the dagging, and changing Josselyn's naps!'

Letty turned pink. 'It's hardly a parallel situation. You talk a lot of nonsense, Nathaniel Pengelly.'

He pinched her cheek. 'And you sound like a reproving governess. And you aren't that, tonight. Can't you get into a Cinderella-at-the-Ball mood, girl?'

'I might,' she said darkly, 'when I see what Mattie's picked out for me to wear.' She was aware that Gideon and Annabel were exchanging meaning glances. Nathaniel was going too fast for her. She felt bewildered. It was so short a time since she first vowed revenge upon him.

Oh, bless Miss Mattie, she'd picked out the emerald green and silver top with the slashed sides and the silver sash. It made the black skirt look twice what it had cost and she'd put in the rope of chunky green beads that went with it, the earrings and bracelet to match. Impossible to believe Annabel had been married upwards of a dozen years. She had changed into a simple cream dress that looked like something out of the gay Twenties, with a dropped hipline and pleats that fanned out from under a golden silk sash.

How lovely to be eating dinner in so leisurely a fashion . . . whitebait fritters from the rivers of the West Coast, evidently deep-frozen, venison done in some delectable way that intrigued the women recipe-wise . . . wine delicately flavoured from the Hawkes' Bay coast of the

North Island holding surely in its pale depths a knowledge
that there the sun touched the earth, and the grapes, first
every day. Then there was the dancing, the first time Letty
had ever danced in Nathaniel's arms. She was surprised,
and said so, naïvely, to find him so expert a dancer. He
raised an eyebrow. 'Why?'

'Because I don't remember you at the staff dances ever.
Your father and brother are always there, and they're
beautiful dancers.'

'Well, even before I took on Mararangi, I was in the
waybacks, learning my stuff. I lasted only a year at the
shop, after college. I like country dances where you know
everyone. This is a fascinating crowd, listen to the different
languages. Tourists all love Queenstown.'

They circled again. 'No wonder,' she said, 'there's magic
in it. Look through that window, you can see the lighted
gondolas ascending and descending for their Million-
Dollar View . . . it's like fairyland and everyone's so
light-hearted. Perhaps because they're on holiday. That's
what holidays are for.' He gathered her a little closer. He
must use cedarwood after-shave. It suited him. 'Yes . . .
holidays can be very necessary. We all need to have
enchanted evenings to remember. Yes?'

Her hand instinctively tightened in his. He laughed. 'It
can't all be lambing and tailing and cutting out foot-rot
and drenching. We've got to make some time for starlight
and magic. Like tonight.'

They came back to the table as Gideon and Annabel did.
Sorbets were brought to them to refresh their palates, then
they went to the dessert tables, with a bewildering choice.
Later, much later, Nathaniel said to the top of Letitia's
head as they circled to dreamy music, 'I usually tire soon
of dancing, get bored. But not tonight. And I'm glad
Gideon and Annabel want to dance with each other most
of the time.'

The music ended, and as they seated themselves a tall,
well dressed and handsome man of perhaps fifty came
across. 'Why, Letty, I heard you were up here,
governessing, to my great surprise. But I didn't expect to
see you dancing—I thought you were right out in the

staying at Drumlogie. I was going to give you a ring. I was speaking to your stepfather in London just before I came here. But oddly enough it was your former boss who told me you were up here. I met him at a dinner in Dunedin. His name rang a bell. How——'

She said quickly, not knowing what he might say or what he might have heard from Tristan . . . who wouldn't be above hinting he had hopes his son might fall for her . . . 'Chester, this is my boss's son, Nathaniel Pengelly, and these are Gideon and Annabel Darroch, of Mount Olivet Guest House, and Glenorchy. This is Chester Burroughs who's in the tourist trade too, owns Burrough's Park Motels in Auckland and a few more scattered round New Zealand, though not in Queenstown.'

'I hope to rectify that in the near future,' he said. And sat down at their invitation. 'I came in with the shuttle service car from Drumlogie.' It was evident he had an appreciative eye for Letitia and news of her stepfather and mother brought a sparkle to her eye.

Nathaniel said to Letty when Chester and the others were exchanging small talk about London, 'Is your step-father in the hotel trade, Letitia? I didn't know.'

'No, he's in a finance company, one that has invest-ments in more than one country. His firm has an interest in some top-notch hotels in Auckland and Chester and he struck up a friendship. He's a lonely sort of guy, rather a pet. He's in a big way, but modest about it.'

Nathaniel had to watch her circling the floor with Chester presently, who seemed to have plenty to say to her. That was the worst of dancing. It was private to two people. He found himself wishing that what Burroughs had to say was being said at the table.

Annabel gave a mischievous giggle. 'Take that scowl off your face, Nat. It doesn't mean a thing. She's being polite, no more.'

He laughed, his brow clearing. 'As noticeable as that, was it? It was just that I was enjoying our foursome. However——'

He supposed that on return to Miss Mattie's, he'd not have Letty to himself, but as they drove home, Annabel said, 'Nathaniel, what a pity to have Letty here and for her not to see the Million-Dollar View by night. Why not take her up? You don't have to eat, you know. I dare say that, like me, you couldn't manage another crumb, but it's lovely on the viewing platform on a night such as this. It's like fairyland, and Miss Mattie's is near enough the terminal to walk home afterwards.'

He didn't hesitate. As Letitia got out of the car, Nathaniel slipped her white stole about her shoulders. 'Miss Mattie put this in. Though it's February and still the last month of summer, there's a triangle of snow on Walter Peak yet, from winter, and there'll be more back in, There are ranges upon ranges stretching back into the never-never behind them. In the interior there are rivers galore, rushing down to the lake one side, to the Tasman Sea the other, and little mountain tarns.'

She said dreamily, 'Wouldn't it be lovely to explore them? . . . little secret valleys and waterfalls . . . but it'd take a lifetime.'

'You've got most of your lifetime to come,' he said.

She didn't answer. A lifetime, yes, but would that be spent here?

They walked across to the terminal at the foot of the piney hill. Naturally, at this time, there were more couples coming down than up. Letty hadn't thought she'd be nervous, but they took their seats facing the heights, and the closed-in, sedan-like gondolas swung right in towards stark cliffs. Instinctively she clutched Nathaniel's hand, and shivered.

He slipped his arm about her, bringing her face into his shoulder so the cliffs were hidden, 'Don't be nervous, darling. It's not as close as it looks, and it's very quick. Haven't you been up before?'

'I was up that new one in Rotorua about eighteen months ago, but that's so open. We went as a whole family, when Grayson and Mother got back from honeymooning, before they went to Britain. They flew off from Auckland, you see, and Grayson thought he'd like us all with him when he did his tour of the North Island. It was partly business. Chester Burroughs joined us. Not all the tour, he just happened to be visiting his motels in Rotorua. That was when he first mentioned he'd like to establish some down here. More of a hunting lodge, to attract hunters from America and Canada. I've a feeling he wants it to gratify his own instincts mostly. To be able to get away from all the pressures of big business.'

'If that's so, it beats me why he wants to keep on extending. But when he joined the family tour, I gather *you* were the attraction.'

Letty forgot her fear, drew her face from his shoulder to gaze at him. 'You've got to be joking! He's twice my age. He's in Grayson's and Mother's age bracket. Besides, I can only take him in small doses, he talks business all the time. You've got to be mad!'

'I'm glad you think it's mad, Letty. Ah, here we are.'

She found herself hoping it wouldn't be crowded on the viewing platform. It wasn't. In fact, they had it to themselves. The rest were inside, lingering at the tables. They went to the extreme corner, drinking it in.

In the light of that pale moon, the immense lake reaching out beyond its many arms, was pearl-shadowed, patched with sable where the peaks faced away from that moon. The slivers of snow, deep-frozen into the clefts of those jagged mountains cast their own light towards them, and were reflected in the awesome depths. How incredible that over and up there should be the sort of temperatures that kept them frozen, yet here it was soft and balmy.

She said so. Nathaniel's voice, when he answered her, seemed strangely moved. 'That's what I so like about you, Letitia Greenaway. You share your thoughts about all this beauty about us. You communicate well. One of the world's givers . . . and you not only use words well but you have all the sounds of summer in your voice.'

She felt a tremor of delight feather over her, an inward pleasure, yet it seemed to touch her skin too, like a caress. She looked down at her hands on the rail, then managed to say, 'What a very nice compliment, Mr Nathaniel! But then you're an articulate man yourself. I've noticed it with the children. You never set their curiosity back, and you treat them like adults. I was analysing it the other night when I was in the schoolroom preparing the lessons. The ability to do that cuts out the generation gap we're always hearing about.'

His hand came to cover hers as it lay on the rail. 'How unexpected. I've never thought about it. But I'll say also, "Thanks for the compliment!" I like it, even if I strongly suspect you were steering the conversation away from the personal to the general.' He laughed. 'Mutual admiration society!' Then he said, and his voice roughened. 'And to think I was such a clot that I put you down as artificial and shallow! And all the time the real you was under the skin.' He added, 'A girl who wanted the rock-strewn passes and the birdsong, and the winds of heaven in her hair.'

She was startled and turned her face up to search his eyes. As she did, his fingers came to each temple, and lifted the fair hair bleached even fairer by the moonlight, then he let it fall back again.

Her voice was bewildered. She said, unbelievingly, 'But—but that's what I once wrote in a poem. How can *you* know it——?'

He said, 'That's why I took you to that pool the other day. It was the nearest I could get to what you dreamed of, Letty.'

'Nathaniel, it's inexplicable. Please tell me how you could know?'

He relented. 'It's a shame to tease you. The long arm of coincidence. You did it under a pen-name, didn't you? I almost blurted it out when I discovered it. But Miss Mattie was in the room with us. Beside, I realised that as you'd done it under a pseudonym, it was private to you. But now . . . '

She said, 'Now . . . ?'

'Now let's say I think we know each other well enough for it not to matter. Only I felt a brute when I read it, knowing I'd judged you by the counter you serviced. Remember that night in the sitting-room I was going through that pile of old magazines in the window-seat? Some of them were ones Mother brought up that time we camped here. This was an English magazine, and I leafed

through it. Suddenly a sentence in Mother's writing caught
my eye. She was a great one for writing in margins, said
that way she could more easily pick up something that had
interested her. There was a whole page of poetry. I looked
more closely because of it. She'd put, "I'm sure this is that
girl at our shop. I'd love to ask her, but perhaps it would
be prying. I'm taken with the way she disguised her name."
You remember the name you used, don't you, Letty? And
the poem?'

'Yes. Oh, Nathaniel, I'm so glad your mother read it.
How strange that she did, and now I'm living—now I'm
governess to her son in the very place where she read it. I
switched given name and surname.'

'You did. Very clever. "Esmeralda Lettington". You
called it "Daydream". I know it by heart by now.'

She looked up again, sharply at that. 'Nathaniel, you
couldn't.'

'But I could. Do you want to know why I could? You
do? Just this . . . I used to have a hobby of doing wall-
texts in Gothic lettering. I started it at school. I've done
one of your poem. Some of the nights I shut myself into
the office. I'm going to repeat it to you now. Look, move
along here into the shadows.'

She thought she'd never forget his voice, with its low but
distinctive timbre, repeating the lines in which she'd written
out all her rebellion against her job.

'I have by now served long apprenticeship,
    In city ways, in commerce, and my feet . . .
My slow, reluctant feet have known no joy—
    I cannot run with eagerness to meet
Each bright new day; once more it will be spent
    Within high walls, shut in from sun and dew;
Nor hear the birdsong in the rock-strewn pass
    Where all the winds of heaven come whistling
through.
These self-same winds should lift my unbound hair
    Back from my temples in wild ecstasy,
And fragrances from mossy forest floors
    Drift up to stir the gipsy heart of me,
Instead of bottled perfumes, soaps and creams,

A hundred aids to beauty, priced too high . . .
The things I barter when I long to splash
    In mountain streams beneath a fair, free sky.
God, in your mercy, grant to me some day
    That freedom that the mountain parrot knows,
And let me live at least one year among
    The forest trees, the dear, high-country snows.'

His voice stopped. Silence succeeded. Letty couldn't speak. His hand increased its pressure on hers. 'Letty, I hope you don't feel I've intruded on your private thoughts and dreams, but . . . but now it shouldn't matter between you and me. Only I find it so poignant and I feel such an unspeakable cad. The way I labelled you in my mind, despised you. It was horribly arrogant. And all the time you felt like that.'

She came to. 'Oh, Nathaniel, that was the way I felt *at first*. I had to come to terms with that job. I didn't live at that pitch of rebellion and unhappiness all the time. You see I was guilty of arrogance too, in despising what I was doing. Then I began to find compensations. I had to turn myself from a tomboy type into someone knowledgeable about things that *could* matter more than I'd dreamed they could, like disguising acne for a special dance to some teenager suffering from an inferiority complex and seeing her confident, even radiant, at the transformation. I remember a woman who'd let herself go, then she got a scare. Thought her husband was taking another woman out. She was most candid. She'd despised outward things. But she came to terms with it, and saved her marriage.'

He gave an involuntary laugh, 'Oh, Letty, you're so full of surprises! So, being you, you flung yourself into it, heart and soul?'

'Yes, something impelled me. I heard that one of our prime ministers had once said that it was more important to like what you were doing than to do what you liked. So I stopped being snooty. And the splendid wage your father gave me saved our financial situation.'

He said slowly, 'And now you are here, and I think you are realising your daydream. But to make it really come true, it mustn't have the time limit of a year on it.'

Again she didn't answer. He waited, then said whimsically, 'Quite a number of folk wouldn't see it as a dream come true. They'd pity you . . . stuck in the wop-wops, on a struggling rundown sheep-station, with very poor access . . . a jack-of-all-trades when emergencies happen. And a godsend to me, because you're the means of my being able to keep a couple like the Mayburys here. Before they came three couples turned down the chance of a job with me, because of lack of access and schools for their children. That's understandable. But The Wilderness is in my blood.'

She said demurely, 'Thank you, boss. It's very gratifying to know I'm giving satisfaction.'

He said, '*Satisfaction!* Oh, Letty, you wretch! It's so much more than that, and you know it. You must know it. Letty, you don't know the half of my earlier and biased opinion of you. What I said when Dad suggested you came up here! I'm confessing it here and now to you, and asking your forgiveness of it. Will you forgive me? My attitude was simply lousy.'

She caught her breath in, and bit her lower lip. Nathaniel heard the indrawn breath and turned her round to face him. 'I'm serious, Letitia. I felt I had to clear the decks before I—well, I've felt such a hypocrite time and again. Will you forgive me?'

This should have been the moment to lead him on, to get him to declare himself, the moment she'd dreamed of, for spurning him. The realisation of that shook her. She couldn't. She said, 'Oh, Nathaniel, I'm not guiltless myself. I—I've felt a hypocrite too. I don't really want to go into it now. It would take too long and they'll be closing down any moment and you could be very angry with me. Very. I will tell you some time, when we're back at Mararangi, and there aren't people coming and going.'

His tone was one of complete surprise. '*You've* felt a hypocrite? Surely not? Why?'

'I can't now, Nathaniel. Let's just say that in coming up here it wasn't just a strong desire to teach in the back-country. Though it saved me hunting for a similar job. Confession is supposed to be good for the soul, so for tonight I'll just say that I had a *very* ulterior motive in accepting the position here. I even misled you into thinking I'd make it permanent. I did intend to stay just a year. The school year. And I *knew* it was ulterior. The Sunday before we left for here our minister prayed for us to be saved from meanness of motive. And mine *was* mean. Dirt mean. Since coming up here I've rid myself of that. I can't do what I meant to do. Mean and paltry things don't stand up to the quality of life lived at Mararangi. But I don't want to go into it tonight. I don't want to do any more soul-searching. I just want to enjoy the view.'

He laughed. 'I like the view myself, so okay. The closer view!' He was gazing into her face. She lifted her eyes. He said, 'Your colouring is exactly right for here, tonight. That moon is bleaching your hair to silver, above your silver tunic. It's quite something.'

She felt herself tremble and said quickly, 'You absurd man. Last time it was honeysuckle gold. Whatever next?'

He took it seriously. 'I don't know. It could be corn-yellow, in full sunshine, among my standing wheat. You're making a poet out of me, Letitia Greenaway. I hardly know myself. You know what it adds up to, don't you? It means I'm——'

Her hand came up to his mouth, stopped it very effectively. 'Nathaniel, you're going too fast. Don't get carried away because this particular woman can take the high-country. It's clouding your judgment.'

She took her hand away and he said with vehemence, 'Of all the mad, crazy ideas! Why on earth did we start talking about your value as a governess? That's not what's making my heart race. I'm not doing an analysis. I'm like any man. *You're* stirring me, your nearness, your sweetness . . . the swirl of your hair and the freckles across your nose . . . and a few other things! Letty, don't talk rubbish. Why do you think I wanted to get you away from the prosaic everydayness of the sheep-run . . . wanted you away from the useful and the wage-earning? Wanted you in the sort of man-woman world most would expect?'

He felt the huge sigh rise up in her, he was holding her so close. 'It's as I said, Nathaniel; you're going too fast for me. I *have* to sort myself out. It's so short a time since I rid myself of that ulterior motive. Please leave it for now.'

He smiled down on her, she was looking up at him with such pleading. 'All right, mate.' He added whimsically, 'I liked the feel of your fingertips against my mouth. There's something I've wanted to do all night. Even when we were dancing. *This*. Don't draw away.'

He brought his right hand from her shoulder, gently traced the outline of her lips. She was amazed at the passion of feeling that swept over her, flooded her. How could such a light caress bring this reaction? It was inevitable that he should kiss her after that. And she wanted him to kiss her. It lasted just a fleeting second. There was the sound of doors opening, voices, footsteps, light streaming out. She wasn't afraid on the descent. Another couple faced them and the man's arm was around the girl's shoulders, as Nathaniel's was around hers.

It took them exactly eight minutes to Miss Mattie's. Not a word was uttered. It would have spoiled the sheer perfection of that last hour. He unlocked the door, helped her up the steep stairway, took her to the door of her room, quietly, not to disturb the others, whispered, 'Haven't I been good? But I'm just biding my time!'

CHAPTER TEN

SUNDAY sped all too fast. They woke hearing the mellow chimes of St Faith's, the Catholic Church, ring out over the lakeside town, and later took their way to St Andrew's Presbyterian service in a modern, beautifully designed church where a huge wooden cross hung against massive water-worn stones collected from the lake-shore. The other three were well-known and Letitia was introduced to dozens of people, all so geared to the stranger-in-their-midst idea natural to this tourist town that they turned down half a dozen invitations to midday dinner.

Miss Mattie's forehandedness in freezing steak pies and trays of apricots provided them with all they needed and allowed them to set off early for the hospital. They found Jamesina and Hope full of excitement because they were being discharged on Tuesday and were delighted to inform them that Edward and Fiona Campbell were in Queenstown and would drop them off on their way home.

They were most intrigued to find Nathaniel had walked Letitia over the bridle-path for an evening's dancing. Letty was surprised to find Jamesina so approving of that. 'Quite right. More sensible than some of your ideas, Nathaniel,' she pronounced. Turning to her four visitors, she said, 'This foolish lad's made such a bogey of that Slip. He ought to be ashamed of himself, with the forebears he's got. It doesna make it easy, that I'll grant, but this economic state won't last for ever. I've seen it go up and down on the pig's back like a seesaw times without number. So we'll come up again, I've no doubt. Look at Fiona and Edward. Once they depended solely on the lake for transport, but now they've not only got their own barge on it, but they flip in and out all over the place at the rate of nobody's business. After all, we don't break bones every week and if you've a governess who thinks nothing of walking the bridle-path for a night off, you're in luck, and dinna forget it.'

'I won't,' said Nathaniel meekly. 'And I know I'm in luck.' He grinned at Letty. 'This housekeeper of mine cuts me down to size every time. Just as well I've got Owen back home—I'm coping with a monstrous army of women at the moment. Well, it's good news that Mattie's staying on a week or two. She can help you too, Hope.'

Hope's eyes lit up. 'I've had a stroke of luck too. That cousin of mine who's nursing in Dunedin has a friend there due for a break, and she's arriving here tomorrow. She was coming to Queenstown anyway but told Josie it would save her accommodation if she could come and give me a hand. She'll stay in our house, of course. Okay by you, Nat? I said I'd ask. She'll spend tomorrow night at Connelly's and come in with us Tuesday.'

'Splendid. Well, we must be on our way. Letty and I have to hike back when Gideon drops us. Has Owen rung today, or am I to tell him?'

'He hasn't rung so far. Probably waiting for a progress report from you.' She turned to Letitia. 'I've heard great things about you from him. It's going to make all the difference. Owen says it's just like having the youngsters at school and that you even look after them out of school hours. Hope it's for keeps.'

'My bet is,' said Nathaniel, 'that she'll stay at Mararangi as long as Miss Mattie stayed at Olivet. She's lost her heart to our valley.'

Letty was sure all faces wore knowing looks in common. She said, rising, 'And on that note, goodbye. The children will be so thrilled when we tell them about Tuesday.'

They certainly were . . . there was so much to tell Mother . . . that Dad had, at long last, glassed-in those shelves in the kitchen, how well Hope's beans were cropping, and that the next lot of lettuces were ready, Mum was a great one for salads . . . and Damien had grown a whole inch since last measuring, and Josselyn was walking and saying three words by now, and the Gravenstein apples were ripening and the yellow Shiloh plums ready for bottling!

'Oh, don't tell her anything about fruit right away,' said Letty. 'Miss Mattie and I are going to do the bottling and jam-making. That old orchard's a dream. Your mother must take it slowly at first. We want her just glad to be home and out on the sun-lounger there.'

Owen burst out laughing. 'You don't know my Hope, she'll be just raring to go. Just as well she's bringing this nurse up with her.'

Tuesday came and the whirly-bird, as the children called it, dropped out of the skies. They'd been frantically busy till then, practically springcleaning the Mayburys' house, filling the vases, and the tins. Letty had been glad of it. It had meant that she and Nathaniel had never been alone. She wanted to marshal her thoughts, then tell him she'd overheard all, and of the revenge she'd planned. Would he see the funny side of that? She *thought* he would. She *hoped* he would. She did wonder, though, if she had needed to hint at it at all. She had simply got carried away in that magic hour above the lake when he had abased himself and asked her forgiveness. She had wanted to meet him half-way. Well, perhaps it was going to be for the best, it would clear the air. But now they were going to have a stranger on the property, she wished she hadn't stopped Nathaniel saying what he'd wanted to say. But she was so aware that the skyway restaurant was about to close.

Nevertheless, she was aware of a singing happiness pervading her very veins; a physical awareness and longing in her every time he came near her. This was what she'd dreamed of, all her life, but never met, and it was worth waiting for, this blend of mind, spirit and body, heady, yet satisfying, her sureness that apart from the attraction, here was the comradeship to last a lifetime. With the settling of the helicopter on the paddock, it was the end of a marking-time period. With Miss Mattie to keep Jamesina company, surely she and Nathaniel could find time to be alone.

Fiona and Edward sprang out and the next moment a girl with hair as bright as a newly-minted two-cent piece appeared. Letitia heard Nathaniel, standing beside her with Josselyn in his arms, draw in a sharp breath. He muttered something. The girl, and Edward, turned to assist Hope down, and Fiona turned back for Jamesina. Nathaniel called out, 'Hope, watch this one . . . ' and put Josselyn on her almost steady feet to walk to her mother.

Letty noticed that the coppery one wasn't watching the child, but looking directly at Nathaniel who didn't return the look. She made herself stop watching the pair, and moved quickly so Josselyn wouldn't clutch her mother's legs, bending down and steadying her. 'Who's the clever girl, then?' exclaimed Hope. 'Oh, dear, I'm a goose. I'm so happy to be home I'm crying. I was terrified my baby might have forgotten me.'

Miss Mattie said, 'We've all been saying "Mum-Mum" to her all morning, hoping she might register it and greet you with it. Say "Mum-Mum," Josselyn.'

Josselyn sat down abruptly, gazed astounded at eye-level at Hope's plaster and said in an enquiring tone, 'Leg? Leg?'

The other children were so overcome by this evidence of great intelligence at knowing something was different that the others missed the way Nathaniel greeted the nurse. All except Letitia. The coppertop said with an upward inflection, 'Nathaniel? You're supposed to mutter, "Good heavens, you! What a small world!" '

His tone was a low drawl. 'Am I, Deirdre? I can't think why. It's no great coincidence like suddenly meeting you in the middle of the Sahara. And after all, *you* knew you were coming here. The only surprising thing is that last time we saw each other you were vowing never to come to this God-forsaken spot again!'

God-forsaken? This then was *that* girl. The one *who had mattered*. Letitia's spirits dropped to zero. Enter a complication! She hoped they wouldn't guess she'd heard. It was enough to pretend she hadn't in the commotion of the welcome. Fiona proceeded to kiss everyone in sight and Edward followed suit. He laughed as he came to Letitia. 'Treat 'em all alike is my motto . . . at least it's been that way ever since I wed this mad MacDonald lass here. She's

just like that crowd at Drumlogie. Upset all my preconceived ideas. I'd always thought the Scots were reserved by
nature, but she upset more than one of my cherished ideas.
Everybody's kissing-kin to Fiona.'

Nathaniel laughed. 'Did you suffer from preconceived
ideas too, Edward? I never heard a whisper of such a
thing.'

Edward grinned. 'There's a treat in store for you then.
When Fiona arrived in New Zealand after a disastrous
meeting we'd had in Scotland, we were at daggers drawn;
added a spice to life, though. Shook me out of my
complacency.'

'I know exactly what you mean,' said Nathaniel meaningly, and draped a casual arm about Letitia's shoulders.
She was sure he'd done it to annoy Deirdre. The girl who'd
despised this place. She managed to move away without
being too abrupt, said, 'Don't keep these two standing
here, come on in, we've got something ready. Less steps
here than in the homestead.' She turned to the nurse,
'You'll be here, of course, in their spare room. I've made
up the bed. And I think there's an introduction due.'

Deirdre lifted heavy coppery lashes from sparkling grey
eyes. 'I don't need an introduction to Nat and
Jamesy . . . though Jamesy didn't find that out till this
afternoon.'

Jamesy . . . and Nathaniel had said she didn't like her
name shortened. Deirdre added, 'And I've heard of Miss
Mattie, though I haven't met her till now. Tell me,
Nathaniel, how come you've got two governesses?'

His tone was nonchalant. 'We haven't. Miss Mattie's
been a friend-in-need. Letty's so likely to be called upon
for tailing or drenching or a thousand-and-one other things
as well as her strict timetable in the schoolroom, somebody had to be at the domestic helm and see to Joss.
Mattie's not on the payroll. Angels won't accept salaries.'

Hope was walking quite well, rocking on her heel and
very happy to be home. Jamesina had only a slight limp.
Owen scooped a ginger kitten out of their way. 'Tiger Tim,
I'm shutting you up in the shed. Nice if they came a

cropper over you the moment they're home.'

Miss Mattie served the afternoon-tea. Everyone talked at once. Edward and Nathaniel came in with the luggage. Nathaniel said, 'I'll put yours straight in your room, Deirdre. This way. This house was only just started when you were here.'

She said quickly, 'Of course I could sleep over at the homestead if it's crowding the family.'

He said coolly, 'Hardly, you'll be wanted here to give Hope her early morning tea, help her dress and so on. And look after Josselyn. Owen's coped well at nights till now. It won't be crowded in any case. Damien and Roberta are at the homestead. They like it better for games. They can come back when you go home. Besides which, nobody plays cops and robbers better than Letitia, according to Damien. Never thought I'd find anyone to equal him in imagination. She ought to write detective novels, not just poetry. What's more she's up with all the jargon. Comes from being so much with a young fiend next door to her in Dunedin. He's coming up for the May holidays.' He added, 'What's more, the cops have to be the heroes. Damien used to fancy being the robber, the stick-up man, but our Miss Greenaway is a stickler for law and order.'

He disappeared with Deirdre. They were away some time. Letty wished she knew what they were saying. Hope said, 'I don't think my cousin had any idea this one knew Nat. I suppose it's okay, is it, Jamesina? It makes me wonder.'

Jamesina evidently felt Hope mustn't be worried. 'Of course it's all right. Must be two years since she was up here. Giles and Lucinda came in one day with a crowd of tourists. Three of them stayed on. We did it as a favour to the Drumlogie folk. They were chockful. They walked the bridle-path to the road and hitched a ride back. But Deirdre, on the way, turned her ankle and didn't go on. I must say it healed up sooner than mine. She was appalled at the remoteness. Perhaps she was curious to see how much had been done here. Now, we'll get away up to the homestead. Oh, here's Nathaniel now. Fiona and Edward don't want to be late.'

As they walked towards the helicopter, Edward said to Nathaniel, 'I met a chap yesterday, don't know his name, because he got called to the phone before I found out, who was asking me about the practicality of access through Big Slip. He was chance-met, sounded like some big business tycoon, and heard I was a consultant. He had been up the Glenorchy road. Saw the Slip, wondered about its history. He asked what it would lead to, if a road was made through. I was just on the point of asking him did he know it was all private land through here, being farmed, when he was called away. I thought he might have been thinking it was Crown land. Queenstown's full of chaps looking for sites for accommodation these days. But perhaps it was just that his curiosity had been piqued.'

Nathaniel nodded. 'And from the road Big Slip gives no indication of how extensively it sprawls. It looks as if there are just a couple of hills to circumnavigate.'

At eight o'clock wild shouts and bangs were issuing from the old orchard when Deirdre appeared at the homestead. Jamesina was on a sun-lounger on the pillared patio sipping home-made lemon squash with Miss Mattie beside her, enjoying a yarn about some of the old identities at Olivet, Nathaniel in a garden chair beside them, with the papers Edward had brought. Deirdre looked cool and elegant in buff linen, the skirt buttoned with large brown buttons and a cream blouse, spotted in brown, over it. She came up the steps and said, 'I was about to explore, to see the improvements—like to show them to me, Nathaniel?'

To the delight of Miss Mattie and Jamesina, he said, 'No, I'm on call for the bunch in the orchard. I'm just about to go to find out what my role is tonight. I'm usually just the watch-house cop.'

Deirdre pulled a face. 'Not telling me you really want to? Most men have to be dragooned into that.'

'Oh, I'm a very willing victim,' replied Nathaniel suavely.

Alarmed shouts rent the air. 'Take cover!' yelled Damien. 'Down, you fool, *down! You* haven't got a bullet-proof vest on . . . *I'll* take the risks. And aim low if you must shoot . . . '

'Poor Letty,' said Nathaniel, laughing. 'She's only a constable. She has to take orders. Damien loves that—he's chief detective. She'll be lucky if she doesn't finish up in a patch of thistles.'

Deirdre said, 'Doesn't sound ideal for discipline in the schoolroom. If I were Hope I'd take a dim view of that. Still, I dare say you have to take what you can get as a governess. They're usually teachers who've failed to make the grade.'

'Don't you believe it. She's the calibre of Miss Mattie here. Those kids can't put anything across her. They have great fun with her, after hours, but they respect her. There's a certain tone in her voice and they know they've gone far enough. My mother had it. She had the best of all reasons for not finishing her training. Her father died and she needed to earn money immediately. There were twins, younger, both at university in Britain now. Their mother married again, a London business man, so Letty was able to leave the shop.'

Deirdre dropped into a spare chair and poured herself a glass of squash. 'The shop? You don't mean she worked for——'

'For Dad? Yes. Head of the cosmetics counter. You know Dad's passion for alliterative names? And his aptitude for picking winners? But she'd always longed to teach in the high-country, so when she no longer had responsibilities she came up here with me. How lucky can a man get, as Jamesina remarked on Sunday? To acquire *Letitia for Loveliness* on a remote place like this! Beauty *and* brains. You'd never think that once she used to swan it around Pengelly's with hair piled up, never a tendril out of place, lashings of make-up, the lot. You knew her, didn't you, Jamesina?'

'Aye, and grateful to her. She used to send up my hair-tints by mail order. Even my family didn't suspect. Not that I ever thought a governess lurked beneath that glamorous exterior!'

Deirdre said, 'As Jamesy said on Sunday? Were you in Queenstown, Nat. Wish I'd known. I'd have come up sooner.'

Nathaniel's voice was careless, 'Oh, Annabel and Gideon Darroch from Glenorchy were having a night on the tiles, so Letty and I joined them. We went down to the road verge. We all stayed at Miss Mattie's, and came home next day the same way.'

'Picked you up at the road verge. Really? Does that mean you can get a vehicle through now? Have you bull-dozed a track through to take a four-wheel drive? How marvellous. That makes all the difference.'

He burst out laughing. 'How naïve can you get? Take more than a bulldozer. That ground's horribly unstable. It's a major undertaking. Edward said for a property like this it couldn't be justified in profitability. We still do a twenty-five-mile roundabout to Drumlogie. We walked it.'

'Walked it? And then went dancing? You've got to be joking.'

He chuckled. 'Our Miss Greenaway didn't miss a dance all night. And she and I were up at the Chalet afterwards till midnight. Ah, there's my signal.' A scout whistle had sounded from the orchard. 'Reinforcements are needed. Come on, Deirdre, if you want company back. Only you'll have to run or I'll be on the mat. Anyway, Hope might need you by now.'

When they were out of earshot, Jamesina said with a satisfied sigh, 'Well, it looks as if he's not minded to look in that direction again. He soon came to his senses about her. She was only carried away because he was a Pengelly. Told him the sooner he got this farming bug out of his system the better. Not to ruin himself in the meantime. But I wish she'd not appeared on the scene right now. It's not as derelict as it once was.'

Miss Mattie said drily, 'Not to worry, there's a powerful antidote at hand this time.' They enjoyed a shared chuckle. 'I hoped for that while I was in hospital,' said Jamesina, 'because I always liked Letty in the shop. But I could wish that Deirdre elsewhere.'

So could Letty. And she hadn't had the comfort of seeing how Nathaniel had handled her.

It was amazing how her presence seemed to affect every-thing. The excuses she made to appear constantly at the homestead were irksome. Letty was sure she rubbed Hope up the wrong way. One day Letty noticed Deirdre making for the stables and knew why. She'd seen Nathaniel go over there. Letty slipped over to the cottage. She found Hope at the bench, peeling apples. Hope turned round guiltily, looked relieved. 'Thank goodness it's you. If I'm not allowed to do something in my own house soon, I'll scream! She told me yesterday not to worry if my progress was tardy, she'd get extended leave. Not if I know it! But don't want to be unpleasant to her. Though she deserves I should be. She even tries to belittle me in front of Owen. Even he notices it. I sound ungrateful, but we're dying to be on our own again.'

Letty laughed, 'I must have a horrible nature. I was just afraid I was the one who couldn't seem to get on with her.'

'If only I'd not asked Josie to come up. But I didn't want to impose on you. Josie couldn't get away, but read my letter out in a group, and Deirdre seized on it—pretended she'd been granted leave. But after she got away, Josie found out that she'd asked for the leave after hearing I wanted Josie. Josie rang me the other night, said she'd smelt a rat right away when she heard that and what was going on?'

'What was the rat?'

'Nat!' said Hope succinctly, and they both collapsed.

'Oh dear,' Letty controlled herself, 'he'd love to hear you. I shouldn't worry, I'm beginning to suspect Nat can take care of himself.' Well, she hoped he could.

Hope said savagely, 'I very much doubt men really are capable of reading women like that. The way she's harped on about how I must always dread the children being ill and how awful if ever there was a really serious accident, not just broken bones but broken skulls . . . and haemorrhaging . . . when expert help is needed. Meaning a nurse . . . herself, I suppose. Said she'd not blame Owen if he couldn't take the responsibility—that he owes it to me not to be at the chancy availability of the mercy flights . . . I lost my temper with her yesterday, said Owen couldn't be happier with his boss, that the economic climate was bad enough for farmers without leaving a chap like Nat battling against the odds, single-handed! That I adored it here now we've got a good governess. So she predicted you wouldn't stay!'

'Wouldn't stay? Nobody has a chance of winkling me out of here. It's a dream come true. The Garden of Heaven . . . a miniature Eden!'

'Exactly. Trouble is, *she's the serpent*. I'd send for my mother if she wasn't looking after an elderly cousin just now. But never mind. It's only another four or five days to go. And she's not making much headway with Nat.'

Letty stayed awake that night mulling over it, and wishing she hadn't checked the eager words on Nathaniel's lips. Deirdre was taking a different tack now, cooing over the improvements, but sighing over the tough time farmers were having, with subsidies dropped, fertiliser prices rising, wages and killing charges, and, above all, lower returns and shrinking markets. In all, a good deal of the joy of life at Mararangi, for Letty, had gone. But she can't stay, she thought, she'll be gone soon. But would she have done any harm by the time she left? Had it stirred anything in Nathaniel? Once this girl had mattered.

One evening Deirdre came over, sang out, 'It's just me,' and entered the sitting-room. 'Nat, I thought Hope and Owen needed some time on their own. Josselyn's down, so I came over here.'

Nathaniel said, 'Well, they'll be back on their own by the end of this week when you go back.'

Deirdre looked thoughtful. 'That's just it. I'm not altogether happy about the leg. I've been massaging it. I wondered if I might ring the Campbells at Wanaka, and if they happen to be coming here in the next week or two, I might ask for extended leave and just fly out with them then. Otherwise it means you taking me to Drumlogie and on to Queenstown, and you seem too busy for that.'

Nathaniel said, 'Oh, I was going to come across to tell you tonight. I knew you had just two weeks' leave and you might want a day or two in Queenstown to enjoy yourself, so I've arranged things. I've something to see Giles Logie about, so I'll take you down on Friday. Stella's going into Queenstown then and if we get an early start, you can go in with her. Suits everyone that way.'

Letitia's spirits soared still more when he added, 'Miss Mattie's going to supervise the children's lessons that day, because I'm taking Letty with me. She's only been off the place once so far.'

There was nothing Deirdre could do about it. Letty thought of the drive back on that beautiful, unspeakably rough road . . . all twenty-five miles of it. They could stop somewhere, be alone. It would be worth every bump, every rut and ford. Deirdre no longer mattered, that was evident.

It was a very happy moment, carefully disguised, when they waved Deirdre off with Stella. The guest house was only slightly less crowded than before. It had been a wonderful tourist season. They once again had a meal with the family and were lingering over coffee when Rob Adair said, 'By the way, Nat, there's a chap here who knows your father —at least he met him recently in Dunedin. Knows Letitia too and said he met you at Tyson's Hotel a fortnight or so ago. Bags of money, owns motels all over the place. Since being up here he's been in touch with your father by phone and your father would like him to see your place, and even the country further in. He asked me about the chance of getting out to see you. Offered to make it worth my while to take him out there if you could have him. And he'd charter a chopper to take him out again. I said why not drop him in too if you could have him, but he said he wanted to see the terrain closer at hand. He's interested in Queenstown of course, from a tourist point of view. Name of Chester Burroughs.'

Nathaniel scowled. 'Oh, heavens, we've only just got rid of Deirdre. What on earth of interest would a chap like that find in my farming venture? It's not exactly a show-place yet!'

Letty's indignant voice broke in. 'It *is* so! It's beautiful! What more could you have? A smiling valley with a dream of an old homestead, the Gate Beautiful to guard its entrance, a thousand trees, I predict that in time to come it will be known as the most exquisite homestead in the

Lake County. You don't do it justice, Nathaniel!'

He cocked a rueful eye at her. 'You could be biased. But if you want this friend of yours to see it, okay.'

'It's not because he's a friend of mine. It's because your father wants him to see it. In spite of all his opposition, Nathaniel, he's very proud of what you've done. But if you can't stand the thought of another visitor, I daresay we can rake up some excuse.'

'Such as what? I hate to sound churlish and Dad could be hurt. Oh, I suppose a few nights won't hurt us, but I'd like to get back to normal. We've plenty of room. The children can go back home, Miss Mattie could have Roberta's room, and Chester Burroughs have hers. The master bedroom's not furnished yet.' Letty looked away quickly. Nathaniel sighed, said, 'All right, lead me to him and I'll play the genial host. Hope he's easy to entertain, that's all.'

Rob said, 'He's interested in everything up here. Particularly, of course, the tourist accommodation. Went up to Glenorchy and scouted round there to see if there's any area suitable for a sort of millionaire's holiday ranch. You know, for overseas people who want to go fishing, hunting, tramping.'

Nathaniel groaned, 'Nothing's sacred now. People used to come here to get away from it all, come here for the solitudes. Now high-rise buildings rear up everywhere and wrangles galore start about conservation. Views get blocked out. Time was, long ago, before the Glenorchy road went through, they used to take our Governors-General uplake by steamer to get them away from everything, where no one could reach them.' He stopped. 'I'm being selfish. We can't keep it to ourselves. But if only they'd keep it simple. Not luxurious.'

Letty said, 'I remember Chester talking about this when we were at Rotorua, and in fairness to him, I believe that was what his first idea was. His dream. A sort of retreat in the wilderness.'

'Well, not in our wilderness,' said Nathaniel. 'However, if Dad wants him to see the place, so be it. I'm always squashing Dad's ideas.'

It was stupid for Letty to feel guilty about it merely because she knew Chester. As it was her spirits had dropped to an all-time low because they wouldn't be alone on the drive back.

They both managed to sound and look cordial when they met Chester and he was in high gig at the prospect. 'Don't imagine I'm looking for the sort of cuisine I provide at my restaurants. My tastes are simple, really.'

'Just as well,' grinned Nathaniel. 'At times it's all hands on deck and no time for frills.'

The country they drove into interested Chester greatly. 'What magnificent scenery! Pity so few see it. Its potential is boundless.'

Nathaniel said quietly, 'It's good grazing country, good agricultural land, and farming will pick up again. We're diversifying greatly and the venison trade proving high export value. I've got quite a few on my back paddocks.'

'How far back does your property go?'

Nathaniel named it in miles. 'Interesting terrain, because when the gigantic slip occurred, the river changed course and flowed off to link up with another stream that finally joins the Shotover. It's a less turbulent river. I always fancy it could, in time, be stocked with trout. Then where it banked up on an elbow, we've got a lagoon and some wetlands, that are a refuge for wildfowl. That's staying a refuge if I've anything to do with it. I'd rather have bird-watchers than hunters.'

'I'm a bird-watcher myself,' said Chester. 'I'd like to see that. Any chance?'

'Not for a few days. What sort of a rider are you?'

Letty said, 'The best. He was brought up on a Waikato stud.'

Chester seemed gratified. 'I'd no idea you knew. Oh, now I remember. I took Grayson off to one, from Rotorua.'

Chester said, 'I believe your father would like to help you develop your place but you want to go it alone.' Letty, squashed in between the two men, felt Nathaniel stiffen. Oh, dear.

Nathaniel said, 'I'm not letting my father risk any of his capital in my venture. If I don't expand too quickly, I'll surmount the present-day hurdles. I will not jeopardise his business. If Dad pulls out any capital, it might make it too easy for a take-over and that would break his heart. It's a family business and it's going to stay that way. I'm breaking even and I've no big ideas.'

Chester said, 'I might have a yarn with you some night. There might be some way round it.'

Nathaniel's jaw set. 'If that's what he sent you up for, you can forget it. The Wilderness is mine, entirely, and it's staying mine.'

'I like a man who knows his own mind,' said Chester.

Letty was thankful it was the weekend. She'd better keep Chester out of Nathaniel's hair. They both, however, warmed to his delighted appreciation of the view from the Gate Beautiful. His eyes swept the valley, lifted to the hills, the far mountains. 'It's so self-contained,' he said, 'a kingdom all its own.'

Nathaniel and Owen were very busy and Nathaniel, impressed by Chester's horsemanship, was glad enough to let Letty go along with him, after warning their visitor she wasn't an expert yet. Nathaniel said to Letty on the Sunday, 'I simply can't spare the time. He's dying to see that patch of wetlands. I rather like him being so interested in the wading-birds. Would you find it much of a chore going along with him? It's about a mile and a half past our little rock-strewn pass, remember?'

His eyes held hers. He said quietly, 'Soon, after he's gone, we'll find an hour or two to ourselves, Letty, and you can do your spot of confessing, whatever it is. Knowing you, it won't be much. I really suppose you've just got a tender conscience. Okay, pal?'

'Okay, Nathaniel, but I wish you were coming along.'

He bent down and touched his lips to her forehead. 'So do I.'

She and Chester didn't get back till late in the twilight. Nathaniel was looking for them along the trail that led from the head of the valley. 'Sorry if you were anxious, Nathaniel, but we rode up that hill beyond the lagoon to see what sort of view and there below us were the Beaumont boys. Strange that I've spoken to them on the phone but never met them. They called us down, and invited us to see their place.'

Chester said, 'I was quite impressed. I like to see young chaps taking on a tough proposition like that, with the hopes of getting enough out of it to buy in a more accessible place.'

Nathaniel nodded. 'Yes. I wish times were better so someone might buy them out. But, like us, their access is against them. Oh, much worse than us. Only our track in from Drumlogie makes it possible at all for them.'

Chester said, 'Letty made some tea for us, while they showed me over some of their buildings. Those shearers' quarters were old but well built. And there must have been an old English stonemason there in the early days, to have such fine walls here and there. Good examples of old-style arches.'

Three nights later Chester said to Nathaniel, 'Any chance of a yarn with you in your office?'

Letty was sure Nathaniel groaned inwardly. Chester was apt to talk big business all the time and Nathaniel wasn't really interested. She and Miss Mattie washed up, Jamesina watching them and knitting. Letty said, 'I'll go and change, I think. I was up the big plum tree getting the fruit from the top branches with Roberta and Damien, and it hasn't improved my jeans one bit. Not that they were much to start with.'

She came back in a brown linen wrapover skirt tied at the waist, with a thin cream silk blouse tucked into it, a green tie loosely knotted under the collar. Even her fair skin had taken on a faint brown now, and a greenstone pendant fitted into the deep V of the neckline, earrings to match swung with every movement. Her hair had been brushed till it shone, and it swung to one side across her creamy forehead. The deep swirl of it at the back suited her far more than ever the lacquered topknot at the shop had done. She had one of Roberta's green bone bracelets on one wrist. 'It's too big for her,' she said. 'So she gave it to me. I love the gifts children think up for themselves.'

She felt happier tonight. Chester had said he must be ringing the helicopter service soon. Oh, to be on their own again!

She heard Nathaniel calling her name. 'Would you come to the office, Letty?' She darted a laughing glance at the two women. 'Sounds ominous, doesn't it. As if I'm to be put on the carpet.'

'Not much chance of that,' said Miss Mattie fondly.

She couldn't read Nathaniel's expression. He said, 'Sit down, Letitia. I want you to hear this. Chester, would you mind repeating exactly what you've just said?'

Letty felt uneasy. 'Why? Is it something that concerns me?'

'Very much your concern,' said Nathaniel. 'Go on, Chester. I want Letty's reaction.'

She blinked, moistened her lips, said, 'Yes?'

Chester looked very much the big business man and, to Letty's apprehensive gaze, very confident. He crossed one leg over the other, settled back, and said in the most ordinary tone, 'I want to buy this place, lock, stock, and barrel. The whole valley and the grazing hills beyond it, the wetlands, the lagoon, all of it. Even Big Slip. The setting is just what I've always dreamed of. It could be the peak of my career. The exquisite old homestead on its terraces, properly restored, of course. The clock over the stables, the cobbles in the stable-yard. I'd keep the homestead as a showpiece. There would be extra cottages built for the staff, chalets to harmonise with the forested area. Long low quarters for guests. I'd stock the river with trout. I'd have to get access put through Big Slip, of course. It would make this place as a tourist attraction to have the lake at its front door . . . launches, canoes, the lot. I'd have a dramatic entrance there to match the Gate Beautiful. I've got every chance of an overseas company being interested in the investment. I've looked a long time for the ideal place and now I've found it. I'm prepared to offer Nathaniel here a fabulous price for its potential. Far, far more than he'd ever get for it as a farming venture. He could farm anywhere then.'

Nathaniel was watching Letty closely. As Chester linked his hands together and settled back more, she sprang to her feet, the most astonishing light in her eyes. 'Oh, no, Nathaniel. *No.* You wouldn't! You *couldn't!* There could never be *another* Gate Beautiful. Ellen built that with her own hands. Your mother wanted those pillars. She saw them placed there.' Then she stopped, and vivid colour rose up into her cheeks. She said, 'What am I saying? What is it to do with me? It's your decision, Nathaniel Pengelly.'

The stern look left his face. He looked across at her and smiled. 'It's everything to do with you, Letty.'

His eyes held hers. She began to smile her slow smile. Chester sat up, looked from one to the other, said, 'Like that, is it?'

'It's like that,' said Nathaniel firmly. 'It's very simple, Chester. *It's not for sale.* Not now or ever. You see, I had a dream too. And I've realised it. To farm the land of my forebears. My mother wanted it, as Letty said. I want my sons to inherit this place. I may not see access to the lake in my time, but they'll see it in theirs. I hope you realise your dream, Chester, but not on my land. Tourism is good and we need that trade, but fundamentally our future still depends upon our agriculture, though we need to diversify. It's a hungry world out there and we have to alleviate that. There's a lot of land across the lake, for instance. Why not try that? Only access by water, certainly, but that could be a big draw for what you have in mind. But this valley is mine.'

Chester had the air of a man who enjoys tough discussion, and is confident of success. 'I'm thinking of a price beyond your wildest dreams. A chance like this may never come your way again. Is this any sort of a place to coop up a girl like Letty, reared in a city, with a barrier like that lakewards, and a horror of a road, if you can call it that, twenty miles and more long, that would be a nightmare in snow . . . when a woman is having a family, producing those sons you talk about? This isn't anything you can decide off-hand, like this. Take time to think it over. Let reason have its way with you.'

What an incredible conversation!

Nathaniel lifted a tawny eyebrow at her. 'What do you say to that, Letitia?' His tone was confident, his eyes glinting.

She gave him look for look, shrugged, then said, 'Ellen Nathaniel had it worse, but wasn't she ninety-odd when she died? And all *she* had to reach a doctor was an open whale-boat.'

His eyes held triumph. 'Then we don't sell, love?'

She lifted her chin. *What a moment!* 'We don't sell,' she said simply.

That was it. Chester Burroughs knew when he was beaten. 'Well, that's it. It was worth trying. And thanks for the hospitality.'

Nathaniel said, 'You're very welcome to stay on a few days, or would you find it too tantalising?'

Chester grinned. Letty thought she'd never liked him so well. He said, 'Your father didn't mention that you were engaged to be married. Perhaps you've not had time to shop for a ring yet. How long since it happened?'

She saw the mischievous light in Nathaniel's eyes again. He looked at his watch. 'At a guess,' he said, 'about seven minutes, give or take a few seconds. I took a risk, but she had to be consulted. I started to propose that night after the dance in Queenstown, but the lady said I was going too fast. Chester, you might slip along and tell Miss Mattie and Jamesina the glad tidings. Tell them to give us a quarter of an hour, then we'll celebrate. I think we should ring my father, and I—er—have a few things to finalise with Letty.'

'I guarantee you have,' said Chester, and went to the door. He paused with his hand on the knob. 'I've been extremely unscrupulous . . . might as well confess it. I just had to make a bid for this, for there isn't anything lovelier in the whole Lake County. But I had the Beaumont brothers to myself while Letty got the afternoon tea ready on their property the other day. I put a proposition to them. It was clinched last night, when I came into your office and used the phone, remember. They've got no sentimental feeling for their property. It was just a means to an end for them. I'm offering them a good price and they'll be able to buy an easier property to work. I'd have liked this too, of course, but I'll build a ranch-style lodge out there. The only thing is——' He paused.

'Yes?' said Nathaniel, obviously wanting him to go. 'I'm quite glad about that. It's splendid country for what you've got in mind. And those boys deserve it.'

Chester said slowly, 'I need easier access. If you grant me the right to put a road through Big Slip, I'll grant you the right to use it. It could serve both properties. But take time to consider it.'

Nathaniel said deliberately, 'It's a deal,' and looked at Letty for confirmation. She said, strangely they thought, 'And when you tell Miss Mattie about our engagement, tell her that mountains are about to be hurled from their seats. She'll know what I mean.'

The door closed.

Nathaniel looked at her. He said, 'It was mean, I know, to play that trick on you, but you did stop me, you know, when the setting *was* right. The moon, the lake, the mountains . . . the whole Million-Dollar View. And you don't need to make a confession, now I know . . . that's why I was so confident about asking you if we should sell . . . I knew from what you'd said that night, you no longer entertained that mean motive.'

She gazed at him in bewilderment. 'I don't know what you mean . . . but Nathaniel, do we have to discuss that now?'

He looked just as bewildered. 'But isn't that what this is all about? Chester Burroughs had told you what he wanted, and you were looking the area over for him? But felt because of the children you must stick it out for the school year and then . . . you fell in love with the place . . . with the Garden of Heaven . . . and, I hope, I *know*, in love with me?'

She swallowed. 'I have a feeling I ought to be furious with you. But I'm not. But you may easily be furious with me in a moment, when you hear what my mean motive really was. Oh, dear!' He stepped towards her, grasped her elbows, shook her and said, 'Letitia, come on, get it over, I want——'

She said, in a quick rush of words, 'I came up here determined to make you fall in love with me . . . to lead you on . . . to get you to the proposing point, *then turn you down!*'

She'd never seen Nathaniel Pengelly look like that before, utterly astounded. *'Then turn me down?'* he repeated. 'Why? In the name of fortune why?' Then, 'But why determine that in the first place? You didn't even like me.'

'That was why. Oh, Nathaniel, don't you remember I said it was Eavesdroppers' Day? There isn't such a day. I made it up on the spur of the moment, because—earlier—I'd eavesdropped too. You and your father came into the outer office and I was in the inner one, under his desk. It was all Popeye's fault.'

'Popeye? That's as clear as mud.'

'Your father's tame pigeon. He'd got shut in all night. I was picking up paper-clips after I'd got him out, and I heard every word you said. That I'd make more mischief in the high country than a flock of *keas!* That I wouldn't know B from a bull's foot on a sheep-station, that I looked like something out of a sheikh's harem, that I'd be a menace, that you couldn't imagine me on speaking terms with a grin, that you got enough cold weather in your valley without introducing a human icicle into it . . . *that* I resented most of all. So when you took your revenge on Portia Latimer by saying you were taking me up here as a governess, I made up my mind that I'd make you eat your words, and make you fall for me.'

'My God,' said Nathaniel Pengelly. Then he began to grin. 'And what happened to that fine resolve, sweetheart?'

She said, 'You know very well what happened to it.'

'Yes,' he said softly, 'but I want you to say it. You must, Letty, you must.'

Her eyes came up to his, a tender light in their green, no reserve left. 'You know exactly. Then I fell in love with you.'

His hands drew her to him, closely. 'Oh, Letitia, this is to be the moment when you prove to me you're not and never were an icicle!'

She felt herself shake in that moment of surrendering proof, the feathering of delight run once more across her skin, quicken her pulses. She raised herself on tiptoe and his mouth found hers.

There was so much to say, to exult in, to anticipate. Reproaches because they'd not been as candid earlier, confessions, revelations.

Nathaniel said, 'You shouldn't have stopped me that night at the Chalet. Then we'd have met Deirdre, that shallow girl I was once misguided enough to have a fancy for, as an engaged couple. I was terrified she'd complicate things.'

Letty, from the haven of his arm, looked up and traced his lips with her finger. 'I was terrified of her too. I'd guessed who she was. But I was even more terrified when I realised you were going to ask me to marry you, that it was because I was so obviously a girl who could take this sort of life. I knew that was necessary, but I wanted to be loved without rhyme or reason, too.'

His astonishment was so great it completely convinced her. He said, 'But—against my will—I loved you long before that. I couldn't believe it. It was before you proved yourself.'

'How could it be? I proved myself so soon, Nathaniel . . . when?'

'As we came into Drumlogie. Some moments can seem an eternity. It rather rocked me. You remember the little boy who shouted that he was King of the Castle? And you said, "I hope that child remembers this moment all his life, whatever time does to him. There was all happiness in that sound." I liked it, Letitia, oh, how I liked it! You didn't know that your echoing laugh had held the same note of pure joy. And in that moment it positively flashed across me that I'd like to spend the rest of my life with a woman who thought like that. I was almost scared of the force of that feeling . . . that was why I didn't leap at the chance to take you through the Moon-Gate. I didn't trust myself. But I'm glad you came, alone, not knowing. Now, do you believe I loved you without rhyme or reason? Even though I still fought against it?'

Her eyes were astar. 'How could I not believe you?' She pulled his head down, and kissed him. His fingers played with the greenstone pendant at her throat. He said, seemingly inconsequentially, 'New Zealand jade. It suits you, my green-eyed witch. Would you—oh, no.'

She stirred a little in his embrace. 'Would I what? And what do you mean, no?'

'I shouldn't have thought of it. Every girl deserves diamonds. And diamonds you shall have.'

Letty said, 'Anybody can have a diamond ring. You've got to tell me.'

He said slowly, 'I don't want you to have it just to please me.'

'You mean, idiot, *dear* idiot, you'd like to buy me a greenstone ring. Nathaniel, I'd rather a ring that is made from part of this very earth of our own, than anything. What does value matter?'

'You're sure? Because Grigor had a very beautiful piece of greenstone given him by a Maori friend in the early days, and had it made into a ring for his Ellen. It's still in my mother's jewel-case.'

She was in raptures. 'Because Ellen and Grigor had so little when they came here to carve out a homestead, I didn't dream there'd be an heirloom like that. I won't be satisfied with anything less.'

She thought of something. 'I know it will be a wonderful day for you when Big Slip is no more, and the lake will lie in our view in all its shimmering blueness, but I'd like one memento of that night, that wonderful night we walked it. I wonder would it be possible to have Kitty's Picnic Table stone prised out of the hill, and brought beside that clump of poplars just at the beginning of the bridle-path? To me that symbolises Kitty making the best of a bad thing. There'd hardly be a path there at first, so they'd have to climb to it. I like to think they rested on the way, and got some joy out of that catastrophe.'

'It shall be done,' said Mr Nathaniel. 'Ellen's Gate
Beautiful, my mother's pillars, Kitty's Picnic Table . . .
and all the traditions we'll create for us and ours in the
years to come.'

He added, 'They'll be thinking it's a very long quarter
of an hour . . . come.' She linked her hands in his. 'No,
Nathaniel, we must ring Tristan first. It's all due to him.
What's his Dunedin number?'

Nathaniel's eyes lit up. 'Try to get him at the Drumlogie
number. Yes . . . it's true. He rang me from there earlier.
Said he couldn't wait any longer to find out how you were.
Not how I, his son, was, mark you, but how Letty Greenaway was. That was when I made up my mind to propose
to you tonight—though not exactly in the way I did. Will
you forgive me for stampeding you into it in front of
Chester?'

Two minutes later, when she'd got her breath back,
Nathaniel was dialling a number, one arm holding her close
against him. Then he heard his father's voice, and said,
'Dad? Your future daughter-in-law wants to speak to you.'

Outside a wind sprang up off the lake, ruffled the dark
waters briefly, swept inland, touched the tussocks among
the rocks of Big Slip, said in passing, 'You've had your
day. Your dominance is over,' and passed on to die away
where Ellen and Grigor, Joseph and Kitty, and Nancy
Pengelly slept among the sights and sounds they had loved
so well on earth.

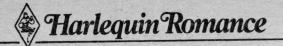
Harlequin Romance

Coming Next Month

Available in January wherever paperback books are sold, or
through Harlequin Reader Service.

In the U.S.
901 Fuhrmann Blvd.
P.O. Box 1397
Buffalo, N.Y. 14240-1397

In Canada
P.O. Box 603
Fort Erie, Ontario
L2A 5X3

Harlequin Intrigue

In October
Watch for the new look of

Harlequin Intrigue

...because romance can be quite an adventure!

Each time, Harlequin Intrigue brings you great stories, mixing a contemporary, sophisticated romance with the surprising twists and turns of a puzzler... romance with "something more."

Plus...
in next month's publications of Harlequin Intrigue we offer you the chance to win one of four mysterious and exciting weekends. Don't miss the opportunity! Read the October Harlequin Intrigues!

Deep in the heart of Africa lay mankind's most awesome secret. Could they find Eden . . . and the grave of Eve?

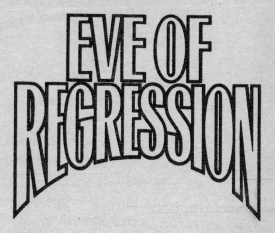

JOHN ARTHUR LONG

A spellbinding novel that combines a fascinating premise with all the ingredients of an edge-of-the-seat read: passion, adventure, suspense and danger.

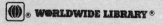